Praise for *The City Beautiful*

"Chillingly sinister, warmly familiar, and breathtakingly transportive, *The City Beautiful* is the haunting, queer Jewish historical thriller of my darkest dreams."
—Dahlia Adler, creator of *LGBTQ Reads* and editor of *That Way Madness Lies*

★ "Polydoros seamlessly blends a murder mystery with Jewish folklore in this haunting historical fantasy." —*Publishers Weekly*, starred review

★ "A gorgeous, disturbing, visceral and mystical experience."
—*BookPage*, starred review

★ "A wild ride of a queer gothic fantasy that's a must-have for YA fantasy collections." —*School Library Journal*, starred review

★ "*The City Beautiful* is a triumph, showcasing queer love, illuminating historical events, and guiding readers to an enthralling ending that will leave them satiated yet desirous to return to the world in which they have become immersed." —*Booklist*, starred review

Praise for *Bone Weaver*

"A heart-pounding adventure. Magic and monsters lurk in every corner."
—Chloe Gong, #1 *New York Times* bestselling author of *These Violent Delights*

★ "Superb." —*Booklist*, starred review

"A dark and thrilling tale." —*Kirkus Reviews*

"Polydoros crafts a magical world that readers will revel in exploring… Fans of Justina Ireland's Dread Nation and the Shadow & Bone series will love this dark fantasy with a touch of horror."
—*Bulletin of the Center for Children's Books*

"*Bone Weaver* is a bloody and unflinching fantasy that balances its darkness with an unwavering cascade of love." —*BookPage*

Books by Aden Polydoros
available from Inkyard Press

Young Adult

Wrath Becomes Her
Bone Weaver
The City Beautiful

Middle Grade

Ring of Solomon

ADEN POLYDOROS

WRATH BECOMES HER

ISBN-13: 978-1-335-45803-2

Wrath Becomes Her

Inkyard Press
22 Adelaide St. West, 41st Floor
Toronto, Ontario M5H 4E3, Canada
www.InkyardPress.com

Printed in U.S.A.

CONTENTS

This book contains content and themes that may be difficult for some readers. For a list of content warnings, please visit adenpolydoros.com.

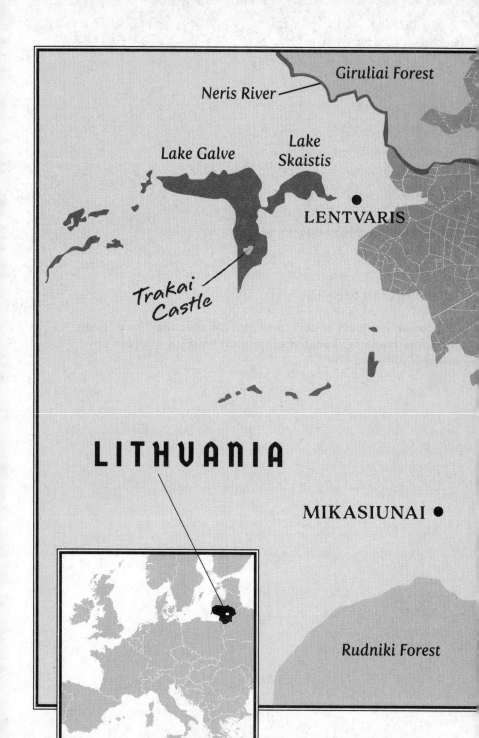

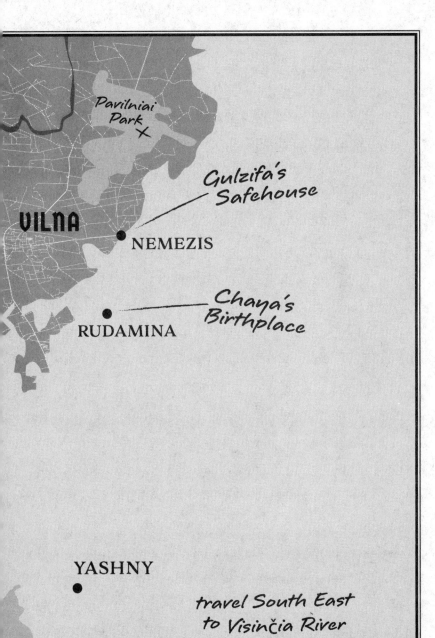

Dedicated to those of us who've emerged from darkness
to find ourselves changed.

PROLOGUE

July 1942
Rudniki Forest, Lithuania

FIREFLIES BOBBED THROUGH THE NIGHT SKY, their greenish glow adding to the low, banked radiance of the fire. Resting against the log, I felt in my pocket for the smooth metal wire left over from the mine I had nestled between the train tracks. We had been nearly a kilometer away by the time we'd heard the crash, but even now, hours later, I felt like I could still feel that explosion slamming through my body in the excited drum of my heart and the nervous jolt of the blood in my ears.

My heart only pounded faster when Akiva sank down next to me, close enough that his hip brushed against mine. Discs of firelight danced across his ice-blue eyes, stoking them with a violet flash when he leaned forward to shrug his rifle's sling from over his shoulder. He propped the gun against the log and stretched out his legs by the fire.

"We did good tonight," I said, lightly tapping my foot against his. Our secret signal.

"You did good, Chaya." A smile curved his lips. "Which reminds me…"

He reached into his pocket and unveiled a small rectangular slab wrapped in blue wax paper. My mouth fell open. It couldn't be.

"A way to celebrate more dead Nazis," Akiva said with a chuckle.

On the log next to us, Kuni leaned forward, the younger boy's eyes gleaming in awe. "Is that what I think it is?"

"Chocolate, yeah." Akiva broke the bar into four, a square for each of us.

"Where'd you get this?" I asked, hardly able to believe it. Food was constantly on my mind, as much a part of our nightly discussions as which train routes and military bunkers we should target.

"When we ran across Volkov's men a few days ago, I traded it."

"So you're telling me you've been warming it with your ass all week," I said, and Akiva rolled his eyes.

"Since when did you ever have a problem with my ass?"

I shoved him lightly in the side, chuckling helplessly.

He gave a piece to Kuni, and when Yael came over, handed her one as well. But when it came my turn, he hesitated and smiled at me, holding it to my lips. A challenge.

Rolling my eyes, I leaned forward, took the morsel of chocolate in my teeth. His fingertips brushed against my lips, calloused but gentle, teasing.

Yael shook her head, rising to her feet and brushing the dust from her pant legs. "While you two lovebirds enjoy yourselves, I'm going to get some sleep. Try not to offend the child now."

"I'm no child," Kuni protested. "I'm almost twelve!"

"She's right," Akiva said, pulling away. "You should probably go to sleep, too, kid. We have a busy day tomorrow."

Sighing, Kuni rose to his feet.

"Kuni?" I said.

He looked back.

"You've got a bit of schmutz on your face." I pointed to the chocolate smeared by one corner of his mouth.

Kuni wiped his mouth with the back of his hand, a blush already creeping across his cheeks. He made it no more than five steps before the night's peaceful quiet was shattered by a gunshot in the direction of our dugouts.

For the briefest, perfect moment, we froze simultaneously. It couldn't have been more than a split second, a single moment when the clock stopped ticking, and the night went still, and the silence that poured into place in the echoing reports of the gunshots was as heavy as a deep-sea void. And then I found myself on my feet, the taste of chocolate lingering on my tongue. Even as I reached for the revolver nestled in my coat pocket, Akiva was already jacking a round into his rifle's chamber.

"Yael!" Kuni screamed out as more gunfire shattered the night, and Akiva and I lunged for the cover of nearby trees.

Kuni just turned and ran from the glade, the pistol Akiva had given him forgotten beside the fire.

"Kuni, wait—" Akiva began.

The boy didn't even reach the tree line. A gunshot took him off his feet, drove him facedown. Akiva ducked behind the cover of a tree. As another gunshot echoed through the forest, I followed his example and pressed my back against a thick pine.

"Kuni, get up!" Crawling on my hands and knees, I tried to reach him. I hardly made it more than a meter before a volley of shots sent me scrambling back against the tree.

The firelight illuminated Kuni's face in garish detail— hazel eyes wide and sightless, an ooze of blood spilled down his cheek, the top of his head—

Bile flooded my mouth.

His *head*.

As Akiva crouched behind the tree next to me, his gaze met mine. Panting breaths pushed through his gritted teeth, his eyes burning like pale fire. A slick, muddy shadow had bloomed across the front of his coat, and slowly, it dawned on me.

This was the end.

CHAPTER 1

I WAS BORN ON SCRAPS OF PAPER. LOOSE PAGES, torn parchment, holy scrolls severed from their dowels. Before Ezra gave me a tongue, he taught me how to read.

Aleph. Mem. Taw.

"There is a mark on your forehead, and it means truth."

Aleph. Mem. Taw. *Emet*. Truth.

I felt the word thrum in the empty space where Ezra would sculpt my mouth. With my fingertip, I traced the three letters he'd jotted across the floorboards, copying them into the dust.

The corners of Ezra's lips twitched upward in a smile. It meant he was pleased or amused. The expression seemed ill at ease on his face, in conflict with his severe cheekbones and hard gray eyes.

"Yes, Vera. Very good." Ezra wiped away the first letter,

making אמת into מת, *met*, dead, before blotting out the rest into a ghostly smear nearly as pale as the breath that left his lips.

Even with the walls insulated by old horse blankets, the winter chill still managed to intrude into the hayloft. From how he shivered, I could almost believe the cold had found its way into his bones as well, like the way I felt ice crystals form and crackle within me on the most frigid winter mornings, veining my insides as sharp and fine as splinters.

Clay and chalk sullied Ezra's hands. On his right hand, he was missing his pinkie finger and the last two knuckles of his ring finger, his leather gloves snipped and sewn to fit. Not unfinished like me, he had explained, but torn from him by the same shrapnel that had turned his right leg to wood and leather from the knee down. He fumbled with the stick of chalk as it dwindled into a nub. Even so, my handwriting was a spidery scrawl compared to his.

Truth. True. Trust me. Trust that this is for the best.

When the sun set, our lessons came to an end. Ezra curled up on the pallet in the corner, just a shadow in the darkness. Candles were precious things, reserved for Friday evenings or when he woke deep in the night, biting his own arm to stanch his wrenching sobs.

To soothe himself from those haunting dreams, he would explain to me what he had seen. A tide of smoke rolling across a pockmarked field, or soldier boys without limbs or innards, or his daughter before he had buried her. It helped him to give his fears a name and face, as though only by talking about them was he able to convince himself they weren't crawling through the stalls below.

Ezra slept with his back to me, buried beneath layers of

blankets to keep out the cold. He had taken off the leather leg and rested it on the floor beside him. From my nook across the room, I couldn't stop staring at it—*Prosthesis, Vera, it is called a prosthesis*—thinking of how my own legs must have looked before he had attached them to my body. Had he shaped them in pieces, first the feet and then the calves? And if it had taken him several months to do that, how long would it take for him to sculpt my mouth?

The thought made me restless. Ezra had given me my second leg less than a week ago, and I had spent plenty of time pacing the room since then. He had even allowed me to venture into the hayloft once, although I had been too frightened to clamber down the ladder to the stalls below. As I rose to my feet, I was pleased by how smoothly I stood. Walking was getting easier every day.

There was scarcely enough room to move. All along the walls were moldering scrolls and prayer books, stacked so that whenever Ezra climbed through the hidden doorway into the greater hayloft, he was forced to step over them.

A desecration, he would say, both to leave them on the floor and to step over them, *but necessary*.

He used the same phrase when talking about his creation of me.

Bats chittered in the rafters above, stirring like black handkerchiefs. They were my only companions aside from Ezra, and I longed to have their freedom. Some nights, I imagined climbing up to their perches and following them through the cracks between the roof slates on wings made of parchment and scroll dowels. I would soar past the fields and forests, and follow the twists and turns of the Neris River until it flowed into the Baltic Sea.

With the hidden panel wedged firmly in the hayloft's northern wall, I was confined to this room. For now, I could only hear the outside world. It was quieter at night, but not silent. The lowing of the cows below; their wet snuffles and shifting bodies. Squawking chickens and barking dogs.

The noises both seduced and taunted me. They sounded so close. If I could just speak, maybe I could shout loudly enough for someone else to hear me, for someone to *answer*. Anyone would do. The man who Ezra chatted with while tending to the livestock, or the girl who called the chickens by name. Even the cows and horses would make welcome companions.

Unlike Ezra, I had no need to rest, and the only time he put me to sleep was when he sculpted my form. To pass the time and distract myself from the temptations of the outside world, I plucked a book from the stack nearest to me and flipped idly through it. A commentary on the midrash. My thoughts strayed and the words buzzed through my mind like gnats. The verses were meaningless to me, as was the rest of the scripture. Even the passages which marked my own limbs.

I had seen Ezra peruse most of the books in our hideaway, and every week the strangers below brought him newspapers or Polish language novels with colorful paper covers. But he refused to touch the loose parchments in the corner, the ones heaped in a crudely hammered lead box so old the metal had turned white and chalky with age. Hebrew and Aramaic, and another Semitic dialect that I couldn't quite place, even though I could read its letters. He wouldn't let me touch the lead coffer or its contents, but once or twice,

I'd snuck a glimpse, and the sight of the water-stained pages had made me feel vaguely dizzy and unstable, as if my core had begun to liquefy. I couldn't quite put it into words, except that it had felt like looking at the dirty picks and scalpels or the clots of clay smushed into the floorboards. A part of myself, torn free and dripping.

I set aside the book with a sigh, contemplated the volume of poetry beneath it, then continued my lazy search for something else to pass the hours. Briefly, I amused myself by playing with Ezra's prosthetic leg, figuring out how it attached to his hip and practicing buckling and undoing the straps. It interested me to touch it, something crafted so much like myself—just the shape of a leg—and yet unmoving and silent.

I traced the word *emet* into the false limb's calf, half hoping it would jerk awake, that the straps might writhe like the centipedes that had crept from the woodwork before winter had banished them into hibernation, or the blockish foot might cleave into separate toes. But it remained still, just a lifeless husk of leather and wood. I had expected as much, only I couldn't help but feel a twinge of disappointment— and above all, loneliness so deep and gnawing, it seemed to burrow into the center of me.

As I set the limb down, my gaze caught in the small mirror hanging on the wall. Several times a week, Ezra would use the mirror to shave, balancing a bowl of water in one hand and his razor in the other.

The mirror's silvery sheen transfixed me. Every opportunity I had, I loved to touch it, tracing its icy smoothness and the pockmarks of tarnish. As I came closer, I could see parts of myself reflected in its surface—arms covered in black letters lifted from the parchment when my skin had yet to dry; the word for truth, אמת, inked beneath a widow's peak of dark curls; deeply-set eyes the dusky gray of dawn; a nose as sharp as Ezra's; and below all that, the smooth expanse where I felt my mouth straining to be.

Soon, Vera, soon.

Gaze fixed on my reflection, I tried to form my lips myself. My fingers mashed uselessly against my face's cool, unyielding surface. The fingernails Ezra had so carefully laid into my skin were useless. I couldn't even dimple it.

Ezra always put me to sleep before working on my body, but I had once glimpsed the instruments he used to create me. Picks, shears, blades, and awls encrusted in chalky clay. Sponges used to buff my skin until it was as smooth as the mirror itself. Bundles of human hair, braided to keep from tangling.

Maybe I just needed to find something sharp. A snapped dowel, perhaps, or one of the nails studding the floorboards.

No. My fingers curled into fists. Then he'd know.

Ezra had never hurt me, but I was afraid of what he would do if he found out. He might take away my fingers until he knew I wouldn't disfigure myself, and my legs until he was sure I wouldn't run away. If he wanted to, he could turn me back into clay and start anew. He wouldn't return me to the river; I would be thrown out, left to muddle with the horse manure and filth all winter long, then baked to a crisp in the summer sun.

So, no nails or broken dowels. I must bear without a mouth for a little while longer.

I just needed to wait.

I despised the wait.

An icy crackle stirred me from my daze. I looked down to find the mirror spider-webbed to pieces around my fingers. Shards studded my skin, leaving behind pinpricks that sealed up in an instant.

Until now, I had used my hands only for the most mundane tasks, to pick up things or rearrange them, and to laboriously copy Ezra's handwriting. A strange flash of excitement rippled through me as I realized that I could break things, too.

CHAPTER 2

WHEN EZRA WOKE THE NEXT MORNING, HIS face hardened at the sight of the shattered mirror. He picked up the shards one by one, cradling them in his cupped palm.

He turned to me, his gray eyes cold and analytical. "You did this?"

Sitting in my nook in the corner, I nodded reluctantly. In the hours since dawn, I had stared at the mirror in terror. I had even tried fixing it. The painless gashes torn into my palms healed instantly, sucking the splinters of glass deeper inside me, but no matter how hard I pressed the shards together, they refused to merge.

"Why did you break it?" He studied me with disconcerting intensity. "Was it because of your reflection?"

The way he said it made something tighten inside my chest.

He made it sound as though that was the expected reason, the inevitable one. I had seen the way he looked at me when he thought I wasn't looking, mostly with thinly veiled repulsion, sometimes with outright *resentment*, as if by just being alive—or the closest thing to it—I was to blame for what he had done to create me. But for the first time, I wondered if a part of him, however small, wished to return me to the dust.

Shaking my head, I picked up a chunk of chalk left over from yesterday's lesson. On the floorboards, I wrote: *It was an accident.*

"Ah, I see. Of course." Ezra chuckled, shocking me. He discarded the broken glass in the chamber pot in the corner. "You don't yet understand your own strength, but you will in time. And you will only grow more powerful."

From the box where he stored his belongings, he retrieved a small bundle and unwrapped its mud-stained folds. Steel glistened in the sunlight streaming through the knotholes. His tools.

I brushed away my writing and began anew, intending to ask him if he would give me my mouth today. I stopped mid-sentence when he held a slim pick out to me.

He pressed it into my hands. "Try to bend this."

I did as he commanded. The rod held up a bit better than the mirror, but after a brief resistance, the metal bent in my hands. I tried to form it into a circle and succeeded halfway before it snapped in two. The sharp edges cut a gash into my palms, a numb line that began to mend immediately. Within seconds, all that remained was a ghostly imprint, until even that faded away.

"You are truly an incredible creation," Ezra murmured, taking the pick's broken pieces from my grip.

I wrote on the floorboards: *Is it good to break things?*

"Some things, yes. However, it is not the act of breaking that pleases me, Vera. It is your ability. Your strength. My first two attempts resulted in weak beings of slush and water, not even stable enough to rise to their feet, let alone pass as human. But you are perfect. I... I think it is time to finish what I started."

Laying down the broken pick, he returned to the crate and took two glass jars from its depths. One was filled halfway with human teeth. In the other, a tongue floated in cloudy liquid. As he shook the teeth into his hand, sadness darkened his gaze.

"These were hers," he said, his voice low and grave.

When I was still just a crude form, he had told me about her. Chaya. His daughter. She'd been sixteen when the war had begun, and seventeen by the time she'd died. For several months, she had lived with him in this hayloft, until the day a pair of young partisan fighters had taken refuge in the barn below—and she had been lured down by the sound of Yiddish voices. Familiar voices.

"The girl was a friend from school." Ezra spat out *friend* with shocking bitterness. "And the boy was quick to become one. I wasn't able to stop Chaya after that. They came back a second time, because knowing her—knowing that Tomas and his family had given us refuge—meant this was a safe place. That they could expect shelter here. And the second time, she left to fight with them."

She didn't last long. Just months after she vanished with

the pair, Chaya was shot to death a stone's throw from the same town she had been born in. The partisan boy had carried her here in a desperate stagger through a muggy midsummer night, heavily wounded, already dying. But it was much too late to save her.

"She's buried at the edge of the field. It was a sin and a crime what I did, but not as terrible as the one that had put her there. A desecration, but necessary. There could be no other way." Ezra's eyes lifted to me. Their gray color mirrored my own. "The dead must be buried whole. But if God is here, he is not listening. There is only you now, Vera."

As he stepped toward me, I recoiled, my face straining with all the words I couldn't say.

Make me my own teeth, I wanted to plead as he set the jars on the floor. *Make them from river rocks or even clay. I'm not her. I don't want to see this. Please, don't make me see this again.*

He sank to one knee and reached out for me.

"Sleep, Vera," he murmured as his fingers brushed against the three letters written on my brow. The floorboards beneath my knees gave way to—

—*wet soil. Slimy pine needles beneath my fingers, rustling branches overhead. Past the forest canopy, the moon was as round and white as a fish-picked skull, surrounded by a silt of stars.*

Only one thought filled my mind: Akiva. *I needed to draw them away from* Akiva.

I lurched onto my feet. I had burning lungs, and a heart that pounded against a bone rib cage. Dark liquid welled from my scraped palms.

I bled here.

Bushes shuddered behind me. I broke into a frantic run, grasping around me blindly as I bolted through the forest. Tree branches struck out at my shoulders and tangled in my hair. The darkness was not my friend, nor was the river. I emerged from the trees to confront its swollen rapids. The water was as black as a grave. I faltered.

If I fell in, I would sink to the bottom. The fish and snails would strip me clean; the current would tumble my bones.

Gravel crunched behind me. Slowly, I turned.

Two men emerged between the trees, stepping toward me. One wore a navy-blue uniform with red piping, the glossy leather brim of his uniform cap shadowing flinty blue eyes and a cruel twist of a mouth. The other was dressed in gray, and as he stepped forward, terror thrummed through my body. Something about the color or cut of his uniform, or maybe the metal skull pinned to his hat, honed my fear into a needle point. Even more than the first man, I sensed this one was dangerous.

"You must understand, it's really quite pertinent that we find him," the man in gray said in crisp and formal German. *"We* need *him. He is the last step. The key to awakening them."*

The words would have meant nothing to Chaya—she didn't have the language sunk beneath her skin, the way the scribes' ink had done to me when I had been left to dry upon the parchments. All I felt was her confusion.

"Tell us where he is!" the other man barked in Polish.

"I don't know!" I heard myself say. "We were separated after the invasion. He's probably dead."

"I see," the German soldier answered, once the other man translated the response to him. A regretful smile edged across his lips as he drew the pistol from the holster on his belt. "That's a shame. I hate killing women."

I woke with the taste of blood and chemicals ripe on my tongue. My tongue in my mouth. My mouth.

I lay there for a moment, my hands splayed across the worn floorboards. Shifting golden constellations of dust motes spangled the air above my head. I focused on them to center myself. The fear didn't remain for long; I didn't have a pounding heart or a body that bled, so Chaya's memories felt rather distant in the waking world. Within moments, her terror buried itself inside me, out of sight and out of mind.

Sitting up, I tentatively ran my fingertips over the smooth edges of my teeth. In the jar, they had been as white and small as the chips flaking from the salt blocks stored in the hayloft, and seemed just as fragile. But against my fingers, the teeth felt solid and even more substantial than the clay they were rooted in.

Next, I tested my lips by pulling on them and then biting them. My lips and palate were not flesh like my tongue, except they felt no different to the touch. As if the differences between what was mine and what had been Chaya's were already beginning to lose their form.

"Careful now," Ezra murmured, sitting atop the pallet with his chin resting on his folded hands. I jerked my head up in surprise. I had almost forgotten he was there. A wry smile edged his lips. "Don't bite too hard. You don't want to ruin all my hard work."

Clay encrusted his fingers, and his wrinkled flannel shirt was smeared with more of the same. He seemed as insubstantial as the bats roosting in the rafters, his harsh face cast in shadows.

"I have a mouth!" The moment the words left me, I gasped

and pressed my hand over my lips. So, this thrum in my throat—this was to speak. And this frigid *whoosh* passing through my chest, this was air. This was what it meant to breathe.

Ezra's eyes narrowed, and for a long moment he merely regarded me.

"Ah, so no baby babbling. Your Yiddish is impeccable." A faint tremor weaved its way through his voice. "I suppose it should come as no surprise that you would be born fully formed, as Eve was. But tell me, were you born with self-awareness? Do you know what you are?"

"Yes."

He waited patiently.

I struggled to answer him. I was clay and steel and ink and words. I was hair and teeth. But I was also more than just my individual parts.

"I am alive," I said at last.

"No, that is not what I am asking. I asked, what *are* you?"

"A golem." The word tasted bitter on my tongue, as harsh and unnatural as the cloudy elixir it had come packed in.

He nodded and took a deep, unsteady breath, as though my voice had bruised him. "And what is a golem?"

I didn't answer. Merely hearing him say it struck me with a terrible image, the relic of a scribe's daydream—a crude form shaped from clay, all lumpish limbs and misshapen features, its eyes just gouged holes. The word אמת hacked into its brow, each letter as deep and gaping as an open wound.

The memory filled me with horror. I was nothing like that. Ezra had said as much. And yet...

"I suppose it's unfair to expect you to know your true nature," he said.

My mouth brimmed with questions I wanted to ask him. More than anything, I wanted to know about the difference between us. I felt that if I learned a little more about Ezra, I would uncover secrets about my true nature. It would be like revealing memories from my own past, or rather, the past that I had inherited through Chaya's eyes and teeth.

"Who are *you*?" I asked, turning his own question back on him.

His brow furrowed in puzzlement. "I am your creator. Ezra. I've told you this before, have I not?"

"I know, but that's not what I mean." I strained to find the right words. "You...you made me. But I want to know, who *are* you?"

His face chilled over. At first, I thought he meant to silence me. A twinge of acute terror rippled through me. He could do that, I was sure. Either through commands, or simply by disfiguring the mouth he had so carefully built. He had left the bundle of tools within hand's reach.

Just when I began to think he wouldn't answer, he sighed, relenting. Brushing his fingers through his hair, he regarded the clay beneath his nails, the scarred absences of his pinky and ring fingers. Flexed his fingers. Curled them.

"I don't know what you expect to hear," he said at last.

"Tell me anything."

His gaze lifted to mine. I could tell from the firm set of his jaw that he didn't want to, but after another hesitation so long it was almost excruciating, he began to talk.

"I was born in 1896, in a suburb of Vilna," he said, tracing a thumb over the worn floorboards. "My father was a rabbi, who hailed from a long line of rabbis, only I didn't share his acclimation for scripture. When I was your age—Chaya's age, I mean—I was angry. So incredibly angry. I was eager to fight. I didn't know what that meant at the time."

When the Great War broke out in 1914, Ezra had been recruited into the Imperial Army. Once this place had been the kingdom of Lithuania, but at that time, it was part of Russia. Only later would it be claimed by Poland, and after that the Soviet Union.

Near the end of the war, a mortar, a kind of explosive, had landed in his trench. He lost the use of two fingers and a leg, the hearing in his left ear, and his dream of traveling the world. But in the end, upon returning to his hometown, he had found something as well.

"What?" I asked, leaning forward, mesmerized.

A wry smile touched his lips. "Love."

Toiba had been a year older than him, a nurse working in a war hospital. Before he had shown her his heart, she had seen the uglier parts of him—his shrapnel-gouged limbs and the bandaged stump of his knee—and inhaled the biting stench of piss and gangrene.

He described these things so vividly, a visceral shiver swept through me, and I found my left hand straying toward my own leg. A part of me expected to encounter a ragged stump and the leaking reeds of torn arteries, that glint of white he'd realized was his own femur. Instead, my fingers encountered smooth clay. It came as a small comfort to know there was nothing beneath.

The sun had risen and fallen in my long sleep, and with

each minute, the night encroached on us. As Ezra continued his story, his gray eyes tarnished to the color of ashes in the failing glow. Unless he spared a candle, we would be in darkness soon enough.

"Toiba died during childbirth." He took a deep breath, pinching the bridge of his nose. "She never had a chance to watch our daughter grow old, but I suppose in some ways that was a mercy. If she were still alive today, she would have been horrified…"

He trailed off, but all his unspoken words hung in the air between us, as cold as a winter chill. She would have been horrified by me, he meant. By what he had done to create me.

He had killed men before. I sensed it in myself. His potential for violence was a part of me, sunk under my skin like ink. But to take from your own daughter her eyes, her nails, her tongue, her teeth…

That was something else entirely.

"The mystics of legend were said to be so wise and powerful, they were able to create the perfect likeness of a man from clay alone." He said it almost apologetically, as though that explained it all. "But I am no holy tzaddik. I am not even a rebbe. So, I had to resort to other means. Kishuf."

"Kishuf?" The word felt strange and peppery on my tongue, like the shape of something I had nearly forgotten.

"Ancient and profane magic," he said quietly. "What my father would have derided as witchcraft or worse. You do not learn these things in a shul or yeshiva. You do not even speak of them. They are abominations against God."

His statements were defanged by the weary resignation in his voice, as if it was a simple fact of my creation to which he'd had no choice, but I couldn't help but feel vaguely uneasy, as if he had exposed a fissure deep within me. Something prone to cracking.

"Then how did you know to create me?" I asked.

A wry smile touched his lips. "Have I ever told you about the legend of Pardes, the heavenly orchard?"

I shook my head, testing the word *Pardes* silently on my tongue. Its shape felt strange and smooth, like water-worn pebbles.

"It is said that, over a thousand years ago, four rabbis attempted to access the orchard of heavenly learning. Ben Azzai, Ben Zoma, Rabbi Akiva, and Achor. One man died, one went mad, Achor became a heretic, and only Rabbi Akiva survived the encounter, leaving in peace and whole. Why do you suppose that is? What do you suppose they saw there?"

I didn't answer. I was filled with knowledge—it was imprinted in ink on my surface, and had sunk even deeper in the weeks since my creation—but the idea of heavenly knowledge felt as inaccessible as the daily prayers Ezra whispered like repentance.

"According to family legend, my ancestor, Shachna Bar Zemah was obsessed with that question. More specifically, with what Achor saw—what must have been so unfathomable that it had turned him away from his faith."

"Why did he want to know that?" I asked.

"I imagine, for more or less the same reasons that led me to create you," Ezra said, smiling humorlessly. "Shachna survived the Khmelnytsky Uprising and the Russo-Polish War after that. He came of age surrounded by death and suffering. In any case, in his search for answers, Shachna too became a heretic—first driven from his home in Vilna by scorn and hatred, then the Vilna rabbis put him into herem in the late 1600s, cutting him off from the religious community entirely. Over time, his interest turned to other, even stranger subjects of immortality and the creation of artificial life. Mix in a little Kabbalah with medieval superstition, Baltic paganism, and Paracelsus's alchemical writings on the creation of a so-called 'homunculus,' and you will come close to understanding Shachna's particular breed of madness."

Ezra gestured to the stacks of books piled along the walls. Some were bound in flaking leather or cloth, while others were so old, the spines had broken away to reveal stitching like dried sinews. "These texts came from the same temple as the village he died in—the one I grew up in—from the genizah where old texts are stored before burial. When the Soviets occupied our town, they turned the shul into a warehouse."

Soviets. Disjointed memories flitted through my head like a flurry of crows: a star and sickle, red flags, clamoring laborers crowding around a man standing on a platform, a young soldier confronting an encroaching tide of smoke.

Overwhelmed by the visions, I pressed my hands over my eyes until they receded into darkness. For something that didn't belong to me, the scribes' memories felt more substantial than my own short lifetime. Chaya's, even more so.

At times, I wasn't even sure who I was beyond the disjointed memories and emotions that filtered down to me. Was the admiration I felt for Ezra something he had carved into me, was it a residue of Chaya, or was it truly my own?

Where did I begin?

As I lowered my hands, Ezra continued talking. These

books and Torahs constituted only a small amount of the writings from the genizah and shul, he explained. Before the Nazis had invaded, he had smuggled out what he could at his father, the rabbi's, behest.

"Yet I suspect even my father didn't know what the genizah contained," he said.

Buried in a lead box beneath the storage room's floor had been Shachna's magnum opus, texts too unholy to keep outside consecrated ground, and too dangerous to bury in the cemetery lest they spoil the earth. They did not concern the mystical art of Kabbalah. They were something different. Darker.

"An ordinary golem is created from pure elements, the same dust from which HaShem shaped the first man. But to create you, it involved power gained from going against all our commandments—the collection of blood in a vessel, the desecration of a corpse, the desecration of the Torah. Self-mutilation."

Ezra turned his palms upward. Puckering pink scars climbed down his forearms, overlaying the older hatching left from shrapnel. The sight filled me with unspeakable shame. I looked down at my own wrists, circled in ink. The black letters resembled scars of their own.

If a tzaddik was able to create a golem, that meant golems themselves weren't abominations. Only ones made through kishuf. Only me.

Ezra must have sensed my mounting discomfort, because he cleared his throat, offering me a thin smile. "But enough about that. Say more. Say anything. That word on your fore-head. Do you remember what it means?"

"Truth." I savored the sound of the word, *emet*. To show off, I repeated it in Polish.

"Polish. So, you can speak Polish, too."

Without further prompting, I echoed the word in German and Russian.

The different languages came to me the same way that recollections of the world beyond the hayloft filtered through the darkness behind my eyes, like opening the floodgates to another part of myself, a stranger sunken deep inside me.

"Incredible," Ezra murmured. "How do you know this?"

I struggled to find the words to answer. When my voice failed me, I pointed at the scrolls and stacks of papers along the walls then pressed my fingers against the calligraphy trailing down my forearms.

The scribes had left me with more than just the Hebrew printed in ink upon my skin—they had poured so much of their souls into their writing, that I'd inherited their memories and languages, too.

Yiddish. Polish. Lithuanian. German. Hebrew. Russian.

I was the daughter of two dozen different scribes and a murdered girl. I was the daughter of the Vokė River.

"I know it because they knew it," I murmured.

His eyes narrowed. "You have their memories?"

I swallowed, recalling the taste of blood. I shouldn't have known what blood tasted like, considering I had none of my own. It troubled me to experience sensations that didn't belong to me, even though they were all I'd ever known since Ezra had dredged me from the riverside.

"And Chaya's," I said.

When I said Chaya's name, Ezra flinched as if I had struck him. He leaned forward in his seat, his eyes afire.

"Then you must know how she died," he said breathlessly. "You must have seen it."

I nodded. "Not all, but…"

"Tell me everything."

"I… I…" I didn't know how to put it into words. Chaya's fear encroached on me like an inky wave, and before I knew it, I bent over myself and pressed my hands to my face. Recalling the desperate flight through the forest, and the impact of the gunshot, so powerful that it had nearly taken me off my feet. The breathlessness, like I was still just clay in the Vokė River, crushed beneath the weight of surging water.

"It's all right," Ezra said, and though he said it as if he meant to soothe me, he remained at a chilly distance, his chin resting in his hands. "You don't have to say it. Just remember the men who killed her. Remember what they look like. Burn their faces into your memory and hate them with every fiber of your being. That is why I gave you emotions, so that you would hate them as much as I hate them. Because one day, you will do what I cannot do. You will destroy them all."

CHAPTER 3

THE NEXT EVENING, AS EZRA ATE THE MEAL THAT the people below had brought him, he stopped and held out the tin can, fork and all. "Do you know what this is?"

Butterflied fish lay in a broth of oil and their own juices. Their spines were as white as the swirling snowflakes I glimpsed through the knotholes in the barn wall when I parted the horse blankets.

"Fish." The word came to my lips in an instant.

He nodded. "Try it."

Excitement rippled through me. I plucked a chunk of fish from the tin and used my new teeth to bite into it, savoring the remarkable moment when I paired the salty-sweet tang of pickled herring with its savory odor.

"Well, what do you think?" Ezra leaned forward, regarding me.

"It's delicious," I said, and he laughed.

"Ah, I knew you'd like it."

"What happens to it?" I asked once I swallowed. "I can't taste it anymore."

He looked vaguely uncomfortable. "I suppose we'll find out soon enough. I don't believe... You do not have the ability to..."

He meant that I was not like him or even the bats roosting above. I had no blood or beating heart. I wasn't a sum of empty vessels and hollow spaces—inside, I was as solid as a stone, my bones an armature of steel rods and wire.

We didn't talk more about what I was or what I could and could not do. Instead, I asked questions about the strangers I sometimes heard in the barn below. They spoke Lithuanian with each other, but the few times Ezra had ventured down to talk to them, they switched to Polish.

"The man is named Tomas," Ezra said. "The girl is his daughter, Živilė. They are our friends. Soon you will meet them. But you've only just begun to walk. You're not strong enough yet to leave this place."

"When will I be? I have a mouth now."

"Soon."

"I look human, don't I?"

He nodded. "You do. But first you need to learn to act human."

There was plenty of reading material strewn around us, but Ezra didn't want me to read from the Tanakh or Mishnah. The names of God must never pass my lips, even though they were written on my body. He had brought me a book of poetry by a woman named Franciszka Arnsztajnowa. I sensed that my voice disturbed him, because after the first few stanzas he made me stop.

I closed the book. "Is there something wrong with my voice?"

"You just…you sound so much like her."

"Chaya?" I asked, and he flinched as if he couldn't even stand hearing me say her name.

"My daughter," he said in the husky whisper of someone struggling not to cry.

"Am I not your daughter, too?"

He stared at me, the shock in his face as glaring as a red-hot brand. His features contorted, crumpled inward on themselves—first in an anguished grimace, then in a snarl of rage.

"No!" he growled, rising to his feet. "No, you are not my daughter. You are my creation, Vera. Do you understand me?"

Just moments before, eager sounds had been bubbling from my lips. Now, I couldn't even find the words to answer him. Despite my innards of solid clay, I felt hollowed out by Ezra's rebuttal, as though he had reached down my throat and torn out something deep inside me, in the place where a heart would have been.

"I gave you Chaya's eyes so that you could hunt down the men who killed her." Even as Ezra regained his composure, his voice remained whetted into a sharp, icy edge. He was hardening himself, as if he meant to become clay. "Chaya's features, so that her face will be the last thing those men see. Her voice, so that it will be the last thing they hear. But do not think for an instant that you are Chaya, or that you are even human. It is not blood that flows through your veins, child, it is mud from the Vokė River. You cannot die, only be destroyed, and you will never be truly alive."

I wanted to scream at him. Scream because of the hollowness, because he had ripped something from me without even meaning to. Couldn't he see that?

Knowing what I had done to the mirror and the iron pick, I could hurt Ezra if I wanted to. Hurt him badly. Kill him, even. That frightened me, because the only people I was supposed to hurt were the guilty. And this rage that rose up inside me with each word he spoke was *wrong;* it was wrong because it hadn't come from him.

To calm myself, I gripped my arms, dimpling the stained surface. Breathed in the frigid air. It wasn't even breathing though, was it? It was just drawing in dust and cold and pushing it out again. And the worst part was, this urge to breathe was a habit that wasn't even mine. It was Chaya's.

"I can't stand being here. It's suffocating. Looking at you, it's—" Ezra shook his head and stumbled back as though just my proximity to him was intolerable. "Your voice. Your face. Gevalt. Your face."

"Where are you going?" I asked, but he was already freeing the panel to the greater hayloft with the frantic pawing of a cornered barn rat. By the second, his breathing grew harsher, quicker. I lurched to my feet and reached out to him, filled with a wordless desire to help him, but that only made him veer away with a pained groan.

The frantic gasps that shook his frame were no different than those that racked him when he awoke some nights, grasping at the tapered stump of his leg. And as he staggered into the greater hayloft, it slowly dawned on me that I was the reason for this.

I was the monster. I was the nightmare.

CHAPTER 4

I WAITED.

Silence down below, except for the gentle lowing of the cows, and a faint, smooth rumbling that grew louder for a minute or two, before diminishing into a monotonous purr. Ezra's absence put me on edge. The memory of his panic and anger destabilized me even further, animating me with such anxiety, I feared I'd begin fracturing at the joints if I didn't move. I tried to distract myself, first by pacing and then by peering into the broken mirror, just to reassure myself I was still whole, pausing only when I felt a strange sense of displacement in my core.

I pressed my hand against my belly as tiny lumps emerged from the smooth clay beneath my blouse. They crunched against my palm—tiny vertebras and ribs so thin, they were nearly transparent. It took me a moment to realize what I was staring at. The remains of the herring fillet Ezra had given me.

Within seconds, the divots created from the bones smoothed over. I kept my palm against my stomach for a moment longer, trying to map out the exact place the fish I'd eaten had sunk to. Was there a hollow there, or had the clay within me squeezed and pushed the fillet, mashing it into meat and juices, until it simply became another part of me? I wished I knew. I wished my body didn't feel like a grave, with some secrets slowly excavated but many more still buried out of sight.

Sighing, I sat on the sleeping pallet and tested the blanket beneath my fingers, worrying at a loose thread. The memory of Ezra's expression remained seared into my mind. All the repulsion I'd glimpsed lurking beneath his features for months had finally reared to the surface. He had dredged me from the river and molded me into this form, so why did it sometimes feel like he could hardly stand to look at me?

It was rare for him to be gone this long, or to leave the hayloft at all. By the minute, the golden coins of sunlight spilling through the knotholes between the horse blankets began to tarnish to shades of bronze and crimson, and a sour wind scratched at the ceiling slates.

Just as I began to lay down, a hollow bang reverberated through the barn as if something heavy had crashed to the ground far below. Except then two more explosions rang out, and I realized the noises had come from outside.

"Ezra?" I murmured, troubled by the sounds for a reason I couldn't quite put into words, except that they conjured a faint and disturbing memory of fleeing through the forest. I repeated his name once more, but nobody answered, and by the moment, my discomfort heightened into something close to dread. I winced as another loud bang rang out, rising to my feet before I even realized it.

Crossing the room, I stepped over the stacks of paper with care, curling my fingers over the calligraphy marking my forearms. I hesitated at the threshold leading out to the hayloft. Ezra had left the panel ajar, and through the crack, I could only discern shadows and the dusty shapes of things.

Anything could be waiting for me out there. The murky darkness of the riverbed. Crushing airlessness, the abyss on all sides.

I knew I should stay in the room, but what if Ezra was in trouble? He could be hurt even. My mouth went dry, drained of river water. Dead. He could be dead.

Shaking off my unease, I freed the panel and laid it carefully against the wall. There was darkness, as I expected, but not the absolute, smothering depths of the river—thin shafts of crimson sunlight pierced through the gaps in the ceiling, rippling across the hay-strewn boards.

Down below, the barn door creaked open with excruciating slowness. The rusty hinges released a harsh, prolonged squeal.

"Ezra?" I repeated in just a whisper now.

"Help," a voice croaked, not in his familiar Yiddish, but in Lithuanian. A young voice. A girl's voice.

I froze.

"H-help," she repeated, this time in faltering Polish.

Hesitantly, I descended the ladder. The rungs groaned beneath my weight, and one rod snapped in my nervous grip. Even after touching down, I continued to flex my fingers anxiously as I approached the figure slumped at the other end of the barn.

I had only caught glimpses of the girl before, through knot-holes in the outer wall and cracks in the floorboards. But I recognized her voice and the wheat-blond hair that wisped around her soft, oval face. She sat on the floor with her legs spread limply and her back pressed against the barn door, already a puddle of melting snow muddying the dirt and sawdust beneath her. As I drew closer, her eyes slowly lifted, the pupils so dilated, only a thin ring of hazel remained.

"You must be Živilė," I said, offering a tentative smile. Ezra had said she was my friend, after all, or would be soon enough.

She didn't answer. I balked at her silence, conscious of my exposed limbs and the mark upon my brow. Ezra had given me a linen summer dress, but no shoes and no socks. Over the months, the fabric had gotten soiled with dust and chalk.

"I'm Vera," I added helpfully.

Her chest rose and fell in heavy breaths. Closer now, it dawned on me that something was wrong. Something was terribly wrong. Blood bubbled from a corner of her mouth and ran down her chin, and more of the liquid sopped the front of her gingham skirt. I stared, fixated by the dark, glistening stain as it spread lower, gathering in a puddle in her lap.

"What happened?" I asked, sinking to my knees beside her. My voice shook with unease. "A-Are you all right?"

Her gaze slowly lifted to my brow. She reached up, but if she meant to touch my forehead, her aim fell short and her fingers traced over my cheek instead. Trailed down. Pressed against the smooth, still curve of my throat, where a pulse should've been. Hot, sticky liquid dewed on my surface. I swallowed hard. Blood.

"Angel," she whispered.

"No," I said, but her gaze was straying, and her fingers eased downward. Briefly, she snagged hold of my blouse, and I placed my hand over hers to hold her steady, but she was already beginning to tip sideways.

The girl collapsed to the ground, her hand clutched in my own, fingers limp but still warm. Her blond hair spread out in the soiled sawdust, eyes bronzed in the glow of the setting sun.

"Are you..." I trailed off. Her gaze remained fixated on a distant space.

Dead. I moistened my lips, testing the clay of my inner cheek between my teeth. So, this was what it meant to be dead.

"We know you're in there," a man called from outside, speaking in Lithuanian. My body froze in absolute stillness. "It's better if you come out. It'll be quicker."

Something clenched deep within me. A feeling I slowly recognized as rage.

As the barn door eased open, I lowered the dead girl's hand to her side and rose to my feet. Even as the man crossed the threshold, I was already closing the distance between us, barely even registering his features—closely-cropped gray hair and hard blue eyes, a mouth so thin and bloodless it could've been a gash carved in stone.

That mouth fell open as I came in close. As I reached him, he veered against the barn door with a low cry of surprise and raised his hand.

He held a pistol. The sight jarred a memory free—a dark-haired boy holding a weapon much like this one, not aiming it at my body, but extending it to me by its barrel. An offering.

A gunshot rang out as the man pulled the trigger. No pain. Just immense pressure, and the dimpling of my flesh. I looked down.

The bullet had torn through my dress and left a bloodless hole in the clay of my stomach. I could feel it still inside me, a hot wedge of metal pushing against my insides.

Slowly, the bullet emerged as the clay began to fill the hole. I caught it in my cupped palm—a misshapen lead slug slick with mud.

"What in the world?" the man whispered hoarsely, the gun trembling in his hand. He pulled the trigger again, but his arm was shaking so badly the bullet shot harmlessly over my shoulder and punched a hole in the barn wall.

Rage rose in my core at the sight of his terror. I strode forward. This. This was why I had been created.

He tried shooting me a third time, but the hammer fell on an empty chamber. Before he had a chance to reload, I had covered the few steps between us. He dropped his gun and reached for a sheathed dagger on his belt. As he began to draw the blade, I seized his wrist. He tried prying my hand off. I grabbed his other arm and drove him against the wall.

His head slammed into the wood with an audible crack. Once, twice, three times, I hammered him into the wall until warm droplets splattered across my face. I tasted them in my mouth. Blood. When I released him, he collapsed to the floor as though he were nothing more than clay himself, his mark blotted out.

Some remnant of Chaya's instinct remained inside me. Her

rage had been what drove me to ram the stranger into the wall, but it was her wariness that made me slip his black overcoat from his body and draw it around myself. The hem was so long, it nearly dragged to my feet. I tore the silver pins from his lapel and stuffed them in my pocket with the white shoulder band emblazoned with the words *Pagalbinės policijos tarnyba*. Auxiliary Police Service.

His shoes were too big for me, but I took them anyway and stuffed the toes with the man's socks. Something told me that I needed to conceal myself. Though Ezra had shaped me in human form, no one in my inherited memories had Hebrew inked upon their brow or lines of text snaking down their limbs and torso. The marks, I sensed, were something completely unique to me.

Outside, snow dappled the barren earth. I stopped in the barn's threshold and craned my head upward, stunned by the sky's vastness. It stretched on farther than I could have fathomed, dappled with a mist of stars.

I had never seen it like this. It looked so much different compared to the fragmented memories I inherited, so much bigger.

Veils of fog screened the night. No lights. A forest cradled the field to the east, the pines crested by a scimitar of a moon. To the west, a small log building crouched low against the earth.

Near the paddock, a massive, wheeled machine purred quietly, wisps of smoke wafting from the pipe protruding from its rear. It was half wood and half metal. Not a sleigh or cart, but a...

A *truck*. The word came into my mind suddenly, from the

dark. Yes. A truck. Chaya had seen them before, driven into town by soldiers.

A second man leaned against the cab, his back facing me.

"Why two gunshots, Lukas?" He spoke in low, drawling Lithuanian. "Were you that lousy of a shot? Come on, let's get searching. The sooner we find those books, the sooner we'll be able to get out of this damn cold."

With a chuckle, he began to turn. His smile slipped from his lips at the sight of me, but by then I was already closing the distance between us, arm cocked back. No hesitation.

My fist drove against the side of his head with a gristly crack, and I felt the surface of his scalp give way beneath my knuckles, crater inward. The blow whipped him sideways and his face struck the metal door, leaving a bloody smear. Before he hit the ground, I was already striding to the truck's cab. I yanked the door open and leaned inside. Empty.

"Ezra?" I called to the night, turning back to the log building. "Tomas?"

Nothing.

A fourth man lay near the edge of the field, facedown in the snow. His hair was several shades lighter than Ezra's, slick with blood.

"Tomas," I whispered.

Swiveling in a circle, I scanned the field for another motionless body. There were two pairs of wheel tracks in the mud, and the overlapping crescents of footprints. But no Ezra. Just silence, and the night closing in on me.

Anxiously, I hurried toward the only other structure in sight, the farmhouse. Painted flowers adorned the shutters, the petals peeling off from age. Ice encrusted the metal roof and gathered in points along its eaves.

Within the home, dark and deserted rooms confronted me. I traced my fingertips over the masonry stove's still-warm surface. In my mind's eye, I recalled another kitchen, smaller than this one but with a similar farmhouse stove. A phantom taste rose on my tongue, something sweet and yeasty, and I closed my eyes, trying to pair a word or image with the memory. No luck. The only thing to come to me was a feeling, a warmth in my chest that faded the moment I opened my eyes again.

A cast-iron pan of porridge had been left on the stove to cool. I remembered Ezra eating kasha in the hayloft, wisps of steam snaking from the bowl. At the memory of him, fear folded over me like the wings of ravens. I lurched through the house, his name tearing from my lips. The sound of my voice—*her voice, hers*—bounced off the walls, echoing through me as wild as the roar of the Vokė River.

It was a small, scrunched house even tinier than the barn. Two rooms rested across from each other, the beds made and unused, now never to be used. A rickety wooden ladder led to the attic. By the time I reached the space above, my fear had grown into a nameless, howling terror. Wooly darkness pressed down on me, the cold air heavy with the musk of wood rot and dust.

I wanted Ezra back. I wanted to see him so badly. I wanted my—

"Tati!" I barreled through the heaps of boxes and crates, gagging on the dust that coated my tongue. Strange that the dust should smother me; it was just more of what was inside me.

At the end of the attic, I splayed my palms over the hewn log walls and twisted around. Not here. He wasn't here.

"Tati!"

I don't want to die.

This panic and desperation, and the name for father that welled like blood from where the tongue was rooted to my lower jaw, they did not belong to me. They were Chaya's, some remnant of a childhood terror, waking from a nightmare and searching for her papa in the night. Yet the fear seized me just the same, spurring me from the attic in such a frenzy the ladder rungs splintered beneath my grip. I cracked the final rung in two with my heel, landed hard on my rear, twisted onto all fours, fled.

I loped across the ravaged wheat field, my ankles and wrists buried deep in the mud and snow. As I reached the tree line, I remembered how to walk on two feet and stumbled onto my legs. The glow of the nearby homesteads grated at me like steel picks, and I forsook the light for the forest's shadowy depths. No sooner had I passed under the pines' quaking limbs than I darted out again, gasping for air I didn't need, harried by the memory of being hunted.

I crossed through one field then another, scaling over the rickety fence dividing them. My hand strayed to my chest. Though the bullet had torn through my stomach, I expected to encounter a second hole over my left breast, only this one guttering hot blood. Somehow, feeling my skin, as smooth and cold as the layer of snow cast over the fields, calmed me.

The farther I strayed from the barn, the more the terror dissolved into a black, silent place inside of me, until I collapsed to the ground in an exhausted heap. I could keep going until

I wore down my boots into scraps, but it was my mind that ached from the strain of it.

Everything was so large and searingly bright, even in the darkness. Stars sprawled across the clear sky, and the moon hung as sharp and flinty as Ezra's tools.

Lights glinted from the windows of houses in the distance. Now that my initial panic had faded, a part of me felt drawn to the glow, but I couldn't bring myself to do much more than kick out my feet, making a hollow for myself in the brush. The ice-coated branches cradled me, lulling me into a vague, dreamless haze. I wanted to find Ezra, but I was content to stay here awhile.

Hours later, a rumbling drew my gaze skyward. Thunder? It couldn't be. Instead of fading with the passing moments, the noise only grew louder.

An immense form skirted through the night, barely visible against the outer darkness. Spread wings, the gleam of a metallic underbelly.

Trembling, I tucked my body even deeper into the earth and pressed my palm over my forehead to protect my mark. Not a bat. It could only be a bird like in the storybooks Tati—*no, his name is Ezra*—had once told Chaya. The Ziz with a wingspan even greater than the sun.

I waited until the rumble of the creature's flight died in the distance before clambering to my feet. Knee-deep in the cold damp, I lurched forward and rushed from home to home, seeking relief in the puddles of candlelight cast upon the snow.

The last house had its shutters spread. As I passed along its side, a girl pursued me from room to room. Glimpses of her materialized behind windows as dark and glistening as frozen puddles—ashen face like the barn owl that had roosted in the hayloft, dark curls in a wild frenzy, teeth bared, eyes afire with refracted lantern light. I shied away from her, and only when she flinched back as well did I realize I was peering at my own reflection.

I kept going. Over time, the darkness peeled away to shades of gray and dusty pink. A blood clot of a sun surfaced past the trees. In its light, the barrier between the soil and spread branches lost their distinction, like ink running down a page.

As dawn broke, I found refuge in a storage shed built against the outer wall of a barn, a slanted lean-to with a ridged metal roof dripping with icicles. When I squirmed my way over the piles of firewood and barrels, the icicles broke against my back. I curled up in the corner, under the wary gaze of a tabby cat.

The familiar scents of hay and wood shavings should've comforted me, but instead, I stirred with unease. Maybe it was the feeling of running from something, or the crunch of sawdust beneath horses' hooves, but as I settled back against the woodpile, a memory jarred free—*a woman stepping down a barn's dirt aisle, immersed in her lantern's warm golden glow. Not Tomas's barn, but a smaller one, with chickens pecking the floor at her feet.*

A dark-haired boy trailed behind her, tall enough that the woman hardly reached higher than his shoulder. His gray-green twill coat was streaked in dirt and one slick maroon patch of blood on the hem of his sleeve. Fresh blood.

"Keep dragging your feet, Chaya, and the Nazis will catch you," he said teasingly, and the way his voice shaped those Yiddish words, lending them a low, cutting edge, made my face prickle. Even the

more sibilant syllables came out sounding crude and intimate, like a hissed obscenity.

"Akiva, are you sure this is a good idea?" I heard myself whisper, but no, that might've been my voice, but those weren't my words. I'd never seen the barn before. It was her. Chaya.

Though his vague smile remained, it lost its warmth.

"Careful," he said softly. "You don't want to offend our host."

He fell back a step, and the woman continued on.

"Maybe this isn't such a good idea. I mean, we don't even know Mara."

"Don't tell me you're scared. You're supposed to be the greatest among us." His bright blue eyes pierced into me, his gaze burning with an emotion I couldn't name, couldn't put into words. "Chaya the Fearless."

He was close now. Close enough that I could have reached out for him, and I began to even, but then—the scent of damp earth and wood rot collapsed in on me, and I found myself alone again, the memory dissipating like dust, leaving behind only a heaviness in my throat and the unshakable conviction that something precious had just been taken from me. And there was no returning from that.

"Akiva," I whispered, testing the name on my lips. The only time I had heard it in my short life was in Ezra's recounting of the legend of Pardes—four rabbis who entered the orchard of divine knowledge, and just three who left it, and Rabbi Akiva the only one who emerged whole and in peace. Chaya's Akiva might've been named after the rabbi of lore, but something told me that he didn't take after his namesake.

It scared me to know that there was so much inside me, buried out of sight, waiting to be discovered. It felt like disinterring a grave. These memories didn't belong, but they struck me as important. Essential even.

Snow had fallen all night, sometimes in curtains and other times in just trickles. I would never be able to find my way back to the hideaway. By now, my footsteps would be erased, and even the bramble I had crushed in my frantic escape would be lost beneath the smooth, soft mounds.

I felt petrified by uncertainty. I wanted to find Ezra, but what if he had fled the barn at the first gunshots, only to return later in the night? Maybe I should just stay here and wait for him to find me. He would be looking for me, wouldn't he?

Eventually, he would have sent me out into this world, but I wasn't ready yet. He had said so himself.

Hours passed, or perhaps it was just minutes. I wished I had Ezra's pocket watch to track the passage of time, instead of relying on the shifting colors of the sky or the slow, arching ascent of the rising sun.

My stolen coat was encrusted with a camouflage of mud and burrs. I drew empty burlap sacks and handfuls of hay over myself to conceal my body further.

A young brown-haired girl emerged from the house and approached the shed. She passed by me close enough that I could have reached through the gaps between the wall's slats and seized her by the ankle. As she retrieved several split branches from the stack of firewood, I froze in absolute stillness.

The girl's gaze flicked over my hiding place. Her eyes were the color of the sky I had studied for hours through knotholes in the hayloft's walls, a soft and warm blue. I waited until she went back into the house before relaxing my locked limbs.

Later she returned with a pail, and as she passed, she reached inside the container. Without looking at me, she tossed an object in my direction. It landed in the straw, soft and brown, and dented at one end from the impact. As she went to the chicken pen, never once looking at me directly, I picked up the object. Bread. It was the heel end of a loaf, studded with seeds and whole grains. I broke it apart, inhaling the sour, earthy scents of caraway and rye.

The scent awoke an aching need inside me, my limbs quaking from hunger that seemed to pierce all the way to my core. I crammed the bread into my mouth, tearing off massive chunks until I felt my teeth shift from the strain of containing the food. After I swallowed, my jaw eased back into place.

The sensation and slick *pop* of clay jarred me enough that I took smaller bites after that, afraid to test the reliability of this form. Ezra had shaped my features with care and fastidious detail—perhaps even with a bit of the same kishuf his predecessors would have decried as witchcraft—but at some point, even clay must submit to its true nature.

Once I finished, I placed my hand over my stomach. I couldn't feel the bread inside me anymore or even taste it, but the hunger remained, a low and needling urge that scraped away at me. It wasn't hunger in the human sense, not driven by survival, but by a desire that went much deeper. It was the same reason I had yearned so desperately for a mouth, to the point where I would have carved it myself, if I could. I didn't even have a name for it, other than that I ate because I wanted to *be*.

On the way back from the barn, the girl left a pail of water by the stacks of firewood. Our gazes met through the hay.

I'd scattered my bangs over my forehead and cinched my coat collar tight, but I tensed anyway, afraid something else in my features might give away what I was.

She smiled, paused to look around, then stooped under the shed's sloping roof.

"Who are you?" she asked softly. It wasn't until strange sounds bubbled from my lips that I realized she had been speaking—and I was answering—in Lithuanian.

"My name is Vera." I tested the words under my breath once more, my tongue prodding at their sloping form. "Màno vaȓdas Vera," not "ikh heys Vera," or "mam na imię Vera." It felt strange to know I had all these words inside of me, just waiting to resurface like the ink beneath my skin.

"I'm Janina. Are you a Jew?"

I didn't answer at first. I wished that Ezra had given me the words to describe myself, other than golem, other than mere clay and scrap metal and hair and teeth.

"I'm looking for Ezra," I said, once I realized Janina was expecting a response. "Have you seen him?"

She shook her head.

She was very young, younger than Chaya had been when Chaya had died. I doubted she would reach much higher than my armpit. I was even younger still, but it didn't feel that way. My mind brimmed with memories and so many words I struggled to describe. They drifted through my head, shifting and half-formed, like fish underwater.

"You must be cold," Janina said.

"I'm not."

"You'll freeze to death out here."

"No."

She didn't look convinced. Combing snowflakes from her hair, she glanced at the house. "I'll be back. I'll get you a blanket."

As she left, I brushed the hay off me and settled onto my haunches. I rearranged my hair until I was sure it hid my brow then waited. Minutes later, the door to the home opened. I expected Janina to appear, but it was only a man. Instead of approaching the barn, he went down the road.

To pass the time until Janina returned, I tore off slivers of firewood, testing my strength. It was easy to break entire branches in half without meaning to, and more difficult to control myself.

Janina appeared soon after. She was accompanied by a boy who appeared somewhat older, his hand around her shoulder. As she neared, my body tensed. Tears streaked down her flushed face. Upon her cheek, the red imprints of fingers.

I rose to meet them, my hands tightened into fists.

"You need to leave now, Vera," Janina cried, breaking free of the boy's grip. She raced toward me but froze as I stepped from the lean-to.

"Did you do that to her?" I asked the boy. "Did you strike her?"

"No, it was…" His face slackened with shock. "That coat… That's a policeman's coat."

Swallowing hard, Janina continued forward. "I'm sorry. I'm so sorry."

I couldn't tear my gaze away from the welts on her face. I raised my hand to my cheek, jolted by the memory of a forest. As Chaya had run, bramble and low-hanging branches had gouged open her cheek, torn her sleeves, snatched her hair out in fistfuls. She had reached into her pants pocket, fumbled with something hard and cold. Metal. Small slick cylinders had rolled around in her palm—what? What? I could almost visualize them now.

Fingers curled around my arm. I lifted my eyes to the boy's face, stirred from my daze. There was pity in his gaze, but also a hint of distaste. He held me at arm's length.

"She told me you were looking for someone," he whispered, nodding toward the sleet-gray haze mounded on the horizon. "Head south. Head for the Rudniki Forest. I've heard rumors of Jews there."

It wasn't a command, but it compelled me just the same. Frost-caked grass crunched beneath my feet as I took off across the field. There was a kind of joy to be found in the fluid motion of my limbs, the winter chill, the glistening of sunlight across the snow. In the golden midafternoon haze, it was easy to slip free from Chaya's residual terror, like a moth shedding its cocoon. Within time, I felt nothing at all.

CHAPTER 5

THE SUN BEGAN ITS SLOW DESCENT, THE SKY
darkening to shades of blood and egg yolk. A sour wind
picked up, scudding steel-gray clouds across the horizon. I
had avoided the forests as best I could, even the stripped or-
chards. The roads and villages seemed equally dangerous.

Something told me that Ezra would have kept to the fields
and swampland, and that Chaya had, too, when she had still
been alive. I felt as though I was following in the wake of father and daughter, and that buried beneath the fresh snow, I
would find their footprints preserved in the frozen soil, clear
as though carved there.

When night fell, I found shelter in the underbrush, because
that was what Ezra would have done. I didn't know what forest the boy had meant, but on the second day of travel, I forced

myself to enter a small woods when the sun had reached its peak. Not far at first, close enough that I could see the field beyond. Shadows dappled the forest floor. Pine needles glistened with frost, sharp as thorns in the gilded light.

Fear weighed down on me, growing heavier with each step. I expected something to happen, that I would hear footsteps behind me as I descended farther into the woods, and that they would grow louder as the canopy grew thicker. If I reminded myself to breathe like a human being, I might feel a heart hammering beneath my chest, or my searching fingers might encounter a ragged entry wound cratering my right breast.

But the only sounds to greet me were birdsong and the rustling of pine needles, and even in the deepest part of the woods, it wasn't fully dark. The sunlight still managed to find its way between the boughs, passing over me in golden pinpricks.

My dread slowly lifted, until a branch snapped behind me and I swiveled around, palm splayed against my chest, over the memory of a wound.

A young deer stood at the other end of the pine grove, all slim legs and nut-brown fur, its antlers velvety with new growth. For a long, unwavering moment, we stared at each other. Set in its slender face, its eyes were as dark as ink.

The sight of the animal conjured a vague memory from the depths of me—sitting by a campfire, a greasy rib bone clutched in both hands. I closed my eyes just for a moment, trying to solidify Chaya's memory into something closer, something physical. And for only a second, I remembered the crackle of crisp fat, and a taste bloomed on my tongue— meaty like the remnants of blood that had dried in the crevices of my teeth, but rich and warm, and so delicious that my mouth puckered with a strange hunger.

As I stepped forward, the deer slipped between the trees, graceful and elusive, its sleek pelt glistening in the sun. Something about watching the animal's lithe strides awoke a desire within me that I couldn't name. Not hunger, but something more, an emotion that was purely my own.

All I knew was that I wanted to move the way the buck moved, with the elegance of muscles and warm flesh, and before I knew it, I had taken off behind it. After several strides, I bounded forward so that I ran alongside the animal. Instead of fleeing from me, it kept pace like a second shadow, as though we were tied to each other.

When the deer disappeared into the forest's deeper reaches, I found myself alone again, left with an ache that, like the same exhilarating impulse that had led me to follow the animal in the first place, I couldn't put into words.

"Come back," I called to the deer, but it was too late. The quivering branches disrupted by its passage had already begun to still. "Come back. Please... Please."

My voice grew fainter with each 23, until on the final plea, it died into a mere whisper. Silence fell over the glade.

For the rest of the second day, I ventured boldly through forests. It wasn't until midday that I recognized something was *guiding* me, a quiet, buried recollection of this path, these fields, that rotting tree. As dusk descended and the blued shadows lengthened into sooty streaks beneath the pines, I reached the ruins.

The half-buried structures gaped at me from the snow like broken mouths—shoddy dugouts hewn from pine trunks and constructed so that only their tin pipe chimneys and busted doors were exposed. One zemlyanka had collapsed under the weight of the hillside, but the others were stable enough that I could enter if I hunched down. Bullet holes peppered the walls of each one, and in the corner of the final shelter, I came across a skeleton still enclosed within a shabby fur coat, the lapels studded with shards of its own skull.

Squatting by the crumpled form, I traced my fingertips along the smooth curve of its jawbone. Coils of golden-red hair clung to what still remained. Even defleshed, I *knew* her.

"Yael," I whispered, testing the name on my lips. For an instant, Chaya's memories poured into my mind. I caught a hint of woodsmoke and roasted meat, felt the rich smatter of deer fat burst on my tongue, and saw her—Yael, radiant in her tawny coat, her strawberry blond hair rippling down her shoulder as she leaned over the fire to turn the scrawny doe on its spit. Then the darkness sank in, and I was alone again, grasping futilely at the memory that had died as instantaneously as a thunderclap.

There had been others around the fire with Yael and Chaya. Others who had hidden in these shelters, talking and dreaming and laughing and sobbing. Two males—one a child with light-brown hair and laughter like the pealing of cowbells, and the other as old as Chaya or slightly older, and tall enough that even in memory I felt dwarfed by him. I shivered at the recollection of resting against a log wall much like this one, the bark gritty against my back as the older boy leaned over me, his breath hot on the side of my throat.

"Chaya," he had said in a low, husky murmur, trailing his lips down my collarbone. His unkempt hair brushed against my cheek, as dark and soft as the stroke of raven feathers, and all I could do was grasp onto his back and dig my nails in, like if I let go, a force more powerful than gravity would rip us apart.

The memory struck me with such brute weight, I swiveled around, my fingers pressed over the side of my neck. I half expected the boy to be standing there behind me, with his rifle slung on a strap over his shoulder and his ice-blue eyes piercing into me. Moonlight cascaded through the zemly-anka's opening, falling on barren earth.

Not here. He wasn't here.

Just the memory broke something inside me, and before I knew it, I had fled from the dugout. I didn't know if I wanted to find the dark-haired boy or escape from the memory of him. Whatever the compulsion, it drove me just the same. I would've loped on all fours again if I had to. The night seemed even blacker than before, the trees closing in like the jaws of a behemoth.

I had been here before. Not while immersed in the flood-waters of the Vokė, but in the body of a human. In *her* body. Pounding heart, sore muscles. I could feel it swelling—desperation and terror, exhilaration and primal desire, all rising within me in a muddled tempest.

I broke into a run, scraping my fingers over the bark of the surrounding pines, digging up clods of dirt in my wake, driven by an urgency that bordered on delirium.

Here. *It happened here.*

My tongue traced over the rounded edges of my teeth. The taste of blood gnashed in the back of my throat, sour and abrupt. This was wrong. This was all wrong.

Something happened to me here, I wanted to scream. *Something* happened *to me*.

I missed Ezra. I wanted to curse at him and slam my fists against his chest until he *understood*. He should have done better. He should have known that emotions and pain were not necessary for vengeance, that I could have carried out his will just as easily if the memory of Chaya's death hadn't been rooted to my scalp and gumline.

I broke free of the tangle of pines and emerged into a field. I froze ankle-deep in the snow. My chest rose and fell in shallow gasps, and I clenched the space above my left breast until I was nearly certain that a pounding heart lay buried beneath the smooth clay.

Just as my terror began to diminish, the night's silence was disrupted by the grating roar of the metallic-winged Ziz.

Fires appeared one by one in the field ahead. For a moment, it seemed as though they had manifested by their own will, like lightning. Then my eyes adjusted to their flickering glows, and I made out three figures. Two stood over small piles of kindling they had set alight, and the third held a horse by its reins as it shuffled uneasily, steam hazing from its flared nostrils. The Ziz's rumble heightened into a roar.

My limbs locked in place. Were they *calling* it?

The Ziz that appeared in the sky was smaller than the first, and its wings were shaped differently. As it descended over us, it vomited a spew of rubble from its underbelly, shapeless forms that unfurled white blossoms as they fell.

I stared. No. Not blossoms, toadstool caps, or torn parchment. Those were fabric sheets, each one roped to wooden boxes. They were…

"Parachutes," I heard myself whisper. I tested the word on my tongue twice more before committing it to memory. An unspeakable relief came over me. Yes, those were parachutes, and that wasn't a Ziz at all, was it? It wasn't even alive.

"Airplane," I blurted out uncontrollably, and laughed. Somewhere deep inside me, all these words were waiting to be found, thanks to Chaya.

Even before the first parachute landed, the strangers were already burying their fires beneath wet earth and snow. They wore shapeless white cloaks smeared with mud, mimicries of the winter forest that could have just as easily been sewn from the same parachutes that crumpled to the ground.

Once all the fires were snuffed, the men hurriedly loaded the crates into the back of the sleigh. The containers must have contained something precious for the strangers to rush like that. Curiosity piqued, I walked to the crate closest to me, an outlier that had landed only meters from the forest's edge.

"Hey!" a man shouted.

As I turned, he opened fire.

Gunshots whizzed past me. I threw myself to the ground and pressed both hands over my forehead. My inked mark was the only thing of importance. He could make piecemeal of my limbs, but as long as the word for truth remained, I would be bound to this world.

As the gunshots ceased, I remained where I lay. If I pretended to be dead, they would move on or get close enough for me to attack them.

"Someone was over there," the man said. "I saw him."

"We need to leave now," another said.

"Boy, check it out."

Footsteps crunched through the frosty soil. I remained in absolute stillness, until I sensed the boy standing close enough for me to touch him. I lunged to my feet and snatched his rifle by its barrel, forcing the muzzle toward the ground.

He froze at the sight of me, his fingers loosening from around the gun's barrel and trigger guard. Dark hair streamed over his chiseled cheeks and brow. The full moon emerged from behind the clouds, exposing a face that could have been handsome, in another life, in another time. Instead, its frosty glow revealed all the cruelties enacted against him—a narrow nose crooked from a recent break; one jagged scar twisting down his cheek and another splitting his left brow; lids bruised from sleeplessness, framing eyes such a pale blue they were almost lupine, with the same feral sheen.

At the sight of his face, my entire body went slack, and my raised fist slowly unfurled.

I recalled crouching in a dark dugout, sharing a cigarette and a small bottle of rank samogon; my mouth puckered in memory. His own mouth had been swollen, his lower lip split; now, only a hooked scar remained. Then, as I took a step toward him, I remembered a biting winter night, wind and snow tearing at the soil-covered walls, and his body curled around me, his hand fluttering against me. Against *her*.

And his name. His name was—

"Akiva," I whispered.

CHAPTER 6

AS PALE AND SHARP AS STEEL PICKS, HIS EYES
pierced me to the core. He stood motionless, staring at me
with his features petrified and his rifle hanging loosely on its
sling, finger still curled around the trigger.

"You're dead," he whispered, and the spark of joy I'd felt
at the sight of him snuffed out in an instant. Of course, it was
Chaya's emotion. It was her tears that welled in my eyes, her
tears that trickled down in my cheeks—so little water, but I
was afraid they'd wash my skin away and expose to him that
there was nothing beneath.

"Kiva, what are you doing?" one of the men demanded.

"Don't shoot!" Akiva turned around suddenly and stepped
in front of me, blocking me with his body. Letting his rifle

hang on its sling, he raised a hand in the air, palm out. "I know this girl. She was a member of my otriad."

"Step aside," the man growled, stepping forward.

Akiva's shoulders stiffened, and his raised hand fell. "But—"

"She's a witness. If the Nazis catch her, she'll tell them the direction we went."

"She can join us, Dukov. She's a skilled fighter and one of the best shooters I've seen."

"I thought you said that everyone in your otriad was killed," Dukov said, and my nails dug into my palm reflexively. Akiva's jaw tightened. The tension in the air thickened with each word. "Were you lying to us?"

Memories pulsed through my mind like the flash of muzzle blasts: the skeleton lying in the corner of the zemlyanka, its furred collar scattered with shards of its own skull; Yael laughing at a joke as she dressed a deer, her hands wrist-deep in the glistening viscera; the boy-child fleeing through the trees until a gunshot flung him forward, drove him to the earth, head coming apart, motionless; the bullet holes studding the shelter's hewn-log walls; pressed against that same wall with my fingers tangled in Akiva's unkempt hair and his mouth drawing a burning trail of heat down my midriff, lower, lower...

The past felt so close now, as if it were suspended in the air around us, frozen still. These were the memories Chaya had clung to, the ones that had survived after everything else decayed. This was what it meant to feel alive.

Akiva's eyes hardened into ice, his hand now lowered to his side, fingertips hovering over the stock of his rifle. "I'm not shooting her."

Dukov stepped forward. "Are you disobeying orders?"

Akiva shifted his rifle into a firing position, his chin raised in defiance. The two men responded by drawing their own weapons as the horses shuffled in agitation, straining on their leads.

"Run," Akiva said without looking at me, his finger curling around the trigger.

Gunshots shattered the night. I couldn't tell who shot first, only that the crate splintered as bullets pierced it, and another slug passed close enough to Akiva's left arm that it *embedded* in mine. With their frantic neighing rising into an almost humanlike shriek, the horses bolted, dragging the sleigh erratically behind them.

Dukov collapsed to the snow, a slick shadow already blooming across the front of his white cloak. As the other soldier opened fire and Akiva's rifle clicked like a dry throat, I lunged in front of him.

My body moved on its own, driven by the same muscle memory that had caused his name to form on my lips, but something about this felt *right*. Felt like it belonged to me.

Bullets pierced my limbs and back. I buried my face against his shoulder and closed my eyes. In the darkness, the violent impacts felt inconsequential, as though the lead slugs were nothing more than stones skipped across the river's surface. They could not touch me down below. They could not harm me.

A gunshot rang through the air, so deafeningly that I thought one of the soldier's stray bullets had caught me in the head and clanged against the metal plate that formed the bowl of my skull. Then I caught a whiff of an acrid odor—

burnt gunpowder—and as I pulled back, I saw the revolver Akiva held in a white-knuckled grip. Smoke trailed from the muzzle.

The night had gone dead silent, as if the gunshot had torn an entry wound into the night itself, creating a breach into some deeper void. Slowly, he lowered his hand to his side.

"I've got you. Hey. I've got you." With his other arm, he reached out to steady me, like he thought I'd fall at any moment though my footing remained firm. I swiveled around, prepared for more violence, except the second man had joined the first on the ground. Unmoving except for a black line of liquid inching across the snow. When I turned back to Akiva, confusion darkened his gaze.

"What were you thinking?" he demanded, and the anger in his voice took me almost as aback as the way it *hurt* me, like his question had actual physical force to it. The bullets had been easy to ignore, even now as they emerged from my back and plopped to the ground, but his razored words pierced somewhere deeper.

His hand slid down my arm. His skin was shockingly warm to the touch, so warm I had to resist the impulse to pull away, as if his heat alone might crack me.

"Are you hurt? Were you shot?"

A hint of fear blunted the anger in his voice. But it wasn't for himself. It was for me, wasn't it?

The realization made my tongue feel thick and heavy. I searched for what to say, but I couldn't even speak.

"This is so like you, Chaya, to—" His words caught in his throat, and his jaw latched tight in an instant, as if he'd said too much, or not enough.

For a long moment, neither of us moved or spoke, as though

the simplest gesture might shatter us. Then he released me and stepped back, his movements stiff and abrupt. His wolf-pale gaze took me in—the stolen coat, my exposed hands, the tangled curls that hung over my brow, the ribbons of calligraphy twined up my collarbone.

"No," he said. "You're not her."

That wasn't entirely true. There were parts of Chaya still inside me. It was her tears that caused moisture to well in my eyes. When I swatted the droplets away, my fingertips came back streaked with muddy water.

"You're not her." He said it one more time, firmly now and slow, as if reminding himself of the fact. "She's dead."

"My name is Vera," I said at last, which felt like the safest answer. I wanted to lay claim to my identity, and just telling him my name meant taking a step away from Chaya. Even if it was her tongue and teeth that formed these words.

"That's an old SS coat. Who'd you take it from—a Panzer tankman or someone from the Schuma? More importantly, why do you look like Chaya?" He narrowed his eyes. "Do you know her? Are you related to her?"

His barrage of questions disoriented me, leaving me feeling as though I was tottering on uneven ground. The only question I could truly answer was the last one.

"Yes. No." I took a deep breath, just muscle memory, but it soothed me anyway. Something told me I could trust him. Chaya did. I *had* to. "I'm a golem."

"Yeah, and I'm the Messiah." Akiva chuckled—a dry, mirthless sound. He returned his revolver to the holster on his belt and drew a small metal box from his coat pocket, switching it out with the one attached to his rifle.

"It's true," I insisted.

"Sorry, but I don't believe in golems any more than I believe in dybbukim." His gaze bored into me, colder than ever. He had hardened himself, buried his shock beneath apathy. "Who are you, really? Some sister or cousin? How did you know my name? And what's with those tattoos? Did someone do that to you?"

"Like I said, I'm a golem."

"There's no such thing."

Akiva's blunt refusal to acknowledge my existence filled me with rage. I felt smothered by his words, like if he said them enough times, they would become true and I would collapse into a pile of lifeless dirt. I wanted to seize him and shake him until he looked at me and saw me for what I really was. Because once I hurt him, he would not be able to deny my true nature.

"I am right here," I said tightly.

"I'm not arguing that you don't exist," he said. "Only that you're not what you say you are."

He was about to say more when a low purr interrupted the forest's stillness. It was a noise softer than the rumble of the airplane, but something about it must've alarmed Akiva, because he swore under his breath and turned away from me.

I stiffened as I recognized the sound. It was the same noise that had preceded the gunshots on Tomas's farm.

As a pair of searing lights riffled through the trees like parting hands, the purr's source dawned on me. It was a vehicle. And that noise…

"Engine," I whispered, testing the new word the sound

had drawn from my tongue. Yes, that was the sound of an engine, wasn't it?

"We don't have time for this. Someone's coming." Akiva crossed the field at a run, stopping only long enough to pry the rifle out from beneath Dukov's body. He snagged the satchel slung over Dukov's shoulder and stole the man's cap as well, even though the rabbit fur glistened with drops of blood. When I came to a halt beside him, he pushed the rifle into my hands. "Take this."

"What about the horses?" I called as Akiva raced toward the tree line.

"There's no time!"

Shifting the rifle's strap over my shoulder, I followed him into the forest, crunching through the snow. Like all humans, he was aggravatingly slow, and if I hadn't made a conscious effort to meter my pace, I would've overtaken him. The rifle's wooden stock slapped against my back with each powerful stride, its weight familiar and strangely soothing. Akiva's harsh breathing and footsteps was even more so.

Somehow, knowing Akiva was ahead of me, knowing he was still alive, made it easier to enter the forest once more. Besides, I wanted to put some distance between myself and the scatter of ruined dugouts.

Snow pooled in sporadic piles beneath the frost-rimed canopy, and a fine grit sifted from the pine branches. I lingered several steps behind him, glancing back only once to make sure we weren't being followed. When I turned back ahead, he had lurched to a halt, gripping onto a tree as he panted for breath.

"Are you okay?" I asked, stopping beside him. His pale eyes locked on me.

"I'm fine." He wiped his mouth with the back of his hand and righted his fur cap, which had begun to slip sideways. "Let's just keep moving."

"Are we going home?" I asked as we continued through the trees, not at a run like before, but a brisk and urgent walk. It took a moment for the words to dawn on me, and I locked my jaw, feeling betrayed by my own tongue. Home to the dugouts, I meant. To the home Akiva and Chaya had made for themselves.

Akiva flinched as if I had struck him, and then laughed, faintly and in clear discomfort. "Oh. You mean to the Soviet outpost?"

I nodded, grateful for his assumptions.

"No. They have a camp in the forest to the south, along the Visinčia River, but I can't go back there. Not with Dukov and Kairis dead, and not without the supplies the Red Army air-dropped to us. There's a shelter not far from here. We can wait there until this storm blows over."

"You want me to come with you?"

"Assuming you don't want whoever was back there to kill you," he said blandly, before adding with a touch of newfound wariness, "That is, if you even can be killed."

I didn't answer. It felt like bad luck to talk about that, and besides, I didn't want him to get any ideas.

"So, you're a...golem," he said as we continued into the forest's depths. The underbrush cleared out, the pines' black trunks rising around us like charred pillars.

"That's right."

Akiva gave me nothing, not even a smile. He was like me,

I sensed. Hardening himself to clay, because there was power in feeling nothing.

Just when I thought he wouldn't respond, he reached out and placed his hand over mine. The sudden motion startled me so much, I nearly jerked my hand away. His fingers lingered against my bare palm, tracing over the calligraphy that wound its way up my wrist.

"Your skin is cold." His ice-blue eyes shifted to me. "Do you even have a pulse?"

I didn't respond. He kept his fingers against my inner wrist for several moments longer, and that was answer enough.

"There are bullet holes in your back, you know," he added nonchalantly, as if he scarcely thought it important to point out. But I could tell from the way he looked at me that he was taking everything in, creating an understanding of me a piece at a time, like sculpting a shape from clay. "I saw them as we were running."

"It's all right. I felt the bullets enter, but there's no pain." There was just the memory of pain and the vague, disconcerting knowledge that I *should* feel something. "The holes will close up soon."

"I see." Akiva turned his gaze back ahead, and a tense silence fell over us. I could tell from the way he scanned the trees, he felt unsettled. I just couldn't tell if it was because of me or our surroundings.

"So, you believe me then?"

"I think it's hard to argue with bullet holes and no pulse." He took off his hat and held it out to me.

I stared at it, arching an eyebrow dubiously. "Do you want me to hold that for you?"

He sighed. "It's for the 'emet' on your forehead. So the snow doesn't wash it away."

"It won't." I traced a finger over the letters to show him. "The ink's already set."

"But in the stories…"

"The aleph has to be gouged or broken." I knew I shouldn't be telling him this, but I couldn't deny the trust I had in him. Chaya would've been just as forthcoming. "It can't just be rubbed off. Same with the rest of the calligraphy."

He nodded slowly, seeming to process it. "So, you're basically a giant porcelain doll then."

The comparison jarred another one of Chaya's memories free—a perfect little French doll with blond corkscrew curls and real lashes, resting in Ezra's outstretched hand. His face was softer than I'd ever seen it in my own short life, his cheeks less angular. No wrinkles; the only lines to bracket his mouth were the dimples his smile cut into his cheeks.

"Happy birthday, Chaya," Ezra had said, and even now the memory of her disappointment hit me like whiplash. As she'd taken it from him, she'd whined—

"It doesn't even look like me," I whispered, testing her words on my tongue. Ten years past, maybe more, and even buried in my clay her fingernails still recalled the doll's icy smoothness. I tried to remember what had happened to that birthday present, but already the memory was beginning to sink out of sight, and the emotions along with it.

Akiva frowned. "What?"

"I'm not made of porcelain."

"Good thing, too, or else those bullets might've shattered you." A dry hint of sarcasm colored his voice, only to disappear as he stopped and studied me. No humor now in his gaze, just a cold, almost feral wariness, like one predator try-ing to sniff out another. "If you're a golem, then why do you look like Chaya?"

"Ezra, my creator, was her father," I said.

"He built you in her image."

I nodded.

"Tell me everything," Akiva said, as we kept going. I did, and he listened in silence, his features unmoving.

I *could* have told him everything, including where my eyes and teeth had come from. But then I thought back to when Ezra had given me my eyes. My first sight of his face was a visage twisted in disgust and horror.

He had turned away from me and covered his eyes behind his hands. Sobbing, he'd called his creation of me repugnant, an abomination, a disgrace, a crime against God.

Ezra had given me ears, but he must have not realized I could understand him, or maybe he just hadn't cared. Each word had pierced me like a blade.

Compared to him, Akiva appeared undisturbed by my presence. If anything, there was almost something *hungry* in his gaze, as if he was taking in every word I said and wanted more. When I got to the part about the soldiers at the barn, he chuckled.

"Shame you weren't created sooner. Just think about the body count you could've racked up back in '42."

That wouldn't have been possible, at least not last summer, when Chaya had still been alive. I hated to think how Akiva would react if I told him the truth about my creation. There was nothing bad about ordinary golems, those created from only mud and water, but I was something else entirely.

There was so much I wanted to ask him, but at the same

time, the past terrified me. It felt like retreating into the Vokė River's floodwaters, being washed away, held under. I sensed that the more we talked about Chaya, the more I would erode parts of myself—the long summer days spent in the hayloft, Ezra's wry smiles, the agonized sobs that racked him deep in the night—until my identity was replaced with her memories and the sad, bitter longing that persisted even now.

A harsh gust swept over us as we continued forward. Akiva's body trembled ever so slightly, and his teeth clicked together until he clenched his jaw, stilling the movement. His face was so pale, even his lips seemed blued.

It dawned on me he must be cold. The winter's chill was delightful to me, but unlike him, I didn't have blood or a beating heart. Even though I heard ice crackle within me as I moved, the deep-freeze didn't slow or stiffen me.

I unbuttoned my coat and slipped it off. Akiva just stared at me. At my arms. At the calligraphy winding down to my dress collar.

אֵל-נְקָמוֹת ה' אֵל נְקָמוֹת הוֹפִיעַ

"'O Lord, Thou God to whom vengeance belongeth, Thou God to whom vengeance belongeth, shine forth,'" he read softly, the Hebrew faltering on his lips. "That's from Tehillim, isn't it?"

I nodded, pleased he recognized the verse.

"Those letters… They cover your entire body?"

"Almost. Ezra had brought the Torahs and documents from his shul into hiding with him. When he laid me out to dry on the papers, the ink set into my skin." It wasn't part of the ritual that had created me, as far as I was aware, but I sensed it hadn't quite been just the result of inattention either. When Ezra had pulled back the layers of vellum to discover the calligraphy had imprinted itself on my surface, he could have simply sanded it away to reveal the unblemished clay farther beneath. But he had left the ink there.

And it wasn't just religious texts. Any written materials evoking the name of God had been stored in the shul's genizah for eventual burial, so in the sprawl of calligraphy left upon my body, I had discovered other fragments as well—on my ankle, part of a marriage contract, adorned with a Lion of Judah and floral motif that snaked to my heel; on my side, an incomplete love note from one stranger to another; running down my back, a Kabbalistic tree of life, the ancient ink faded to sepia in places.

"He never wanted you to blend in, did he?" Akiva asked, as if sensing my own suspicions.

"That wasn't what I was made for." I held out my coat. "Take this. Your cloak doesn't look warm."

"It's not for warmth, it's for camouflage." Akiva hesitated for only a moment before taking it from my hands. Underneath his cloak, he was wearing a coat of his own, but he drew the stolen garment over his shoulders like a blanket. "Thank you, Vera."

Thank you. A smile twitched on my lips. I turned back ahead, embarrassed to show how his gratitude pleased me. I had never been thanked before.

No sooner had I taken two steps before Akiva said my name again. I looked over to find him cupping the handful of pins I had torn from the coat's lapels and shoulders and stowed in its pockets. He had picked one from the pile.

"The man you took this coat from," he said, studying the badge in the moonlight. "He was a member of the Schuma, the Auxiliary Police. Some still wear the blue police uniform, but a lot of the newly commissioned officers wear these old black Schutzstaffel uniforms, now that the Schutzstaffel has switched to the gray ones. But this badge is…new."

ᛗ

The symbol taunted me, embedding itself like a splinter in my mind. I took it from him, turning it around in my palm. With a shiver, I recalled the dream I'd had after Ezra had put me to sleep—the German soldier in gray, the pistol pointed at my chest, its muzzle like a gaping wound. The badges on his jacket collar had glinted in the moonlight.

That's a shame, he'd said, stepping forward. *I hate killing women.*

And then he'd pulled the trigger.

"Vera?"

I flinched, looking up at Akiva.

"Your hand," he said.

I had gripped the badge so tightly, the pin back had driven into my palm to its base. When I tore the needle free, it took only a second or two for the puncture to fill in. Akiva just watched, his expression muted. He'd probably seen worse, and at least this was bloodless.

"What does the symbol mean?" I asked, handing it back to him.

He licked his lips absently, still staring at my palm. Slowly, his gaze lifted to my face. "I don't know, but I don't like it. The last thing we need is another division like the Einsatzgruppen lurking around here."

"Einsatzgruppen," I echoed softly. The word felt oddly familiar on my tongue, like the shape of something that I had once forgotten. But there was no history of the word in my memory, not in a dozen memories, and even Chaya's associations came back blurred and half-formed.

"They're the Nazi death squads," Akiva said, and though his face remained cold and composed, his voice dripped with hatred. "After the Soviets retreated, they came on the heels of the infantry. The Lithuanians welcomed them as liberators."

Something in my face must have betrayed my confusion, because without prompting, he told me of what Ezra had only hinted at. Instead of sidestepping the issue, circling it as warily as a stalking wolf, Akiva went straight for the throat, laying down the facts with the brutal swiftness of a killing blow.

Nearly two years under Nazi occupation, tens of thousands of Jews missing and yet more executed. Talk of mass graves in the Ponary Forest, graves the victims had been forced to dig themselves. Even before the Nazi forces had assumed control, pogroms and massacres had spread through Lithuania, instigated by their own countrymen.

I had only known the area's Jewish community through the scribes' memories and Ezra's own stories. And yet, upon hearing about the deportations and murders, I felt as though something had been ripped from me and smashed underfoot. I clenched my teeth, raked by bitter anguish for what had been, for what was no more, for what I had never known.

"It used to scare me, knowing I might not survive this war," Akiva said, his lupine eyes boring into mine. "But now, what keeps me awake at night, is asking myself 'what if I do, what if I do, what will be left?'"

CHAPTER 7

WE TOOK SHELTER IN AN ABANDONED FISHING shack along the Merkys. During the summer, it must've been a pleasant spot, but the river was frozen over this time of year, and even after latching the shutters, the windows rattled with each gust. There was no stove, but Akiva built a small blaze in the fireplace using newspaper and twigs.

The moment the fire was burning steadily, he settled heavily on the floorboards and turned his attention to the satchel he'd retrieved from Dukov's body. He pawed through it, snagged a dented tin flask from its depths, and took two urgent gulps before continuing his search.

After hitting the bag's bottom, Akiva upturned its contents onto the dusty floorboards—a few coins that rolled into the shadows, a bottle of oil, another small metal tin. He searched through the jumble and shook his head in disgust, swearing under his breath. "No medicine. Great. Not even ointment."

But there was half a sausage wrapped in some grease-stained brown paper, which disappeared down his throat so quickly I wasn't even sure if he'd chewed it or just swallowed. The heel of black rye bread he found soon followed, though not before he used the crust end to sop up some grayish lard from the tin. He washed the food down with another shaky sip from the canteen, rubbed a dollop more of the tallow into his chapped lips and wind-chaffed cheeks, then stripped out of his camouflage cloak. His brown quilted jacket and sweater quickly followed, set to warm with his gloves by the fire as he rolled up the shirt beneath.

My teeth clenched as the firelight glazed across his naked skin. If the scars on Akiva's face were bad, they had nothing on the marks that covered the rest of his body. A patina of bruises crawled across his rib cage, dappled yellow and purple. Scars carved a warpath down his lean torso—puckered shrapnel marks, a burn the size of my palm, the sunken knot of a bullet hole.

A pad of bloody bandages had been stuck to his side with thin strips of fabric—*tape, it's medical tape*—and the skin around the area was so bruised, it was nearly black. The trembling in his fingers had died down somewhat, but began anew as he peeled back the tape slowly and with care, rolling each strand up like tiny Torah scrolls.

Beneath the gauze, there was a wound in his side as long as my middle finger, crudely sutured. Blood had hardened along the line like an encrustation of rough garnets.

The sight of it mesmerized me. I had watched Ezra cough

up blood, and in the barn, been rewarded with the brittle crunch of the soldier's skull giving way. But this was different. This was what it meant to be human—to have parts of yourself always at work, always in movement. Pumping blood, healing. Rotting.

Clenching his jaw, Akiva shook some of the flask's contents onto the wound. The liquid ran down his side, diluted pink with blood. From the way he hissed, I could tell it hadn't been just water in the flask.

"Are you okay?" I asked, and his eyes flicked up at me. He stared at me, and then a harsh, short laugh escaped his gritted teeth, so breathless and abrupt that it came out nearly a wheeze.

"I'll survive. It's just, there was probably medicine in those crates. Food. Actual winter gear. And we just left it all behind back there."

"We can go back?" I suggested, but he shook his head.

"No, that horse would've never made it out of the field. It'll be gone now, the air-dropped supplies, too. And if we return, the only thing we'll get is a bullet to the gut—or worse, we'll be captured."

"How's that worse?" I asked.

He licked his lips, turning his gaze back to the fire. "I've heard stories. A member of the Polish Home Army passed through the Soviet outpost a while back, raving mad, ranting about how he'd been captured. Tortured. He'd managed to escape, but he was missing an eye and arm. Apparently, some kind of Nazi experiment. And if they treated a Pole that way, I figure they'll treat a Jew even worse. I'd rather just be killed quick."

He retrieved a roll of medical tape from his coat pocket and tore off strips with his teeth, using them to secure the bandage back in place. As he rolled his shirt down and put his extra layers back on, I kept my distance, but even standing at the opposite end of the shack felt intimately close. My gaze trained on the steady rise and fall of his chest and the way his fingers drummed anxiously against the stock of his rifle.

The tallow had left a soft sheen on his lips, and I found my eyes drawn there as well. A faint residual shiver rippled through me as I recalled the vision that had returned to me in the dugout—the heat of those lips on my mouth and downward still, leaving a burning trail from neck to navel. I had never known that kind of touch, but my tongue and nails remembered it.

"I came across your hideout," I said as he warmed his hands by the flames, giving voice to something that had been lingering on my mind since I had first fled in terror from the collapsed dugouts. "There was a body left behind."

His gaze remained on the blaze, but from the way he stiffened, I could tell my words had struck him with the violence of a blow.

"Yael," he said, rubbing his hands together. When he finally shifted his head to glance over at me, his eyes were bluer than ever, as if the fire had lent them some of its light. "And Kuni is somewhere in the woods. They shot him as he tried to run away. You didn't know him, but he'd always been..." Akiva moistened his lips, and I realized how difficult it must be to sum up the whole of a person in just a sentence or two. "He was so *small*."

You could've buried them, I thought, and would've said so out loud, but something held me back. Something in Akiva's face or the way his voice thickened with each word.

"I should've gone back there and finished the job," he said, as if in this moment our thoughts were linked. "But I didn't have the right tools, and I was injured. By the time I recovered, the ground was already beginning to freeze over. Besides, the whole idea of burial, or tahara, or even just sitting shiva, they don't mean anything when you get down to it. They're pretty gestures, but the truth is the only thing that matters in our world is what we can accomplish in life. Fact is, there are forests all throughout Lithuania strewn with the bodies of dead Jews. The true way, the *only* way to honor Chaya, to honor Yael, to honor Kuni and the rest of the dead, is to make the Nazis and their collaborators suffer for what they have done. To pay back our agony sevenfold."

In his gaze burned the same anger that I felt coil in my core, tightly clenched as a fist.

"Tell me how they died," I said.

So, he did.

The evening it had happened, Chaya, Akiva, and the two other members of their small otriad had been pinned in the forest by members of the Auxiliary Police.

"They're supposed to be our countrymen," he said tightly, "but they're just the Germans' bloodhounds. I don't know how they found our hideout, but I have a good idea who might've pointed them to us. Anyway, the point is, they weren't there for the whole otriad. They were there for her. Chaya."

I blinked. "What do you mean?"

"They caught us by surprise while we were in our camp. Yael was the first to die, Kuni the second." His jaw tightened, and he glowered into the embers. "They had more men than us, more guns, and I'd been shot in the shoulder. Chaya and I

were just about out of ammunition when their group leader—
Matis Kazlauskas, a bully of a deputy before the war—said
he'd spare me if she gave herself up. I don't think he realized
how many of us there were left, and he wanted to avoid a
prolonged gunfight."

"Why her?" I whispered.

"I don't know." He racked a hand through his hair. "I've
returned to that day in my head, over and over again, and
although I suspect how they might've found us, I can't figure out why *her*. We'd derailed a train earlier that day, but it
wasn't as though they could've known it was us. Even if they
had, then they'd have been looking for all of our otriad."

Soft curls parted beneath my fingers. My own hair. I recalled the way the branches had scratched at me, gouging at
my hair and face. I closed my eyes. I just needed to get a little
closer to Chaya, even if her memories terrified me. It would
be better to face them here, when I was with a boy who had
cared about her. It felt safer that way.

"I must have passed out at some point from the pain or the
blood loss," he said. "When I woke, she was gone, and I was
lying there alone. So, I searched, and then I found her. Shot.
Dying. She didn't go with them, I guess. She fought back. It
was so much like her. Except in the end, it didn't matter. It
was too late. She wanted me to take her to her father. She'd
been worrying about him for months, ever since she left. I
think she wanted to warn him, but I don't know why. I just
did what she asked and carried her all that way... I think she
was dead before I arrived."

I understood it now. Chaya hadn't just been running. She

had been luring the policemen deeper into the forest, away from Akiva. Until the end, she had wanted to save him.

"I had to," I heard myself say. "I mean, she had to. There was no choice."

"We all make our choices, don't we?" His gaze steeled over. "I know I probably won't see the end of this war. I've made peace with that. But I'm not going to go like a sheep to slaughter. If you have come searching for vengeance, you should know—I want the same."

I wasn't sure what I wanted, other than to find Ezra. Except, wasn't vengeance what he had created me for? Wasn't that my purpose, my entire reason for being? To spill blood for blood?

Now that I knew the purr of an engine, it dawned on me that there'd been the noises of two vehicles approaching, outside the barn back at Mikašiūnai. Two sets of tire tracks in the mud. If the two policemen had stayed behind, who had been in the second car?

"Could Kazlauskas be the same one who killed Tomas?" I asked.

"This area is under his jurisdiction, so I'd say there's a good chance he's involved."

"Tell me about him."

"He's a hunter. Before the war, he hung the heads of prized bucks on his wall. If he could do it now, he'd probably do the same to Jews."

"It sounds as though you actually knew him."

"We're from the same town. Yashny. Not far from here. Just outside the forest, to the northeast. We were neighbors." His gaze shifted to the hewn wood wall behind me, as though imagining the heads of deer floating disembodied. "My father was a zoologist who worked at the university before the antisemitic policies started back in the '30s. Kazlauskas would poach in the Rudniki Forest. He even shot the swans that would come to nest at the town's manor. My father thought it was profane."

The way Akiva said *father*, sharply, quickly, as though he was spitting out a shard of glass, made me realize that his father was likely dead now. Something in my face must have given away my shock, because he smiled mirthlessly. No. He was just baring his teeth.

"Now Kazlauskas hunts Jewish fugitives and partisans," Akiva said. "From what I've heard, it's sport for him."

I gave it some thought. "So, let's give him a hunt."

CHAPTER 8

DUSK DESCENDED OVER YASHNY, BRINGING
with it a sour breeze that tore at my coattails as I fled through
the snow. Ice and twigs snapped beneath my heels, and a flurry
of gritty snowflakes scoured my cheeks like sand.

Ahead, a farmhouse emerged past a row of trees. The warm
glow of candlelight beckoned me closer, until I landed on the
brick step, my limbs trembling half from exhilaration and half
from the memory of being hunted.

I knocked on the door, pulling back at the last moment
to avoid accidentally punching a hole through the pane. The
lace drapes stirred in the wake of a hand, and through their
gauzy layers, I caught a glimpse of a wan and narrow face.

When the door creaked open, the older woman on the
other side was holding a pistol. Bathed in candlelight, her

features appeared eerily greenish, as if on the verge of putre-
faction. As I stepped into the yellow glow radiating from her
threshold, she flinched and nearly lifted the pistol, only to
catch herself at the last moment.

"Please, don't shoot. I'm not armed." My Lithuanian came
out awkward and unwieldy, edged with a trace of genuine fear, although not *my* fear. "I was told you can hide me.
You're Mara?"

A shiver raked her thin frame, and the blood drained
from her face so rapidly, I thought she might collapse. Had I
botched Akiva's directions and gone to the wrong house? No.
She swallowed hard, and at once, I recognized the look in her
eyes as shock and terror, as if she'd been visited by a dybbuk.

"Y-yes." She tucked back a frizzy brown curl and forced a
trembling smile. "Come with me."

I waited for her to put her boots on, staring at the ground
because I was afraid that if I looked her in the face, I might
try to kill her. I could already feel a crimson rage simmering
at the edges of my vision. Her expression when she'd caught
sight of me had been as good as a confession—just as Akiva
suspected, she was guilty.

I followed her out to the squat barn. Behind the hay bales
in the corner, she had made a nook that was dry and sheltered
from the brutal wind. She took a horse blanket and gave it
to me wordlessly, her gaze sweeping from my borrowed fur
ushanka down to my boots. I'd traded Akiva's coat for the
one I'd taken, and the voluminous folds of wool enveloped
me, the hem dragging to the floor.

"Have we met before?" she asked as I drew the blanket
around myself.

"No."

"It's just…" She moistened her lips anxiously. "You look familiar. Are you from Jašiunai?"

"No, but last year, you helped give shelter to a cousin of mine. She told me that you could be trusted."

"Ah. So that's it." Her lips pressed in a tight smile. "Please, don't look so worried. You'll be safe here tonight."

"Thank you." The words burned like acid on my tongue.

Once she left, I settled into the hay and waited. Her footsteps grew softer and softer until they faded away entirely. When all I could hear was the howling wind and rasp of snowflakes against the walls, I climbed to my feet and opened the barn door just a crack.

Darkness reigned past the fields, where the forest blackened the horizon as though it lay at the rim of the world. I didn't want to look at it for long. Chaya had been shot somewhere within those pines and black alders, had bled in its dirt, and found her death there. The land felt poisoned to me.

A light flashed within the trees. Once. Twice. I sighed in relief. I needed to remind myself, I wasn't alone here. Akiva waited on the other side of that lantern, pacing the woods to warm himself.

On our hike over, he had told me about Mara. He'd thought he could trust her because she'd given Soviet partisans refuge, and only after Chaya's death had he begun to actually consider how helping Soviet fighters wasn't the same as helping Jews. Hatred ran deep, and it wasn't uncommon for even the Red Army's partisans to betray their Jewish comrades for the reward of ten rubles. Dukov and the other members of the Volkov Brigade had joked about it more than once, but until tonight, their bigotry had been limited to delegating the most dangerous tasks to Akiva.

"So, the Soviet partisans are different than the Jewish ones?" I'd asked, after he had explained it to me.

"It depends. Some Soviet partisan groups, like Dukov's, have Jewish members. Other brigades, they'll just shoot you outright if they can't sell you out to the Germans. That's why most Jews form their own otriads to fight back. It's why I did back then, with Chaya and the others. Because in the woods, you're not just fighting the Nazis and their collaborators. You're fighting the cold. You're fighting hungry villagers. You're fighting Soviet partisans. And everyone wants you dead."

I returned to the hiding place and settled into the hay once more, drawing Akiva's coat around myself. A faint medley of scents rose from the damp wool as I buried my face against it—dirt, and sweat, burnt gunpowder, and machine oil, and all I could think was it smelled like *him*. And it soothed me.

The minutes dragged on. In some way, those long months in the hayloft had been a blessing. They had taught me to still my mind and sink into the monotony of waiting, so that the passing of hours felt like minutes and time lost its distinction.

As dawn bled across the eastern horizon, I was stirred by the brittle crunch of footsteps through snow. I edged from the nook and hid behind a stack of grain sacks in the corner.

"Go back to the house," a man said quietly from outside the door. The sound of his voice chilled me to the core, my hands curling so tight that my nails dug divots in my own palms.

Outside the barn, ice snapped beneath a man's heavy tread. I listened carefully, sinking even farther into the shadows.

One set of footsteps. Just like Akiva had anticipated, Kazlauskas had come alone. If there had been two of us, he might have brought backup, but one policeman was more than enough to deal with an unarmed girl, a girl who had fled here in terror.

The barn door groaned, swinging forward on rusty hinges. Kazlauskas swore softly. There was a low click. The sound of a gun being cocked.

As Kazlauskas headed deeper into the barn, I glimpsed him through a gap between the grain sacks. He was a solidly built man whose graying hair was hacked short against his scalp, his face broad with a jaw that looked heavy enough to crush walnuts. My body tensed. In the months since Chaya's death, he had exchanged his blue uniform jacket for a heavy black coat, but I recognized him in an instant as the man who had accompanied the German soldier in gray.

Kazlauskas advanced toward the nook with his gun drawn, his pale eyes flicking restlessly. Something about the way he approached the hideaway made me realize he had been here before. The nook was placed out of the way, so that whoever hid in there wouldn't have been able to see the door. It sickened and enraged me to think about how many people had come here seeking shelter, only to be betrayed by someone they thought they could trust.

As he stopped in front of the nook, I came at him from behind. He swiveled around with a groan of shock. I grabbed the gun's barrel and drew it downward, just as he pulled the trigger. One slug caught me in the side, then another slammed into my thigh.

Kazlauskas's gaze widened at the sight of me, and the cruel

sneer that had enveloped his face dissolved into a gape of horror. "No. You're dead."

Ripping the pistol from his grip, I was greeted with the gratifying snap of his finger breaking in the trigger guard. He stumbled back with a cry.

"You killed me." The words welled on my tongue of their own accord. They weren't mine, but the rage that rose within my core still felt as if it belonged to me.

I was about to say more when a third gunshot erupted in the barn's echoing confines. I twisted around. There was a second policeman, this one with a rifle. He took aim, and I clapped my hand over my forehead and darted for the cover of the crates on the other side of the room. No sooner had I taken shelter behind them than the *whish* of metal swept through the air above my head. I rolled out of the way just as a pair of pitchfork tines sank into the soil at my feet. Breathlessly, Kazlauskas tore the pitchfork free and advanced toward me.

I lifted the gun to shoot him. Nothing happened. Too late, I realized that I had curled my finger over the guard instead of within it. I reached for the trigger, but as I touched it, he drove the pitchfork through my chest, knocking me off balance.

Using the pitchfork as a lever, Kazlauskas slammed me against the wall. The tines grated sickeningly against my steel core, going deep enough in me that if not for the rebar, they would have likely come out the other side.

I reached up and seized hold of the pitchfork's wooden handle, but he thrust it even deeper still. The tines broke through my back and sank into the barn wall.

"Laumė, or ghost, or devil, I'll kill you just the same," Kazlauskas growled breathlessly.

As the second policeman approached us, a gunshot rang out. He collapsed to the dirt.

Swiveling around, Kazlauskas released the pitchfork handle, the blood draining from his face. "Wh-what? How?"

Akiva ducked through the barn door and pointed his rifle at Kazlauskas. "Get down now! Hands on your head!"

Instead, Kazlauskas darted for the gun I had dropped at my feet. I swung my leg up, catching him in the chest and hurling him several meters across the room. The crunch of snapping ribs was gratifying. He screamed in pain, and in that same instant, a savage roar ripped from my throat as though we were linked.

As he struggled to hoist himself onto his hands and knees, I tore the pitchfork free, snapping the handle in the process. Mud welled in my throat, flooding my mouth and spilling from my lips. I spat it out at him.

"What are you?" Kazlauskas whispered, staring up at me in shock and—what was that? Awe? Terror?

"Vengeance," I said as I strode toward him.

"Retribution," Akiva added. Snowflakes clung to the wool fibers and gathered in his thick dark lashes.

"W-wait. What happened wasn't my fault." Circling on his hands and knees, Kazlauskas twisted toward Akiva. "You. I know you. You're from Jašiunai. We were neighbors. You must believe me, I had nothing—"

"You butchered my family!" Akiva slammed the butt of his rifle into Kazlauskas's back as the man tried to stand, driving him back into the sawdust. "You killed Chaya! And Yael! And Kuni!"

With each name, he brought the gun down once more. The third time, we were met by a hollow *crack*. At first, I thought the rifle's stock had splintered, but when Kazlauskas screamed out, I realized it was the sound of breaking bone.

"No." Kazlauskas coughed violently, long strings of blood oozing from his mouth. "It wasn't—We were just following orders."

"Whose orders?" I snarled, wrenching Kazlauskas up by his shirt collar. As I rammed him against the support post, dust sifted down from the ceiling, stinging my eyes. Or maybe that was tears. "Who ordered you to find Chaya?"

"Rot in hell." He spat a thick gobbet of blood in my face.

"Vera, hold him still," Akiva said, and turned to regard the tools hanging from pegs on the wall. Picking up a pair of pliers, he gave a dry smile. "You know, this last year has given me a deep appreciation for the many uses of farming equipment. Say, Matis, do you happen to have any favorite teeth?"

"You're bluffing," the man said, even as a faint tremor worked its way into his voice. "I know you. I knew your father. You're both weak, spineless. You may be able to pretend to have an ounce of bravery in you, but let me assure you, you're no different than he was. Sniveling. Weak."

Akiva turned slowly. "Don't talk about him."

Kazlauskas leaned forward, straining against my hold. A cruel light shone in his eyes, and he bared his teeth. "Would you like to know how he died?"

Akiva stiffened, still weighing the pliers in his hand.

"He didn't fight back. You know that? He just laid down and died like an animal."

"No, I don't think this will quite do the job," Akiva said, returning the pliers to its hook. He lifted a hammer instead. "Vera, what do you think about this?"

"He died—" Kazlauskas began, but already the confidence had begun to leach from his voice.

"Oh, no, this is a good one." When Akiva turned back to us, he was holding a pair of wicked shears with short, curved blades. "If I'm not mistaken, they use this one to geld cattle."

Kazlauskas gulped. "W-wait."

"So, do you want to start with your fingers? Or maybe your toes?" Akiva squeezed the shears. The rusty blades groaned as they came together, squeaking like ungreased hinges. "The way I see it, why not save the best for last?"

"F-forgive me," Kazlauskas stuttered.

"Sorry, Matis. Only God can forgive you now." Akiva stepped forward, shears in hand. "All I can do is make sure you meet him a bit earlier than intended. And with a few missing parts."

The blood drained from Kazlauskas's face. "Okay, I'll tell you! It was Brandt. Dr. Brandt. He was searching for her father, and he thought if we found the girl, we'd find him, too."

"Why?" Akiva asked.

"I don't know. All I know is that we were supposed to find the man. And the papers."

"So, where's Ezra?" I demanded. "Where did you take him?"

"I don't know, I swear. We handed him off to the gestapo." He swallowed hard. "But I can tell you where the papers are.

We came back for them when—when my men didn't return. They're in the archives."

"Archives?"

"The old Jewish archives. In Vilnius. So, please, just let me go. I won't follow you. I won't try to hunt you. Just don't kill me."

I looked to Akiva for guidance, loosening my grip, not much but enough that I wouldn't accidentally strangle Kazlauskas. Metal flashed in the corner of my vision. As I turned, a blade pierced my throat, driving nearly up to the hilt before it struck metal.

My hands tightened before I could stop myself. Something cracked inside Kazlauskas, and his fingers slackened around the knife handle in an instant. When I dropped him, he landed face-first into the sawdust, and didn't get up.

"Vera." Akiva stepped toward me, flinching visibly as I wrenched the knife free and threw it to the ground. His blue eyes were no longer as hard and cold as they'd been before; unease stalked like a pair of wolves in them now.

"I'm sorry." I pressed my hand over my throat to hide the hole until it filled in. My voice came out wet and gargled, and I waited a moment longer before continuing. "I know you wanted to do it."

His eyes chilled over, and the fear in them retreated out of sight. He smiled—a thin, harsh line.

"No. It's the same in the end." He bent by Kazlauskas and searched through his pockets, coming up again with a leather ammunition pouch. He stuffed it in his coat pocket.

"What about the bodies?" I asked as I followed him from the barn.

"Leave them." Akiva turned to the farmhouse, jacking another round into his rifle. The lights had been blackened, and the drapes were tightly drawn, as though by keeping out the night, the woman, Mara, could hide from what she had done. "Go on ahead. I'll catch up in a minute. This is something I need to do alone."

CHAPTER 9

FLAMES CONSUMED THE LOG HOUSE, TEETHING the tin roof and licking away the flowers painted on the shutters. With a deafening crash, the roof collapsed inward, releasing a seething curtain of sparks.

I watched from the woods' edge, far enough away that the fire's heat couldn't reach me. Already, the rage and exhilaration were sinking away into a deep place inside of myself. I had expected to feel something more once I avenged Chaya's death, maybe relief or even joy, but what had it even changed? Ezra was still missing, this Dr. Brandt was still out there, and beyond it all, the war loomed like a storm bearing down.

I didn't know what I wanted. I didn't think it mattered. Ezra hadn't considered my own wants and needs when he had created me. He hadn't plucked me from the riverbed, just a dripping handful of clay, and asked me if I wanted to *be*. He had simply molded me into the form he saw fit for vengeance.

Akiva crossed the lawn, backlit by the blaze. With his coattails cast out behind him, and his unkempt hair thorning his face in a soot-black nimbus, it was as if an angel of death from one of the scribes' daydreams had stepped forward, through my inherited memories, into this darker reality.

Two gunshots had rang out moments after he had entered the house, and now as he approached, I could feel the silence those reports had left behind, weighing over us. He carried a burlap sack over his shoulder, and with each step, glass chimed and metal rattled from within the bag.

"No actual medicine, but some food at least," he said, stopping before me. A wry smile bent his lips. "Clean bandages. Extra shoes, since those boots look too big for you. And best of all—" He reached into the bag and flashed a bottle half-filled with clear liquid. "Vodka. The real stuff from Stumbras, not samogon so shitty it'll blind you."

"Blind?" I asked, unsure if he meant it literally.

"You have to be careful with what you trade. Back with the Soviet partisans, some methyl alcohol made it around another otriad in the same outpost. A few men were blinded from it, and a couple even died." He nodded at my coat. "We could probably trade that coat of yours for more than a few bottles of this. German uniforms are worth their weight in gold to the Soviet partisans, and Schuma ones are valuable, too."

He handed the bottle off to me as he scrounged deeper into the sack. I turned it around in my hands and uncapped it to take a whiff. Wrinkling my nose, I replaced the lid quickly. Something about the alcohol's sharp fumes made me think of the chemical odor of formaldehyde, and how the taste and smell had lingered on my tongue for hours after awakening.

"Not even a sip?" Akiva asked, one corner of his mouth folding up in a smirk. "Really? What happened to the whole 'I can outdrink a bear' thi—"

He drew in a sharp breath, and his smile faded into the same shocked grimace I felt slacken my own features.

"Sorry," he muttered. "It's just…it's your face. Your voice."

"It's all right." But the truth was, I felt smothered by his words, as if Chaya still lived inside of me, buried somewhere deep down, and each time he spoke *to* her, she grew stronger. And one of these days, she'd devour me if I let her.

"The thing about losing someone, it's like…" He trailed off, gaze shifting to the sack. "You see something, and you think 'oh, they'll love this once I tell them' or 'I can't wait to share this with them,' but you can't. Because they're dead. So you just store these—these *words* inside yourself, because what the fuck else can you do?"

Silence fell over us as he continued to sift through the bag. It made me uneasy, even more so than the faint crackling of burning wood that reached us as we retreated into the forest. So, to bury my discomfort, I said, "To be fair, *I* could probably outdrink a bear."

He chuckled, glancing up at me. "Probably, seeing as you don't have a liver."

I felt a little better, as if I were reasserting myself. But I didn't want to risk taking a sip of the vodka, afraid my tongue might recognize the drink. Then anything might come out.

"I wish we could've taken more than this," he said. "There was an entire pantry full of food."

"I don't think you could've eaten all that on your own," I said.

"It wouldn't be just for me. We could've brought it to the family camp west of here."

"Family camp?"

"Yeah. A couple dozen refugees who escaped the ghettoes or fled before the massacres began. Back with my otriad, we traded with them sometimes. And after I was shot, I got patched up by the doctor there." Akiva pulled out a knit wool hat. "Anyway, I got you this. Figured you could use it."

I took it from him hesitantly, giving him the vodka bottle back in turn. Fingers working at the embroidered trim, I turned the cap around in my hands. It shouldn't have disturbed me to wear a dead woman's hat, considering that I'd acquired my coat and boots in a similar fashion, but something about this felt different. I didn't want to wear anything that had come from her. Didn't want to be here any longer.

"Do you not like it?" Akiva asked, and I looked up to find him studying me. I swallowed. What had he seen in my face?

"That's not it," I said.

"I thought you might want it to hide your 'emet.'"

"It's hers."

"Yeah, well, she won't need it anymore." He unscrewed the bottle's cap and took a sip, reconsidered, and followed it with a longer swallow. "Anyway, you can give me my hat back now, before my ears freeze off."

I relinquished the fur hat to him, then wadded up the knit cap and shoved it into my coat pocket.

"You want the shoes I found now, or once we stop for the night?"

"The boots are fine for now," I said.

He nodded, putting his hat on. "Let's go."

"Are you all right?" I asked as he turned away. He hesitated, looking back at me. For a moment, the chill thawed from his face, and I caught just a glimpse of it—a hint of vulnerable sorrow, the sheen of unshed tears in his eyes. Then it was gone.

"She was a traitor," he said, building up his barricades again with each word. He turned back ahead, absently fingering the bolt of his rifle. "She looked like my mom."

As we trudged through the forest, snow fell, first in sporadic bursts, and then in a heavy, relentless downpour. Akiva drank a little more vodka, then chased it down with some water from his canteen. When he tried screwing the cap back on, the container slipped from his fingers and spilled across the ground.

When he leaned down to pick it up, he had to stop and grasp at the tree, his other hand pressed to his lower stomach.

"You shouldn't have drunk so much," I said, bending down to retrieve the canteen for him. Then his gaze fixated on me, and it dawned on me suddenly how pale his face was. Faint trembling racked his shoulders, and his lips tightened around the low groan that escaped his throat.

"Akiva?" I reached for him, and he shook my hand away and staggered forward.

"I'm fine." He took the bottle from me, hand trembling so violently that the canteen's cap jangled on its chain, and capped it. Shoved it in his pack. Kept going.

"Who do you think Dr. Brandt is?" I asked as I lingered at his side.

"I don't know. The name Brandt... It's familiar. I think I heard it before, back with Volkov's brigade. But I can't pair it with a face or title. Maybe Gulzifa will know more."

"Gulzifa?"

"She runs a safe house outside Vilna. She might be able to help us get into the ghetto."

About twenty minutes later, when he staggered, I was prepared to catch him before he fell. He leaned against me, panting as if overtaken by a terrible heat, and it shocked me how *warm* he was. Hotter than the night before, like all this time, a fire had been smoldering inside him, gnawing his bones to soot and ashes.

He twisted away from me and gagged with such force, I half expected smoke and sparks to disgorge from his lips. Instead, the only thing to splash to the ground was a mess of liquid and bile. The stench hit me seconds later as he leaned into me—sour infection and rot.

The smell would've curdled my stomach if I had one, but instead it uprooted some vague recollection of a childhood slip, a gashed arm slick with yellow pus, a gray mustached doctor who had joked that if I wasn't careful, I'd end up with one less limb, like my father. Like Ezra. The experience had terrified Chaya enough to imprint its memory in her vestigial remains, and hit me with all the force of a whiplash as Akiva collapsed against me, still clutching his side.

"Your wound," I whispered.

"It's fine. Just give me a minute to breathe. It's..." He closed his eyes, breathing heavily. "It just hurts. A lot. I think I might've ripped out the stitches back there."

"Tell me what I should do." I kept a steady grasp on his

shoulders, afraid that if I let go, he'd fall to the ground. Even as he regained his balance, I maintained my hold.

"Dr. Reznikoff at the family camp, he can help. We're not far. A few kilometers deeper into the forest." He spoke through gritted teeth, each sentence short and abrupt. "We can rest there for the night then continue to Vilna in the morning."

Carefully, he eased himself away from me and continued walking, but didn't protest when I kept at his side, one hand hovering over his back. We made it another half kilometer before he fell again, and this time he didn't get up.

I knelt down and lightly shook Akiva's shoulder. He groaned, turning his face away from me. His fur ushanka slipped to the ground.

"Hey, you can't rest here." I shook him again, but it did no good. Something about the way he moaned, or maybe just his pallor, made me shift uneasily. I rolled my lip between my teeth, testing the clay.

I picked up his ushanka, putting it on my own head so it wouldn't get lost. Falling back on some baser instinct, I wrangled Akiva onto my back. He made for awkward cargo, and I had to stoop over to keep him from slipping off.

Snowflakes swirled down, brushing against my face like Ezra's smoothing fingers. One landed on my lips, and I licked it. Just a patch of coldness that melted onto me, or into me.

Every few trees we passed, I pulled off a strip of bark or broke a branch, making a trail for myself in case I had to loop back.

Three times Akiva stirred against me, and three times he

mumbled incoherently. I only caught a snippet of his words, slurred by sleep or something worse.

Chaya.

"I won't leave you," I said, hoping he might at least be comforted by the resemblance of my voice to hers. After all, it was her tongue that shaped those words.

There was something oddly familiar about drifting through the clammy dark. With wisps of mist snaking between the trees like pale algae, I could almost believe I was underwater. But the illusion was lost as it grew lighter, with the rising sun bleeding red to the east. I caught the faintest whiff of woodsmoke, as though the sky truly were set alight.

I turned as the bushes rustled. A young woman emerged from the underbrush, carrying her rifle slantwise on a sling. Her dark hair was twisted up in a loose bun. A few errant strands had spilled loose to frame her hooded brown eyes.

"Are you two alone?" she asked in Yiddish, her gaze flicking to Akiva then back to me. I realized she must have been watching for a while, so quiet that I hadn't even noticed her.

"Yes."

"Is he wounded?"

"It's more than that. He doesn't want to wake up." I moistened my lips anxiously. "He said that Dr. Reznikoff could help."

"Here, let me help you carry him." She stepped forward.

I stepped back, a low warning growl rising in my throat. "No."

"But you must be tired."

"I'll carry him." Even with my mark hidden by Akiva's ushanka and my calligraphy lost beneath the dragging sleeves of my coat, there must have been something that betrayed me. Just for a moment, a flicker of unease passed over the girl's features, before resolving.

"Fine. But let me know if you need help. It'll be worse to drop him."

The camp consisted of a scatter of huts and buried rooms, revealed by the open doorways and the wisps of smoke trailing from hidden chimneys. At this hour, only a handful of people lingered about, carrying rifles or pistols at the ready. They eyed us as we passed, but no one made an effort to approach.

"My name's Susannah," she said, glancing back at me.

"Vera."

"I'm from Gerviškės."

When she said her town's name, a vague image surfaced in my memory—golden loaves of bread, cookies overflowing with rich poppy seed and cherry fillings. Before I could stop myself, I said, "Does Mrs. Beck still bake her delicious challah?"

She gave me a strange look. "You don't mean Elsie Beck? She was my mom's best friend growing up. Her family left years ago."

My smile slipped from my lips. I should have known these memories weren't recent, that they were something the scribes had left me. But they felt so close, as though they waited just over my shoulder.

"Where do you two come from?" she asked.

"Beyond the forest," I said, which felt like as good an answer as any.

"It's all right," Susannah said. "I don't want to talk about my past either."

She brought us to a sunken zemlyanka at the camp's center, guiding us down the low dirt incline and into a log-lined chamber below the earth. Faint light palpitated from an oil lamp, the flame kept so low it was little more than a spark. A man lay asleep on the lone wood pallet, a rudimentary bed softened only by a pillow and blanket. He stirred as Susannah leaned down and shook him, before startling awake.

Fetching a pair of spectacles from the floor beside the cot, he squinted up at us. His hair cupped the sides of his head in small white curls. Though I could tell he was old, only a handful of wrinkles folded his face, as if time had smoothed out his skin like a waterworn pebble.

"Sleeping on the job, Dr. Reznikoff?" Susannah teased as the man staggered to his feet, one hand pressed to his back.

"Even an old man like me needs sleep." Wincing, he rubbed his lower back. He turned to me with a weary sigh, gesturing me forward as if he had seen this situation play out a dozen times before. "You can put him on the cot."

I did as he instructed, but instead of stepping away, I settled onto my haunches at Akiva's bedside. His head lolled senselessly, labored breaths shaking his body. Sweat glistened in the banked glow of the oil lamp, and more moisture caught in his thick lashes. Tears or melted snow.

Dr. Reznikoff knelt down beside me and placed his fingers beneath Akiva's jawline. Pressed the back of his hand to the boy's brow.

"He's burning up. How long has he had a fever?"

"I don't know," I admitted. I hadn't even realized he had a fever, and only knew vaguely what that word meant; that it wasn't an enemy I could fight. It wasn't an injury I could take unto myself. "There's a wound in his stomach though."

Dr. Reznikoff unbuttoned Akiva's camouflage cloak and the quilted jacket beneath, removing the layers until the oil lamp shone upon Akiva's side.

In just hours, the skin surrounding the bandages had become swollen and inflamed, and red streaks crept up his flank. When Dr. Reznikoff peeled back the bandages, I caught a sour whiff of something, and all I could think was, *this was death.*

The lips of the wound had swollen to such a degree, the threads at one end had split, revealing the glistening maroon inside him.

"This isn't good," Dr. Reznikoff said grimly. "The wound is infected."

"Then do something." The sharpness of my voice startled me. My body was still and cold, but I felt something rise up in me, a feeling even more piercing than anger. I trembled in its grasp.

This was terror, and it too was what it meant to be human. Or the closest thing to it.

"I'm sorry, but we have no antibiotics, no phage, no iodine. Not even garlic. All our medical supplies were 'reappropriated' by a pair of Soviet partisans a few days ago." A humorless smile bent the man's lips, his voice dripping with bitterness. "'For the liberation of the homeland,' they said."

"Do you mean the camp to the south?" I asked, recalling what Akiva had told me about the Soviet partisan fighters stationed in the forest.

Dr. Reznikoff nodded. "What great neighbors, no? I tried to tell them the people here need that medication, that we don't have the Red Army air-dropping supplies to us. They said we should be grateful they didn't deliver us to the Nazis."

I rolled my lower lip beneath my teeth, peering down at Akiva's restless features. His brow wrinkled as a low groan left his lips. "If I get antibiotics, will he...will he be okay?"

"Antibiotics, even phage, would be infinitely better than what I can do now, which is simply clean and dress the wound, and pray that he recovers. But I don't know where you could possibly find medicine."

"I know where," I assured him, rising to my feet. As I left the dugout, Susannah caught up to me.

"You can't possibly be thinking of going to the Soviet camp," she said incredulously. "You're a girl. Do you know what they'll do to you?"

"I'll be fine." I began to turn, but she seized my wrist.

"You'll never get out of there alive."

I slipped off my hat and brushed the dark curls that had fallen over my brow. As her gaze lifted to the letters inked across my forehead, I smiled wryly. "As I said, I'll be fine."

"Emet," she whispered.

"Watch over him while I'm gone, please."

She nodded, her gaze still fixed on the word for truth.

CHAPTER 10

MIST COILED BETWEEN THE TREES, SLUGGISH and serpentine. Overhead, crimson and yellow streaks edged across the sky, as bright and inflamed as an infection. I strode at a brisk walk until the noises of the family camp faded behind me, replaced by tranquil birdsong and the hiss of the wind through the trees. And then I broke into a run.

Some buried recollection guided me deeper into the forest, following the Visinčia River when I came to it. The ground was marshier here, swamp frozen into a black slush. Dead reeds sprouted in brown clumps along the sandy shoreline, the underbrush growing in a wild tangle. Birch trees replaced the pines and spruces, their black-streaked white trunks confronting me like a multitude of eyes.

I smelled the Soviet camp before I saw it. As the wind

changed directions, the faintest tang of woodsmoke reached my nostrils, carrying with it the savory aroma of roasting meat.

No sooner had I caught the scent than a gunshot rang out. Less than ten centimeters from my head, a branch shuddered, raining splinters on my cheek. I slammed to a halt.

"I'm unarmed," I shouted, raising my hands. I resisted the impulse to press my palms over the mark on my brow, not that it would do much good against a bullet. Instead, I simply repeated myself, first in Polish and then in Russian. "I'm unarmed!"

"Stumble a bit off course?" a man called in Russian, and another chuckled, just out of sight.

"I think you're in the wrong camp," the other chimed in.

"Is this the Soviet outpost?" I asked.

For a moment, neither of them answered, and then the pair stepped from the trees. One tall and dark-haired, the other blond with a cheek pocked by a recent burn. Each was draped in the same hand-sewn white cloak Akiva had worn, that I now realized was a staple of winter warfare. As the pair regarded me with half smiles, it dawned on me how they must see me. Not as a threat, just a source of humor.

"What do you want?" the blond one asked.

"Antibiotics," I said.

He cocked his head. "And what makes you think we have antibiotics to spare?"

The other nodded in agreement.

"I know that you took them from the family camp. I want them back."

"Well, you're not getting them back," the dark-haired one cut in. "You lot have no use for them. You're not out here fighting to liberate this country. As far as I'm concerned, you're of no use. So, go. Keep hiding."

"I said, I want them back," I growled, refusing to look away. Something in my voice or my face must've struck the pair, because their smiles faded, and they exchanged looks.

"There's a difference between fearlessness and stupidity," the dark-haired one said, but without much force now, and I remained unmoving.

"Let's take her to the general," the blond said, tracing his fingers over his burn scar. His gaze shifted to me then away again, mouth cocked in unease. As he turned away, it dawned on me that he was just a boy, not much older than Akiva.

I followed behind them, entering a camp not much different than the one I had left behind, although by the amount of barrels and crates stacked around, it became abundantly clear to me that these people had far more resources. And from their faces, I could tell that they were better fed.

Soldiers loitered in the doorways of their zemlyankas, some in khaki quilted jackets and peaked fabric caps, others with ushankas and greatcoats, and yet more dressed in a mishmash of clothing that looked like it'd been salvaged from a variety of different uniforms and sources.

Eyes followed us as we headed deeper into the camp. I didn't care much for the way some of the men looked at me. Although they were no more imposing than the soldiers I had killed in the barn, or the ones I fought at the farmhouse, something about their glances put me on edge, made my fingers curl into fists.

It occurred to me that they were looking at me as though

I was a human, and that in my short life, I'd had few people look at me this way. I didn't like it.

The pair brought me to a man sitting on a barrel next to his dugout, rolling a cigarette in calloused fingers. His flinty eyes flicked up as we approached. His upper lip was cleanly shaven, but a reddish-brown beard covered his heavy jaw.

As we stopped before him, he propped his cigarette between his lips and struck a match off his bootheel. He spared a moment to inhale before slinging a question my way in the same barking tone as an order: "Who are you, girl?"

"I think she's with the Jews, sir," the soldier with the burned face said. "She came asking for the medical supplies you had us take a few days ago."

"I didn't ask you. I asked her."

"Vera," I said, and he took another drag of his cigarette.

"Zhidovka?" he asked, and the word coiled dark and unwelcome in my core. Until this point, he had been speaking to his men in Russian, and the word came across harsher in that tongue than it would have in Polish. He meant it an insult—if that wasn't obvious, the way he spat at my feet moments later drove the slur home.

I didn't answer, although a part of me wanted to tell him yes, to say it boldly, reclaim the word from his filthy mouth. He could call me a zhidovka, and I would show him just how powerful one was—as a Jew, as a woman. I would show him what I was capable of.

"Tell me," he said, "why should I give you these supplies?"

"Because they're not yours. And you took them from people who need them."

"This isn't a charity." Smoke curled from between his thin

brownish lips. His gaze shifted lower, tracing over my body. "If you want them, you'll have to do more than just ask."

I didn't answer, measuring him with my gaze.

"I think you're mistaken," I said slowly, weighing my words. Weighing the distance between us, the span from my fingers to his throat. "I'm not asking. I'm *telling* you to give them to me."

The others chuckled, but he simply studied me, a small furrow forming between his brows. The contempt had thawed in his gaze, been replaced by a faint unease. He looked at me as though I were a puzzle, something to be broken down and rearranged.

"Where did you get that coat?" he asked.

"Off the man it belonged to."

"Take it off. Those boots, too. They'll be an adequate trade." He probably suspected that would be the end of it. If I'd been human, I wouldn't have been able to survive long in this weather without shoes or a coat.

As I removed my coat, his dull mocking smile slowly faded. And by the time I had unlaced my shoes, it had disappeared entirely. The cigarette dangled forgotten between his fingers, well on its way to becoming ash.

I held the boots out to him, and for a long moment, he simply stared. My bare feet were exposed, as were my arms. I didn't mind the cold. I welcomed it.

The general took the boots from me, and then the coat as well. He waited, perhaps expecting me to change my mind. We stood there, staring each other down. He couldn't possibly know what I was, not with my forehead hidden by Akiva's hat, but disquiet darkened his gaze by the moment.

"The antibiotics," I reminded him.

He didn't answer.

"We had a deal."

His jaw worked silently. "What exactly do you need?"

"Medicine to help an infected wound," I said. "One that has caused a fever."

He gave a slow nod. Turning to the other soldiers, he gestured with one finger. "You heard her. Now, go get it."

CHAPTER 11

BY THE TIME I RETURNED, THE OIL LAMP HAD diminished to just a spark, but there was enough light streaming in through the open door of Dr. Reznikoff's shelter that as I descended into the dugout, I was able to discern Akiva's restless features. The doctor rose to his feet, his jaw coming unhinged at the sight of me. I'd endured similar stares entering the family camp, not to mention leaving the Soviet one, and I felt too exhausted to do much more than hold out the bundle of medical supplies to him.

"Will these do?" I asked.

He just stared.

"Well?"

Swallowing hard, he took them from me. Though I could tell he wanted to ask me about my bare feet or, more likely, the calligraphy exposed on my body, he turned his attention to the bundle and unwrapped the cloth with infinite care. Several vials glistened in the candlelight, resting alongside two glass syringes and a pad of clean gauze. It was hard to believe that something so delicate, containing less than a mouthful of fluid, was what stood between life and death for Akiva.

"How'd you get these?" he murmured.

"I asked, and they gave them to me."

He nodded, his gaze straying back to the letters winding down my arms. Clearing his throat in discomfort, he knelt down beside Akiva and administered the liquid. Once he was finished, he set aside the syringe, but kept his gaze lowered to the ground.

"Pardon my intrusion, but I couldn't help but notice that… well, that you don't appear to be breathing." Dr. Reznikoff said it slowly, tentatively, like stepping over broken glass.

I nodded. "It's not necessary."

"I see. I suppose you have no lungs then."

"No," I said.

"No heart either."

"That's right."

"Susannah told me…" He took a deep breath. "That you have a word written in ink on your brow. May I see it?"

I took off my cap and parted my bangs. The breath hissed between his teeth. His gaze met mine, and the faintest smile wavered on his lips.

"You know, I've never been one to believe in superstitions or bubbe meises. I thought the legends were simply just that— legends. But I suppose I can't argue with my own eyes." He picked up Akiva's white camouflage cloak from the ground.

"It's probably better if you wear this. And the hat, too. At least for the time being."

I stayed with Akiva through the day. His fever broke in the afternoon, and he awoke sporadically, drifting in and out of consciousness. The first time, he shied away from me, disoriented, Chaya's name rising on his lips. But the third, or fourth time, when I awoke him to make him eat the grainy porridge that Susannah had brought, he called me by my name.

"Why don't you go out to get some fresh air?" Dr. Reznikoff asked as he came in to check on us as the sun dipped below the trees and the sky darkened to the east.

"No, it's all right. I'll stay here."

"I insist. Hovering over him won't make him heal faster."

I nodded reluctantly, climbing to my feet. I was so used to spending every waking moment with Ezra, and being confined to the hayloft for the rest of that time. It troubled me to realize that out here, I wasn't bound to these walls or to any individual. I could go anywhere.

I slipped on the shoes Akiva had taken from Mara's house—leather boots lined with fur, well-suited for the cold weather—and adjusted my hat over my mark. Stepping out of the dugout, I trailed my way through the camp. The scent of woodsmoke hung in the air, and people milled about. Their pallid faces peeked out from their shabby coats. Hunger hollowed out their features, and the cold chapped their cheeks and noses. Compared to the Soviet camp, the atmosphere was one of desolation and weariness.

At the center of the camp, a pot of gruel cooked over a low banked fire, wisps of steam fading into the indigo sky. Everybody had their own bowl or cup, and I lingered at the edge of the line, watching people go to the cauldron one by one, receiving only a scanty ladleful each.

"Vera!"

I turned. Susannah waved from the front of the line. I walked over to her and was taken off guard when she grasped me by the hand.

"You've been in there all day," she said. "How's your friend doing?"

"Dr. Reznikoff said his fever broke."

"That's wonderful news," she said enthusiastically, but I didn't feel nearly as confident.

Humans were such fragile creatures. I hadn't even used my full strength several nights ago, and I had still struck those two men hard enough to crack bone. And Kazlauskas's neck had snapped beneath my fingers as effortlessly as I'd crushed the herring fillet's vertebrae between my teeth.

"Anyway, you must be starving," Susannah said as we moved up in line.

"No, I'm fine."

She cocked her head. "So, golems don't need to eat then?"

A few people glanced questioningly in our direction. I sighed.

"How many people have you told?" I asked.

"Everyone." She rolled her eyes. "Only no one believes me. Well, actually..."

"What?" I asked.

"There is one person. Rav Oren. He said he wanted to meet you."

"Really?" I blinked. "Why?"

"I don't know. He wouldn't say. Let me just get some food, and then I'll take you to him."

As we reached the cauldron, the woman at the front of the line looked at me wearily, almost bitterly. As she filled Susannah's bowl, she muttered under her breath, "Any more people, and we won't be able to feed any of us."

"It's all right," I said. "I'm not hungry."

That wasn't entirely the truth—there was a part of me, something low and primal, that ached for food, or at least the feeling of eating. To fill my mouth, to tear at meat with my teeth, to feel the hot sting of porridge mash against my palate.

The strangest thing was that I sensed the feeling hadn't come from Chaya. This desire to fill myself, to *actualize* myself, it was truly my own.

The woman furrowed her brow. "Are you...are you sure you're not hungry?"

"See, I told you, Goldy," Susannah said triumphantly, pointing a finger at the woman. "Golem."

"Right," the woman said. "Well, if the 'golem' decides she wants to eat, she'd better get back in line before we run out of food."

Once Susannah got her porridge ration, she guided me back through the camp, trailing in and out between the dugouts. The camp was more extensive than I thought, complete with a livestock pen and a well.

"How many people are here?" I asked as an infant wailed out of sight.

"About three dozen, give or take. It changes every day, as the FPO sends more people here, and others die." She said it so nonchalantly, it dawned on me that death was something she must've been accustomed to here.

I didn't know what to say. Ezra hadn't taught me such things. Death had been something he had discussed in a weary, familiar voice, describing to me the horror of the trenches in no different a tone than he used to discuss grammar or geography. Only when he had spoken about Chaya had his voice taken on a thin, wavering note of grief, or darkened with the deepest rage.

Susannah and I continued on. When we reached a dugout, she paused and turned to me. "He's here, I believe."

"Thank you," I said.

She hesitated, and I suspected that she was waiting for me to keep talking—to ask her to stay or go, or perhaps something else entirely. When I didn't answer, she turned away.

"I'll see you back at the cooking area," she said.

I nodded.

As she left, I turned my attention back to the dugout and descended into the buried room. The only light came from the opening above and the scattered glow of a single candle. A man sat in the corner, weaving rope from strips of bark. His head was bowed, but as he turned to pick up another long strand of bark, I caught a glimpse of dark hair and a narrow face.

"Ezra!" I said, stepping toward him.

He lifted his chin, revealing a face much too wrinkled to be Ezra's. Heavy creases bracketed his eyes and mouth, and the hair that hung down his cheeks was streaked with silver. His eyelids drooped down in the corners, while Ezra's were upturned.

My smile dropped from my lips. All the words I'd learned dissolved in an instant, leaving me grasping for what to say.

"I... I... You're not him..."

"You." Slowly, the man set aside the rope he had been twining and rose to his feet. His eyes confronted me, flecks of gray that gleamed in the candlelight. Revulsion imprinted on his face. "It's been a while since I've seen one of your kind."

"Are you telling me there are others like me?" I asked, unable to contain the shock in my voice. "Other golems? Where can I find them?"

"Come closer."

I did as he asked. He was old, and I could tell it hurt for him to elevate his voice. I didn't want him to strain himself more than necessary.

"Closer."

I leaned in.

His hand swept forward. The candlelight glinted across the dull wide blade he had used to separate the bark into layers. I jerked back. Instead of striking my brow, he cut through my throat.

I caught the knife on the downswing and tore it from his hand, casting it across the room. Gurgling sounds pushed from my throat as the gash began to close. I tasted mud on my tongue, and for a moment, I felt like a girl stumbling through a forest, cupping her blood in her hand to keep from leaving a trail.

"You foul creature!" the man snarled. "Don't you understand? You must die!"

My body moved on its own. I caught him around the throat with one hand and hoisted him against the wall. He struggled, his nails digging into my arm. Weak. He was too weak, and I was much stronger.

"Vera, stop," Akiva shouted from behind me.

His voice took me so aback that I froze, for a moment believing it to be a figment of another shattered memory. But when I turned around, there he was, staring at me with his ice-blue eyes flared in alarm. A fever sweat gathered on his brow, and his lips were parched and trembling, the candlelight turning the scar slashed across his cheek into a jagged shadow.

"Vera, you're going to kill him!" He reached out to seize my shoulder, but I shook his hand off with ease.

"He tried to kill me," I growled, except Akiva's words were enough to give me pause. This wasn't what Ezra would have wanted. This man didn't bear the broken-cross insignia of my enemy. Therefore...

I released the old man. He landed hard on the floor and bent over himself, clutching his throat and gasping for breath.

"Come on." Akiva placed his hand on my shoulder. I followed him to the ladder, my senses prickling. At any moment, I expected to feel the man's bark-scraper gouge into my back, wrenching me apart scoop after scoop.

"Boy," the man croaked. "Boy, listen to me. You understand me, yes? You know what she is? You must kill her."

"You're sick, old man," Akiva said dryly, looking back.

I turned around, too. The old man remained on his knees, his eyes sparks of light in sunken crevices.

"Golems are cursed beings," he said. "And ones capable of living among humans are even worse. Don't you see what she is? What was done to create her?"

"Sorry, I don't know what you're talking about," Akiva answered, coaxing me forward with a light push on the shoulder. "Vera, go."

As I climbed the ladder, the man continued to speak to us in a low, fervent chant. "You will understand one day. There has never been a golem that hasn't destroyed everyone close to it, before destroying itself. They long for what they cannot have, for what they are *not*. And once they realize they will never be human, their admiration for humanity turns into hatred."

Akiva waited down below until I reached the top. As I crawled onto solid ground, he said something to the man, too indistinct for me to make out. Moments later, he joined me on his haunches, his jaw tight with anger.

"What did you say to him?" I asked.

"I told him to just look how we destroy each other, and to tell me who the real monsters are."

CHAPTER 12

PEOPLE SHUFFLED THROUGH THE CAMP, SLOW
and sluggish, like streams of half-frozen water. Akiva tensed
as we passed, his gaze shifting warily over both children and
adults alike.

"How long have I been asleep for?" he asked as we retraced
our steps back toward Dr. Reznikoff's shelter.

"Almost a day. You've been in and out."

"Everything's just a blur," he said, his gaze turning to me.
In broad daylight, more so than in darkness, it dawned on
me how strained he looked, as though he were being held
together by just threads.

"I want to find Ezra," I said, once we had returned to Dr.
Reznikoff's shelter, and Akiva was working his way through
a bowl of steaming porridge. "Kazlauskas said that he took

the papers to the Jewish archives. He must mean the books Ezra had, the ones from his shul's genizah. Why would the Nazis want those?"

"From what I heard, they've been collecting old books and records from all across Lithuania. They even have a dedicated group for it, the Einsatzstab Reichleiter Rosenberg." Akiva gave it more thought. "By archives, he probably meant the old YIVO building. I've met a few members of the FPO, the Jewish partisan organization within the ghetto, and I know that at least a few months ago, workers were being taken from the ghetto to the old YIVO building, to help go through the documents the Nazis were compiling."

That settled it. "I need to get to the YIVO building then. If they took the papers there, they probably took Ezra, too."

Akiva nodded, as if he had expected that answer all along. "Your best bet would be to sneak into the ghetto and get on a work detail. That way, you'll go straight to the archives, straight to where they're holding him. And I can take you there."

"Really?" I asked, surprised. "Wouldn't it be safer if you stayed here?"

"No. This place is no different than a ghetto. It's just people waiting to die. Starving. I don't want to die like that. I decided a long time ago that I want to go down fighting, and take as many of them down with me as I can. I'm coming with you."

"To Vilna," I said.

His lips rose in a dull smile. "To Vilna."

Two days later, we set out for the capital. It was danger-ous to travel in broad daylight, even if we stayed off the main roads, except at this time of year, the night chill could prove even more dangerous for the living. And we had a long way to go.

The people at the forest camp had little to spare, but on the way out, Dr. Reznikoff stopped us and pressed a small cloth-bound packet into Akiva's hands.

"You need to take care of yourself," he said. "Unless you want another infection on your hands."

"You people could use it more than me," Akiva said, and tried to hand the package back, but the man refused to take it.

"We owe it to the dead to survive," the doctor said, his voice firm with conviction.

"What we owe them is vengeance," Akiva answered back, looking at me as he said it.

I wondered what he saw me as—if the reason his gaze was drawn to my features was because of my resemblance to Chaya, or if it was because he viewed me as a way of fulfilling his desire for revenge. Wrath incarnate.

It was what I was made for, so it shouldn't have bothered me. Except I wondered if that was all I would ever be. Who was I beyond the purpose for my creation?

"You won't be able to take revenge if you're leaking pus everywhere," Dr. Reznikoff said.

Akiva didn't argue with that. Sighing, he stuck the bundle into his knapsack then turned to me. "Let's get going. If I have to stay here much longer, it won't be this wound that kills me. I'll be listening to the doctor's lectures."

Coils of mist slunk through the trees, and steam rose from the snow as it warmed in the rising sun.

"We'll have to do something about your clothes before

we make it into the city," Akiva said, glancing down at the white cloak he'd lent me. "You won't make it past the Gate of Dawn looking like a partisan."

"I can take it off," I suggested, and began to unbutton it. He shook his head.

"Those verses aren't going to make you any less conspicuous. Your creator should have thought about that before marking you up like a Torah."

"How exactly do you plan to get into Vilna?" I asked.

"There's a safe house just outside the city. The woman there, Gulzifa, has contacts with the FPO along with the Polish Resistance. She should be able to help us find a way to get into the ghetto."

"Why can't we just break into the archives?" I asked.

"Because they'll be guarded."

"I can kill anyone who gets in my way."

For a long moment, Akiva didn't answer. His fingers drummed absently against the stock of his rifle. Then, at last, he said, "Vera, it's different inside the city."

"What do you mean?"

"The repercussions of warfare. If you fight them inside the city—particularly in the YIVO building, particularly in the ghetto—you're going to get innocent people killed. That's why I don't want to join the resistance movement there, because it's like wrestling with one hand tied behind your back. Anything you do, the Nazis and the Auxiliary Police will retaliate against the people in the ghetto."

His words weighed upon me. There was so much I didn't know about this world. He had lived long enough to make sense of the way things worked, how one person's actions could lead to a torrent of unintended consequences. I didn't know if I'd ever be able to make sense of it that way.

With Akiva by my side, the forest didn't seem as dark or menacing. His agile tread and the even sound of his breathing kept the shadows of Chaya's death at bay. But at the same time, this felt like a calm I didn't deserve. I was dipping into her feelings for him again—this familiar comfort was hers. A part of me wanted to tear it out at the root, until I realized that I probably could—hair by hair and tooth by tooth.

We passed between the centuries-old pines, following the same route of broken branches and gouged trunks I had made several days before. Akiva had a compass just to be safe, along with a weathered map-book. I sensed that even without these tools, I would've been able to find my way. Not because of the memories I had inherited through my ink and teeth, but because there was something within me that felt as much in tune with the layout of the land as with Chaya's feelings for Akiva. Maybe over the millenniums, the shifting of the soil or the slow movement of a glacier had carried soil from this forest into the very part of the Vokė River that Ezra had dredged me from.

A fallen pine blocked our path ahead. Instead of going around it, Akiva swung himself over. When it came my turn, he reached out for my hand as I climbed over. To stabilize me, I realized, except when I landed on solid ground, the weight of my body nearly tipped him over. I had to reach out to support him.

"Oy, you're heavy." Akiva chuckled in surprise, and for the first time, I caught a genuine hint of warmth in his smile. "I should have guessed as much, you being made of clay and all."

"I'm not just clay," I said before I could stop myself.

A trace of puzzlement clouded his gaze. "What do you mean?"

My voice caught in my throat. I wasn't ready to tell him the truth. Not that. "I have feelings, I mean."

"I know."

"And I'm alive."

"Oh, I have no doubt of that." From the way his fingers lingered on my wrist, maybe he felt the same soothing sense of familiarity. Or maybe he felt something else, because as his fingers slipped away, he said to me, "Vera, have you ever heard of beshert?"

"Destiny," I said, the word rising to my lips of its own accord. I could only pin a half-formed feeling to it, a vague and comforting recollection of standing beside a warm body, and the sensation of someone else's hand within my own. I couldn't put it into words, other than to understand that beshert meant much more than destiny when it referred to another person. It was like putting broken pieces of pottery back together. Making the whole out of a fragment. Two people bound by their souls.

"I feel like you and I met for a reason." Akiva turned back ahead. "That we met to avenge her."

The moment the words left his mouth, a sinking disappointment swept over me. Those weren't the words I'd been expecting, or what I'd wanted to hear.

Chaya was long dead and buried. I'd never even known her. But even now, I felt drowned within her shadow.

Over the next hours, we passed villages and settlements whose names stuck like bramble in my throat. I didn't ask to stop. I much preferred the forest and fields, except those too were sullied. Twice, we came across clearings where the earth was disturbed. Winter-starved animals had dug at the earth, rutted through it. Charred bones glistened in the sunlight.

Akiva lightly upturned the dirt with the toe of his boot, exposing a skeletal hand.

"Most of the Jews of Yashny were taken to Voronova and then to Lida," he said, turning back ahead. His voice was languid, collected, as if he thought by steadying his voice, he couldn't feel. "I heard they were shot outside the town, in Balerovski's forest. Stripped naked and forced to lay down in mass graves atop the dead. The ones who tried to run were pitchforked by the villagers. Children and infants. Pitchforked."

I searched for the words to answer, but the only thing to leave my mouth was a low, plaintive groan, a noise more animal than human. We looked at each other, looked down at the scatter of bones. Akiva bent down to smooth the dirt back over them, press his palm to the earth to pat it smooth.

"A few weeks after it happened, we came across a man wearing my father's coat," he said. "A peasant on his way to market. He was the first man I killed."

I thought back to the soldier I had encountered in the barn, and the sound his skull had made as I slammed it against the wall. The taste of blood in my mouth, the warm smatter of it across my face. There was no emotion attached to the memory, as if it was something I had witnessed from afar.

"How did it make you feel?" I asked.

Akiva scoffed, and a dry, mirthless smirk raised the corners of his lips. "It didn't change a thing, and once it was over,

I realized he was just a scared farmer, and that killing him wouldn't bring my father back. I don't think he even realized what he did wrong, and somehow that was the worst of it. He kept asking us, why, why, I didn't do anything. He probably didn't see my father as a person, let alone wonder if he had a family or even a name."

"I'm so sorry."

"I remember, Kuni threw up afterward." Akiva turned back ahead. "He was the kind one in our group."

A memory rose from the depths—a boy even younger than Chaya, with inquisitive brown eyes and a sheepish smile, a bandage crossed over his snub nose.

"He wanted to name our group the Maccabees." Akiva chuckled. "I told him we weren't getting any miracles here."

"What name did you want?"

"Mashit. The destroying angel." He traced his fingers over the stock of his rifle. "But Chaya's idea won. It was—"

"Light." The word formed on my lips of its own accord, shaped from the raw tendons rooted to my clay palate.

Akiva narrowed his eyes. "How do you know that?"

I didn't answer, my throat sealed tight. He wasn't supposed to know that.

"I never told her father that."

I searched carefully for what to say. "I remember things."

"Things?"

"Chaya. The zemylankas. You. It's just part of the creation."

"I see," he said, but from the look in his eyes, I sensed he didn't fully believe me.

"Let's keep going." Turning back ahead, I began to moisten my lips, another twinge of her vestigial remains, then caught myself. Because if he saw that tongue, or if he caught an even closer look at my teeth, or if he glimpsed the humankind gleam to my eyes, it would all come together in an instant. And he would recognize what I truly was.

A monstrosity.

An hour later, through a similar stretch of forest, we came across signs of even more recent violence. Blood puddled in the snow. Except for the haphazard sprawl of footprints the fresh snowfall hadn't yet managed to bury, the gore seemed to have come from nowhere. No body, no trail leading away. Just an elongated circle of blood and a scatter of loose mud.

"Is that from a human?" I whispered.

Akiva jacked back his rifle's bolt, his lupine eyes flicking over the trees surrounding us with wild animal awareness. I found myself similarly on edge, searching the underbrush for any sign of movement. There were two sets of footprints, but one ended abruptly at the puddle of gore, as if the runner had fallen there.

A cold droplet landed on my cheek. Then another. I wiped my hand across my face and came back with a single red line streaked across my palm. Slowly, I lifted my head.

A man hung suspended in the trees, impaled at the stomach and leg with the pines' jagged branches. The weight of his body had dragged him downward, tearing him open from navel to rib cage. His hand-sewn camouflage cloak brushed against his legs, the white silk dappled in a patina of mud and gore like a pair of bedraggled wings.

Akiva stared up at the dead partisan, his blue eyes glazed in cataracts of sunlight and his lips parted in something almost akin to awe. The rifle hung forgotten on its sling, his finger slanted loosely over the trigger guard.

"Akiva?"

He flinched as if suddenly awakening, his chin jerking in my direction.

"What could have done this?" I asked. He rolled his lower lip between his teeth in unease.

"I don't know." His gaze returned to the disemboweled corpse. "Maybe he was climbing up there, and fell, and impaled himself."

"There was more than one person here." I pointed at the second set of footprints.

"Yeah, well, he could have been running from a German patrol or waiting to ambush someone."

"Maybe an animal dragged him up there."

"No bears in Lithuania." He moistened his lips, turning ahead. "And wolves don't climb."

CHAPTER 13

BY THE TIME THE SUN HAD REACHED ITS ZE-
nith, we had walked hours through the countryside. I could
have kept going until the soles of my shoes wore down to
rawhide, but Akiva grew tired even before we left the forest.
We stopped in groves and fields and along the river, out of
sight of settlements and homesteads.

On one such break, as Akiva was examining a map, a name
caught my eye.

"Rudamina." I tested the name on my lips, pleased by its
musical twang. "I know that town."

"Is that where Ezra lived?" he asked, glancing up at me. From
the way his hand hovered over his side, and how he avoided
using his left arm to lean down and retrieve his metal canteen
from his knapsack, I could tell his wound was bothering him.

"I don't know. But I want to go there."

"I don't think that's a good idea. We should keep off the roads until we can't anymore. It's not safe to pass through towns."

"If we go, I might be able to learn more about what happened to Chaya."

"You already know what happened to her."

"I mean, about her final moments."

He froze, staring at me for so long, I knew I had said something wrong again. Given him too much. "So, you don't just know things? You actually have her memories?"

I clammed up. "I meant that I might find someone who knows more about why Dr. Brandt was searching for Ezra."

Akiva didn't answer. I swallowed hard, running my tongue over my teeth. It occurred to me that I should be careful smiling or laughing from now on, that even a flash of tongue against teeth might make him suspicious.

The more I thought about it, the more my body felt treacherous—even just my natural expressions could betray me in an instant. And the worst part was that it'd always be this way. Even after the war was over, if I survived the war—if I didn't just slosh into a puddle of mud and water once my purpose was fulfilled—I'd still be an abomination.

"It's worth a try," I added quickly, trying to keep the conversation moving.

Akiva sighed, running a hand through his hair. He turned his attention back to the map, tracing a thumb along the route he'd sketched in ink. "It's not far from the safe house in Nemėžis. Six kilometers to the south. Only a little ways off course."

I smiled, closed-mouth this time. I knew someday Akiva and I would go our separate ways, but I liked having him at my side. Something about his resolute silence, or even just the subtle human warmth that radiated from his body. But I knew if he saw me, if he *really* saw me, that would be the end of it.

Over the course of the day, the storm clouds that had snuffed out the moon and stars last night had cleared until cottony streaks were all that remained along the eastern horizon. By dusk, even those clouds had lifted. When we reached the town, the sky was a moody maroon and growing darker by the minute.

We kept to the tree line. It was a hundred paces or more across a low slope dashed with streaks of snow. Akiva hesitated at the forest's edge, his expression darkening. He seemed at home in the wilderness, but every time village lights had glinted on the horizon or the faint rumble of an engine reached our ears, he had shied into the underbrush like a wolf with its hackles raised. Even now, his eyes flicked warily around us. "I don't like this. Vera, we shouldn't be here. If someone spots us..."

"It's fine," I said. "I'll go on ahead."

"With that cloak, you're dressed like a partisan."

"Maybe I am one."

He chuckled abruptly, and I could tell from the way a smile quirked his lips that I'd startled him. "You've certainly earned the title."

For a long moment, we just smiled at each other.

"Wait for me here," I said.

He nodded, but from the way he looked at me, I could

tell he wanted to say more. As I began to turn, he cleared his throat.

"Be careful," he added.

"I'll be fine."

"We should get you a helmet after this."

"I wouldn't be against that," I said, before venturing forward alone. Though it wasn't yet dark, the dirt road was deserted save for a few scrawny chickens pecking for insects or spilled grain in the mud. Single-story wooden houses clustered on either side of me, their ridged tin roofs lined with snow.

I found my way to the Jewish section of town, or what had once been that. Where mezuzahs had once hung on doorposts, scars gouged the wood to show where the decorative cases had been ripped free. Doors were missing and windows broken. Only a few of the homes appeared inhabited, with ribbons of smoke trailing from the chimneys.

Chaya had lived here once, and her recollections of the place had sunk beneath my skin. I struggled to reconcile my inherited memories with the scene that lay before me. My memories of the village were bright and vivid. Domestic scenes of lighting the Shabbat candles, singing, and steaming challah bread fresh from the oven. Playing in the streets as a child against a shifting backdrop of seasons, kissing a childhood friend in the shelter of the apple trees.

But the village I passed through was nothing like the one I had patched together from her memories. It was lonely and cold, and though faint sounds of the world beyond filtered down to me, I felt paralyzed with fear and loneliness. Either something terrible had happened here in the months since the invasion, or Chaya's memories had been false to begin with.

Both possibilities filled me with deep unease. If I couldn't trust the memories I had inherited, then what did I have to ground me to this world? Nothing but a hayloft room twelve paces long by eight paces wide, with creaky floorboards and heaps of paper. Or the faint memories of a river.

I crossed my arms and ducked my chin down, falling back on my inherited instincts as I strode down the dirt road. A dog barked nearby. Somewhere in the distance, a rooster crowed.

The temple would be just ahead, past that line of trees. I remembered it clearly. And I knew that I would feel safe once I passed through its broad double doors, that I could lose myself for hours in the brightly painted murals on the walls—scenes from Eden and Exodus.

I stepped under the oak trees' boughs, and through the screen of light snow that had begun to fall, I discerned the building's metal roof, the slates oxidized to a dull red. There it was. It was—

As I reached the courtyard, I came to a halt. The temple lay in ruins, its doors broken down. The walls were charred, the roof collapsed inward, and where there wasn't soot, the aged oak shone like pale bones against the snow layer. The wooden ark had been torn from the wall, leaving behind a crevice like a hollowed chest cavity.

As I stopped before the ruined bimah, moisture filled my eyes. I wiped it away, mud-tainted water that stained my sleeves. The sadness welling up inside me was something I could neither name nor own, its headwaters flowing from a place that went deeper than my identity. I was mourning a community I had never known, and that I would never know, and that I would never be a part of now. I was mourning the absence.

"Chaya," a voice said, and I turned slowly. I had thought it must be Akiva, but the boy who confronted me was several centimeters shorter, his features soft where Akiva's were hard, his smile hesitant but with a warmth I was unaccustomed to. Even before he spoke, I could tell from the way his cornflower-blue eyes darted away from me that he was nervous, afraid even.

"It's really you," he said in faltering Polish.

I didn't answer.

"What are you doing here? I thought you were taken to Katkiskes with the others..."

He trailed off as I stepped forward. Maybe it was the stillness of my chest or something else entirely, but he took a step back, swallowing hard.

Before he could say more, from behind us came the muted click of a gun's bolt being jacked back. I turned to find Akiva standing in the doorway, eclipsed by the glow of the setting sun.

"Turn, slowly," he said, and from his voice alone, I knew that he wouldn't hesitate in pulling the trigger. That perhaps even a part of him wanted to. But I wasn't prepared when he stepped through the threshold, entering the sanctuary's flinty dimness, and without the sinking sun to silhouette him, I could see the frigid hatred riming his gaze.

The boy hadn't done anything, except maybe just living was something. Having warm clothes. Having a roof over his head. Maybe, for Akiva, it was enough to justify pulling the trigger.

The boy must have thought similarly, because he raised his hands in the air as he began to turn, his warm complexion curdling to the color of spoiled milk.

"We were just talking," the boy said.

"Right," Akiva said, and it slowly dawned on me that the conversation they were having wasn't about me, not really. I was just a stand-in for Chaya. Because Akiva knew that I could protect myself.

Hands still raised, the boy looked over at me. "Please, Chaya. Tell him you know me."

I didn't answer. What could I say, when the boy was a stranger to me?

"I'm not her," I said, and while the boy flinched visibly, Akiva stiffened as well, his teeth gritting tight. I shifted uneasily. I'd have thought that it'd be soothing being so close to two people who knew Chaya, that the same sense of security I felt in Akiva's presence would've been extended to this other boy as well. Instead, it made me feel less like a person than like an absence—a hole in the shape of her.

"Chaya's dead," Akiva said bluntly.

The boy's face faltered. Swallowing hard, he whispered something under his breath, too softly for me to make out.

"Speak up."

"How?"

Akiva scoffed. "Use your imagination."

The boy bit his lower lip, gaze shifting to the ground. Fabric crinkled beneath my fingers. I looked down. My hand had strayed to my chest of its own accord, palm pressed over the place where a wound should have been.

If Akiva noticed, he showed no sign of it. His attention remained on the boy, and I realized that for him, this was what life was now—enemies on all sides, always on the move, no one who could be trusted.

Although, that wasn't quite true. Akiva had let me into his life, at least a little. That meant something.

"What's your name?" Akiva asked, and the other boy moistened his lips nervously.

"Syarhey Avturavich."

Akiva relaxed his grip on the rifle, shifting his finger to the trigger guard. "Belarusian?"

Syarhey nodded. "Listen, whoever you two are, I swear, I won't tell anyone you were here."

"A wise choice." Akiva nodded in my direction. "Vera here doesn't take too kindly to collaborators."

"R-right," I said quickly, realizing Akiva was expecting an answer.

The boy's gaze shifted my way. It made me uncomfortable to meet his eyes. Just a glance felt unwelcomingly intimate, as abrasive as nails digging into my clay. "I'm not a collaborator."

"That's what they all say," Akiva said, but lowered the rifle anyway, glancing through the open doorway. "Are you sure nobody else saw us?"

"You'd know it by now if they did," Syarhey said. "Are you related to Chaya?"

Akiva exchanged a look with me. "Cousins."

"Yes, cousins," I echoed. I wondered if I'd ever get used to talking to strangers, or if human words would always feel clunky on my tongue, each one spat out like a pebble.

"We heard that someone was looking for Chaya," Akiva

said, sparing me from having to say more. "Her or her family, specifically. They must have stopped by here, no?"

Syarhey hesitated. "You mean the officer…"

"The officer?" I asked.

"Right. He came back a few weeks ago. Here actually."

I blinked. "You mean the shul?"

Syarhey nodded. "To look through the ruins, and to see if anyone had found any books that were…um, left behind."

"In other words, he wanted to see what people had looted from dead Jews," Akiva said dryly. "Was he a member of the Auxiliary Police?"

"No. He was German."

"Did he give you a name?" I asked.

"No, but…" Syarhey dragged the toe of his boot through the soot and snow, cutting a clear path across the floorboards. Four lines. "On his collar tabs, he was wearing a badge like this."

ᛉ

CHAPTER 14

THE SUN SLIPPED BELOW THE HORIZON, LEAVing in its wake a sharp sickle of a moon and a scatter of stars like an arterial spray. Even after the scatter of houses disappeared behind us and the refreshing aroma of pine replaced the sour tang of woodsmoke, I couldn't escape from the memory of the ruined temple or the look on Syarhey's face when Akiva had told him Chaya was dead.

It hadn't been surprise. Just resignation and sorrow, as if he had been expecting that answer all along.

"Akiva," I said, and he glanced back from where he trudged on ahead. He had seemed in just as much a rush to leave Rudamina behind us as I was. No, even more so. And even now, a kilometer later or more, he kept his harried pace.

"What is it?" he asked as I caught up to him.

"Syarhey knew, right? About what happened to the Jews in the village? I mean, he must have. Right?"

"Vera, you don't think those villagers watched half their town disappear, and didn't hear the gunshots or smell the smoke?" Akiva turned back ahead, a bitter laugh escaping his lips. "From what I heard, even the Americans and the Brits know. It hit their newspapers back in June—'One Million Jews Dead,' only now that the Nazis have made their way to Stalingrad and sunk their claws into Norway, I'd say it's more like 'two.'"

"But how?" My fingers curled into my palms. My shock changed tides, flowed into something thick and ugly. More than just indignation. *Rage.* "How could people know and let this happen?"

"They don't just let it happen. They participate."

We fell into silence after that. I turned Akiva's words around in my head like a puzzle, but no matter how deeply I thought about it, I couldn't understand *why.*

As the sun entrenched itself below the earth, the moon shed an uncertain light upon the meadow. Night slunk over us, and we proceeded in silence, wading up to our ankles in snow and mud.

Akiva knew all the right places to walk, finding solid footing in flattened clumps of brush and clay banks, as if he had been born for the wilderness. But then he stopped. Ahead, lights gleamed in the distance. It was a scatter of low wood buildings.

"I think we've gone off course," he said, after a long moment. "We should have reached Neměžis by now, and I don't recognize this."

"We've been heading in a straight line this entire time," I said.

He looked around us. "Shit. It all looks the same in the dark."

"We'll have to go back."

"No. If we go back, we'll end up spending all night stumbling through the fields, and the last thing we want is to be shot by a Nazi patrol. We'll go around."

As we passed the village, a lone dog began barking furiously from the shadows between two houses. Within moments, a chorus of barking rose throughout the village.

Akiva swore and broke into a run, heading for the cover of a nearby grove. I took off after him. In several strides, I passed him, my hand pressed over my forehead to protect it from low-hanging branches.

About fifteen meters from the tree line, I caught my foot on a taut wire buried in the snow. I fell down, grinding my knees and elbows into the dirt, twisting my head sideways to protect it. A sharp rock cut open my cheek.

"Vera, are you okay?!" Akiva slammed to a halt.

I drew in a sharp breath of air. Moisture gurgled inside of me. Loose clay squelched between my teeth and coated my tongue. I spat it out and pressed my hand over my cheek, terrified of how his expression might change if he caught sight of me before the clay smoothed over.

"I'm fine. It doesn't even hurt." My voice came out wet and thick. I swallowed hard and tried again. "I'm fine. Careful. There's a wire here."

Akiva sank his hands into the snowbank and located the wire. He teased it free and untangled it from around my foot.

It was tipped with razor points, which snagged his fingers and made him hiss. His own blood dripped to the snow, as dark as the stuff that welled inside me, but not nearly as thick.

Behind us, the dogs continued to bark. As Akiva helped me to my feet, a gunshot rang out. Several meters away, a tree shuddered as a bullet pierced its limb. Ducking our heads low, we fled for the trees, stumbling blindly over buried ditches and patches of bramble. I strayed behind and ran so that I was behind Akiva, knowing that my body would become a shield for him. I didn't understand why, but I wanted to protect him. The desire felt like as much a part of me as my need for vengeance.

Gunshots echoed through the glade. We threw ourselves to the ground once we reached the trees, finding cover behind their slender trunks.

I groaned. "Why do people keep shooting at us?"

"That partisan cloak of yours sure isn't helping."

The gunshots stopped.

"We need to keep going. We'll leave one at a time. Head west." He nodded in that direction.

"What's west of here?" I asked.

"Hopefully the railroad tracks, so we can find our way to the Nemėžis safe house."

We didn't have much of a choice. I nodded.

Akiva fired a shot into the dark. Whether he hit something or not, I couldn't tell. As the gunshot faded, a heavy silence fell over the grove.

"Did you get him?" I whispered.

"I don't know. I don't see anyone." He moistened his lips,

gaze flicking across the span of snow and dead grass. "It's been long enough. You make a run for it on the count of three."

"I'm not leaving without you."

"But that's—"

"I'll stay behind. You go."

"You don't have a gun."

"I don't need one." I sank my hand into the gritty snow at the base of the tree. My fingers closed around a rock the size of an apple, worn smooth by time or water. "Go."

He swore under his breath and rose to a crouch. "Don't you dare die on me, Vera the golem."

A small smile touched my lips. "I won't."

As he darted through the trees, three rapid gunshots pierced the night. I leaned out from behind cover long enough to sling the rock toward the sounds. If the stone hit the ground, the snow stanched its impact. The gunfire resumed seconds later.

There was more than one person out there now. Their bullets pierced the trees, the boughs trembling all around me and scattering down snow and dead leaves. A shriveled apple thumped on my knee.

I searched the base of the tree for another rock. Footsteps crunched across the frigid ground past the grove. When I glanced around the trunk, I caught a glimpse of two men advancing toward me, each carrying a longarm.

From between the crook of two roots, I retrieved another stone even larger than the first, hard and full of jagged edges. I leaned out and hurled it at the closest of the two men.

The rock slammed into his head. He collapsed with a low grunt, his gun clattering to the ground at his feet. As his companion turned in my direction, I darted from behind the tree and raced for the pitch-black bowers at the depths of the orchard. A bullet slammed into my thigh, but it barely staggered me.

Even before I found new cover behind a gnarled apple tree, I realized that I wasn't going to follow Akiva. He had the right to run, but if I fled with him, I would be denying my true nature.

My search through the dirt and snow uncovered no rocks this time, only stunted apples crested white with veins of ice. I picked one up and tested it in my hand. Solid, but not hard enough to do more than surprise the man stalking between the trees. It would have to do.

I weighed the apple in my hand as I cocked an ear toward the sound of his approach. His ragged breaths filtered between the trees.

"All out of bullets, you little bastards?" His voice was gruff with age. He had spoken in Lithuanian. "You might've been able to take Jurgis by surprise, but you won't take me."

I tossed the apple in the opposite direction of where I heard his voice. When it struck a tree, it exploded into rotten chunks with a hollow thumping sound.

The man swore and fired. He stopped after the second gunshot and advanced in the direction I had thrown the apple. I couldn't see him, but I heard his heavy footsteps receding.

I gathered apples in my pockets. Easing from behind cover, I crouched low to the ground, my palm pressed over my brow. Though I was certainly as heavy as he was, the snow seemed to soften my footsteps rather than amplify them. It met me at the ankles, sucking gently at the soles of my boots.

We were rather like kin, the snow and I. Come spring, it

would melt into the Nemėža tributary of the Vokė River, taking soil with it. The flow would become a part of what I once was.

Through the forked branches, I caught sight of the man slipping between the columns of trunks. I hurled an apple over his head, so that it landed against a tree a meter or two to his right. He swiveled in that direction and fired blindly, tearing the trees into splinters until his gun made soft clicks like a dry throat.

The man reached into his pocket and pulled out a handful of bullets. As he fumbled to insert one into the top of his rifle, I lunged at him. I landed on top of him and drove him to the ground, my hands on his arms, my full weight crushing down on his spine.

He struggled and swore. I ensnared my fingers in his hair and brought his head down, once, twice, succumbing to the rage that flared inside of me. By the fifth blow, his body went still. I knelt there for a moment atop him, wet warmth spreading over my hand, wet darkness spreading across the snow.

So, this was the power these men had craved.

CHAPTER 15

I EMERGED FROM THE GROVE WITH THE MAN'S blood sticky and still warm on my hands, feeling strangely distanced, as though a vital sense was missing from me. It was the feeling of being set out to dry on old vellum, unable to move, no eyes or mouth or ears yet. And yet aware. And alive.

During those times, I had felt as though I was a part of everything but myself. Somehow, this felt the same. There were emotions inside of me that I could not control, that had been put there by someone else. Rage. Hatred. Wrath.

They made me feel powerful, but they were not my own.

I had taken no more than three steps into the barren field before I froze. Ahead, a child stumbled through the snow, wearing thin flannels. Even I could tell her clothes were unsuitable for the weather.

"Papa?" she called, looking around. "Where are you?"

Images of the dead men tumbled through my mind. I had only caught a glimpse of them. Which one could have been her father? Had either?

She perked as I strode forward to meet her. When I stepped into a patch of moonlight, her face dropped. She took a step back.

"Wh-who are you?" she asked, hugging herself. She tilted her head to look past me. "Where's Papa?"

"You need to go back inside," I said softly, stopping in front of her. "It's not safe out here."

"My papa—"

She had blond hair. Blond like the man lying facedown in the orchard, a corona of blood radiating through the snow.

"He'll be home soon." I reached for her then stopped, conscious of the blood staining my hand. I wiped it off on the camouflage cloak, but that only made it more visible—a streak of garish red against the soiled white silk.

Suddenly, she pushed past me and bolted toward the grove. I let her go. The only alternative was to chase her down and drive her to the cold earth, and I was terrified that the same rage that had goaded me to kill her father might be turned against her in turn.

As I left the meadow behind for the untamed forest to the west, the little girl's screams joined the howling of village dogs. No matter how quickly I ran, I couldn't escape from the image of the two men—one eagle-spread in the snow with a jagged chunk of flint eclipsing his eye socket, and the other facedown in a circle of his own blood.

Those men weren't wearing the emblem of my enemies, but I thought that Ezra would've certainly wanted me to kill them.

The old man's words echoed in my head: *Golems are cursed beings.*

No! What I had done back there was justified. Those men would have shot down both of us without mercy or hesitation, simply because they had suspected we did not belong. Akiva and I hadn't even done anything to them when they had opened fire.

When I had first left the hayloft, I had thought that only the men responsible for Chaya's death were my enemy. Then I had thought the Nazis as a whole were, in that they were equally culpable in her death. But these men had never known her, and yet, to survive, I had been forced to kill them. Even if they were civilians. Even if one was a father.

So, that made them the enemy, too.

I shook the thoughts from my head and turned my attention back to the way ahead. The moon had emerged from the clouds to shed a filmy gray light like the powdery wings of moths. The glow seemed to linger over everything. Ahead, I could just barely discern a slope. Far to my right, another cluster of lights hung suspended in midair, too few to belong to a settlement. A building or two then.

As I descended the low hill, a light skimmed through the darkness in the distance. It streaked past the lit building and continued in a trailing beam. For a disorienting moment, I recalled an inherited memory of watching comets and shooting stars dart across the night sky. This was similar, except at ground level. So, it must be…

"A train," I whispered. "Those are the train tracks."

It came as an immense relief to find the right word, and to be able to pair it by association with the disjointed memories that filtered down to me at random. Train. Railroad. Railroad ties. Railroad station.

I savored the words that passed through my mind, testing them under my breath in Yiddish and Polish. It felt like becoming complete, as though it was my responsibility to recall these things, just as it had been Ezra's responsibility to piece me together.

As the train passed, I spotted Akiva crouched in the underbrush. He hastily gestured for me to come closer.

"Get down before you're spotted," Akiva whispered, and I sank to my knees. "Glad to see you're still alive."

I couldn't speak. I couldn't tell him what I had done. Yet some proof must have shown in my face, because Akiva studied me carefully.

"Are you all right?"

"Yes." The word came out muted, abrupt. It didn't sound like my voice. Yet had it ever been my voice to begin with? "Yes. I… I took care of them."

"Oh. I see."

I looked back ahead. Down by the tracks, several men walked along the line.

"Patrols," Akiva explained. "Partisans target train tracks all the time, so the Nazis have set up bunkers every two kilometers or so."

After they had passed, we continued on our way. With the railroad tracks to guide us, it was only a matter of time before Akiva came to a stop once more.

"Finally," he whispered, his shoulders loosening in relief.

Ahead, a narrow line of fruit trees bordered a farmhouse. It was a one-story building with age-blackened log walls, built upon a stone foundation, shutters drawn to keep out the night. A barn stood nearby, one-story as well and likely only large enough for a single stall.

Hurrying to the home, Akiva knocked on the door, twice, followed by three quick raps. We waited in stiff silence until the door opened.

A woman stood framed by the yellow glow of candlelight. She was the same height as me, but her analytic brown eyes and firm mouth bracketed by deep lines made her seem imposing. Her hair hung to her chin, the underlayer black and the crown streaked with silver. Over her thin gown and woolen bottoms, she wore a heavy wool coat.

She was a stranger to me, but when she looked at Akiva, recognition sparked in her gaze.

"Akiva? What are you doing here?" Her Polish was curt and formal. "Where's Dukov and the others?"

"It's a long story, Gulzifa, and we've traveled a long way. We're on our way to Vilnius. Can we stay here for the night?"

Gulzifa stepped outside in her slippers, her arms crossed.

"Are you sure you weren't followed?" she asked, peering over our shoulders.

"Absolutely," Akiva said.

"And her…" Gulzifa's gaze flicked my way. "Who is she?"

"My name is Vera." Each time I introduced myself, it felt as though the name was becoming more of my own, rather than something Ezra had thought of the moment he had painted the letters on my brow. I hoped that in time, the rest of my body would feel that way.

"Vera," she echoed.

Though my knit hat concealed the mark on my brow and my clothes hid the rest of the calligraphy, her gaze felt sharp enough to chisel away at me. I practiced my breathing to show her that I was human.

She turned back ahead. "You two should come inside."

As she opened the door of the small farmhouse, a shapeless black form hurled from the darkness, growling furiously. I raised my fists, preparing to confront the beast, only to stop in befuddlement when Akiva sank to one knee and allowed the creature to maul him.

No. I stared as the creature's pink tongue slathered across his neck and cheeks. It was…licking him.

"Down, boy." He chuckled, wrangling himself away from the animal. "Down, I don't need a bath now."

A dog. Up close now, I recognized the animal for what it was. Its pelt was all black, except for the rusty-brown smudges over its eyes, lower legs, and muzzle.

"His name is Arslan," Gulzifa said.

Akiva scratched the animal behind its ears. "Aren't you a good boy? I missed you. Dogs are the best kind of creatures."

I studied Arslan carefully. The dog looked nothing like the scrawny, wire-haired animals I recalled from my patch-work memories, but the longer I stared at it, the more other associated images began to fall into place—the lean cropped-eared hounds guided by soldiers; a scatter of mewling puppies curled in a basket; the rounded warmth of a sleeping pup's head against the palm.

Gulzifa led us into the farmhouse. I began to take off my shoes as I had seen Ezra do after entering the hayloft, but Akiva caught my wrist and shook his head.

"Just wipe them off," he said quietly. "It's better to keep them with you."

The floorboards creaked beneath my weight. Down below,

I heard the slightest sound of movement. Rustling fabrics. Shallow breathing. I looked up at Akiva, but he followed Gulzifa obliviously. He settled into the chair at her table with a low groan of satisfaction. In the gloom, his hair had been as black as the night surrounding us. The lamplight coaxed out a bluish sheen like a raven's feathers.

"My feet are killing me." Leaning back in his chair, he closed his eyes. "You're lucky, Vera. You can't get blisters."

As he unlaced his boots and rubbed his ankles, Gulzifa went back outside with her dog, obviously still worried that we had been followed. I eased to my knees and cocked an ear toward the floorboards. There it was again, the faintest sounds of movement.

"Vera, what are you doing?" Akiva asked.

"We're not alone," I whispered. "There's someone down there."

A muscle in his cheek ticked. He looked past me at the door outside.

"Just one person?" he whispered back as I rose to my feet. "Or more?"

"I can't tell."

The strangest look came across Akiva's face. His jaw tensed, and his gaze shadowed over with something akin to dread. But his features remained composed, almost rigid, as if he was building armor. And I realized then that he was preparing himself for the possibility he might need to kill Gulzifa.

"The door to the cellar is in the other room." He reached into his coat, silently slipping his revolver from its holster. "When Gulzifa comes back, keep her distracted."

"No, I'll go." I crossed the room, the floorboards straining with each step.

The next room contained a bed of dark carved wood, a steamer trunk bound with brass braces, and a dresser. Lace curtains flanked the window. I crossed the room, studying the whitewashed walls. There were no seams or knobs to suggest an entrance. Behind the furniture then?

As I stepped up to the trunk, from behind me came the groan of unoiled hinges. I swiveled around, expecting to find Gulzifa standing in the doorway. Instead, the floorboards lifted. It was a trapdoor like the one that had divided the hayloft from the room I had been born in, except this panel was set in the floor rather than the wall.

Could it be possible? Could this person be a golem like me?

I bent down to get a closer look at the stranger through the widening gap and caught a glimpse of auburn hair.

Before I could help it, a smile spread across my lips. "Are you a—"

With a wild cry, the girl lunged through the trapdoor. The candlelight glistened across the slim blade of the tool she held, a pick similar to the one Ezra had me break, except with a wooden handle she gripped in a white-knuckled fist. I stepped back, but not quickly enough. The spike sank into my chest to the hilt, grating nauseatingly against the steel rebar that formed my breastbone.

"Die, Nazi swine!" she snarled in Yiddish, then froze as her gaze lifted. The blood drained from her face, leaving it an ashen gray. She stumbled back and would've plummeted through the trapdoor to the basement below if she hadn't caught herself at the last moment. "You...you're a girl..."

I wrenched the pick free and threw it to the ground. Mud slickened the narrow blade. More of the same oozed down my chest. Maybe it was the fact that she'd spoken in Yiddish, or the panic burning in her gaze, but I didn't feel angry. More importantly, I didn't lash out, didn't want to. She wasn't my enemy.

With a low groan, the girl stumbled back, colliding with the bed. She gripped onto the post to keep from falling.

She had a narrow face and the widest green eyes I had ever seen, made even wider by her shock and confusion. Her skin was flecked with numerous brown spots that I couldn't stop staring at. They looked like faded brown ink, as if maybe her creator had accidentally spilled an inkwell on her when she was still drying. Except, of course not. Her breath left her in ragged gasps. She was human.

"That wasn't necessary," I told her.

"No, no." The girl laughed, shaking her head in disbelief. "No. This can't be happening. I must be dreaming."

"Shit!" Akiva rushed through the door, Gulzifa swift on his tail. "Vera, don't hurt her. She's on our side."

Gulzifa stepped forward, staring at the brown stain surrounding the hole gouged through me. In tearing free the tool, I had also torn my dress down the front, revealing the ink-marked clay upon my midriff.

"We can explain—" Akiva began.

Gulzifa looked at me, her expression haunted by the same fear and wonder that colored the red-haired girl's gaze. "What are you?"

The girl's gaze lifted to the mark upon my brow, and awe overcame the horror in her face. "She's a golem."

CHAPTER 16

BACK IN THE MAIN ROOM, GULZIFA POURED TEA into small porcelain cups. She checked that the drapes were closed and the windows were tightly barred before retrieving a tin of cookies from the lower shelf.

"I keep these for guests." A small smile touched her lips. "They're halal, so you should be able to eat them, Vera."

"I'm not hungry," I assured her as Akiva nearly inhaled a cookie. "But thank you."

He took a second treat, and then a third while the girl introduced herself as Miriam.

"I found her a week ago, nearly freezing to death in the cold," Gulzifa explained, brushing a hand through her hair. Her fingers had stopped shaking, but every gesture of hers sparked with tension.

"I'm on my way to Vilna," Miriam said, drumming her fingers anxiously against her teacup. Her gaze shifted around the kitchen, but each time she glanced away, she immediately looked back at me. "My brother was studying at Ramailes Yeshiva before the invasion. I've been hiding with a friend's family all this time, but if there's a chance my brother's still alive, I need to find him."

I brushed my hair over my face, disconcerted by Miriam's steadfast gaze. Everyone was looking at me now, even Akiva, and I could tell that their awkward back-and-forth was just a screen for what they really wanted to talk about.

"What exactly is a golem?" Gulzifa asked, looking from Miriam to me.

"They're creatures made of clay." Her green eyes grew distant, and the fingers she had been drumming against her teacup fell still. She couldn't have been any older than Akiva, but there was something ancient about her gaze. "They're supposed to protect us during pogroms and massacres. I always thought that they were just legends. Vera—your name is Vera, right?"

I nodded.

"Who created you?"

"Ezra."

"Ezra," she echoed.

"Do you know him?"

She shook her head. "I'm sorry, I don't. I came here from Lemberg with my brother. When the Nazis invaded Poland, our parents sent us here to live with our grandparents in Lentvaris."

"Why aren't you with them?" I regretted the words the

moment I blurted them out. Akiva shot me a warning look and shook his head, while Miriam's mouth puckered as if she'd bitten into a moldy apple.

Miriam looked down instantly. "They... They were taken away with the others in their town. We were told that we were being sent to the ghetto in Vilna. I managed to escape before the liquidation, but they decided to stay behind. Our grandparents... They're probably dead now."

An uncomfortable silence fell over the room with the weight of a lead blanket. Gulzifa scuffed the floorboards, her features darkening in anger.

"After the Soviet troops retreated, this whole area fell into chaos," Miriam said. "Some of my friends' families tried to reach Belarus or gain travel permits. They were carrying valuables with them and kept to the roadsides, so that made them easy targets. Many people blamed us for the Soviet occupation, even though we suffered the same persecution under the regime that they did. They thought we were responsible. And when the Nazis herded us into ghettoes, they told us, this is what we deserve."

As she spoke, tears welled in her eyes. Clear, not inky like mine. She clenched her hands in her lap, biting down on her lower lip so hard, it blanched white. I stared at her in rapt fascination. It was grief she was struggling to contain, or anger. This was how those emotions looked on a human face. This was how people reacted to such things.

"Akiva, there are some spare clothes in my room," Gulzifa said. "Perhaps you can help Vera find something a bit more suitable than a summer dress and—" She gave a skeptical glance at the white camouflage cloak I'd borrowed. "Whatever that is."

"Yeah. Sure." Akiva rose to his feet, glancing over at Miriam once more before ushering me forward with a flick of his hand. He took another cookie from the tin. "Come on."

I rose to my feet and followed him into the other room. Flipping open the trunk, Akiva poked through its contents. He chuckled and turned to me. "Look, Vera, it's you."

He held an old porcelain doll, its hair frazzled in brown clumps and eyes yellowed with age.

"Funny," I said dryly, taking it from him. Now that he mentioned it, he had a point. My limbs were as smooth as the doll's, and nearly as white, without creases or folds, the fingers meticulously molded.

The only difference was that I had nails and teeth. And I wasn't nearly as fragile.

I set the doll aside, senses prickling at the subdued weeping filtering from the other room. The noise gnawed away at me, as abrasive as the flurries of snow scraping at the closed shutters. I knew I wasn't responsible, but it felt that way.

From the heap, Akiva retrieved a brown corduroy jacket and a blue button-up shirt. He considered a skirt before exchanging it for a pair of work pants. "These should do."

I took the clothes from his hands. "Do you think her brother is still in Vilna, Akiva?"

Akiva's expression never changed. "I imagine he's probably dead."

When we returned to the kitchen, the tears had cleared from Miriam's eyes, and Gulzifa had bolstered her with a fresh cup of tea and several more cookies from the tin. There were mostly crumbs left, but when Akiva sat down again, he managed to find a few more fragments at the bottom of the tin, which he shook into his cupped palm and downed dry.

Gulzifa sighed and rose to her feet. "There are some kartoflaniki left over from dinner. I also have beef sausage, but I don't know if the way it was prepared would be considered kosher."

"Gulzifa, it could be pork for all I care," Akiva said with a chuckle. "I don't keep kosher."

Miriam looked vaguely uncomfortable. "So, then you don't—"

"Believe in God? No."

"But Vera's a golem."

"Right, and when HaShem decides to show himself, I'll believe in him, too." He turned his attention to the plate of cold potato dumplings and sliced smoked sausage that Gulzifa brought him, only pausing between bites to explain our reason for wanting to go to the ghetto.

"I might be able to help," Gulzifa said, folding her hands on the table. "I know a way inside, that members of the FPO have taken. But I need you and Vera to do something for me first."

"What?" I asked.

"Perhaps Akiva didn't tell you this, but I do more than just offer refuge. Years ago, I worked as a switchboard operator in Vilnius and Kovno, and since then, I've always been interested in long-distance communications and amateur radio. During the course of the war, I've put it to good use." She smiled wryly. "Five times in the last month, I've intercepted radio signals about shipments from Germany. Normally, they've been scrambled, and I haven't been able to decode them, but a couple days ago, there was a Lithuanian liaison handling the call. And it, well, it was a baffling one. If this shipment contains what they say, it could turn the resistance into a full insurgence."

"Is it weapons?" Akiva asked.

She nodded. "Something, apparently, that could change the tide of war on the Eastern Front."

"Did they say what it was?" Akiva asked, his food forgotten. The excited glint in his eyes made something stir within me, a strange and pleasant tingling.

"No, but from the other signals I've been able to decipher, I think it must be raw materials. I've already informed General Volkov—"

"That's the leader of the brigade by the family camp," Akiva explained to me, and I scowled, recalling the way the bearded man had spat at my feet in disdain.

"—but he refused to send his men," Gulzifa finished. "Apparently, he's stretched thin. He already lost two soldiers recently during a Soviet airdrop."

Akiva and I exchanged a look.

"And another patrol disappeared last night."

"So, you want us to help you retrieve the shipment?" I asked.

She nodded. "It'll arrive in Vilnius next Wednesday at ten on the Warsaw-Hrodna railway."

"That's a full five days away," Akiva said. "We'll have plenty of time to get to the ghetto and back if we leave tomorrow."

"So, you're willing?" she asked.

"To get my hands on a weapon that can kill more Nazis?" He chuckled. "How could I resist?"

Smiling wryly, she rose to her feet. "I'll contact Volkov."

I thought she would reach out to them in person, venturing through the forests and fields like we had. Instead, she went to the masonry stove and knelt on her knees before it, rolling back the handloomed rug at the hearthside and then lifting the floorboards to expose the crawl space beneath. From the crevice, she took out a wooden trunk and several small bundles wrapped in burlap, and unpacked their contents on the table.

"It's called a radio," Akiva explained as she fiddled with the black box's dials.

"I know what a radio is," I said, but that wasn't quite true. I just remembered seeing a similar machine once, resting on a lace square atop a dresser. Chaya had loved to play with it; my fingers curled around the table's edge, recalling the smooth buttons, the flex and tension of the grille cloth.

I was stirred from the memory as a sudden burst of static crackled from the grate of Gulzifa's radio. As we huddled around her, Gulzifa leaned over the device and adjusted the dials until the sound became a voice.

At first, the words were cloaked beneath the buzz of static. Then, slowly, a man's desperate voice resolved from the din: "Is anyone out there? Is anyone listening?"

Gulzifa unhooked the receiver and lifted it to her mouth. "Is this Volkov's brigade?"

"No—it's Plater. Plater Unit in the Giruliai Forest. Do you hear me? Something's happening. It's—" A sudden staccato of gunfire drowned out his frantic cry. From the frequency of the shots, it could have only been from a machine gun. "It's bad. Whatever this thing is, it's moving in complete darkness."

Her brow furrowed. "What do you mean? What is?"

"We were on a recon mission near Trakai when we came across something. Something not human. It took out Łukasz as we reached the forest's edge. Came down on him from the trees. God, it tore out his throat. Ripped it out with its own teeth. It looked—it looked like a man, but it wasn't. It couldn't have been."

Beside me, Miriam shivered. Akiva went to the door and peered out, as though concerned that just by talking about the strange presence, we would be giving it the means to find us.

"We returned fire. I thought we killed it, but we must have only wounded it." The man's voice tightened in terror as another volley of gunfire crackled from the speakers. "It followed us all this way, been following us for hours, and we didn't even know it. It's here."

"Gulzifa, we need to help them!" I said.

She gave me a reproachful look that silenced me in an instant and kept her mouth to the speaker. "Are you sure it is only one person? Could a German patrol have—"

A sudden scream came from the speaker, shrill with fear and agony. Miriam's face turned as white as parchment, and even Akiva's complexion blanched. As the scream died into groans and choking gasps, my body grew cold, as though the clay had frozen within me.

"Plater Unit?" Gulzifa leaned forward in her chair. "Plater? Can you hear me? Come in. Plater?"

Dead silence. Not even the sound of breathing now.

Just as Gulzifa began to lower the receiver, a dull scrape came from the speaker. Then the rustle of fabric. She froze.

"Hello," a man said in German, his voice pleasant and relaxed. He didn't even sound out of breath. "Are you still listening? Can you hear me?"

Gulzifa didn't say anything. She looked at me and mouthed, *What is he saying?*

I stepped forward and took the receiver from her hand. She hastily passed me a sheet of paper and fountain pen.

"Who is this?" I asked.

The stranger didn't answer.

Concerned he hadn't heard me, I placed my mouth closer to the receiver and repeated the question.

"I have no name," he said.

Writing in Polish, I relayed the message to the others.

"Of course he doesn't," Gulzifa muttered under her breath, pinching the bridge of her nose as she paced the room.

I turned my attention back to the radio. "What happened to Plater?"

"Do you mean the man who was sitting here? Let me check." The man paused, and my jaw clenched at the soft, fleshy squelch that came from the other end of the speaker. "Ah, see. He's gone now, I'm afraid."

"What are you?" I asked.

Silence.

"I asked, what are you?"

"Mökkurkálfi."

"I don't know what—"

"I'm so hungry. This hunger. It's as though something is growing inside of me."

My pen stilled over the paper. I opened my mouth to answer then closed it. A sour taste bloomed in my mouth, the memory of blood.

The line went dead.

CHAPTER 17

PAST THE WINDOW, THE SKY LIGHTENED TO shades of pink. The rising sun was the brightest crimson. This close to the city, it was too dangerous to leave when the sun was up, so we settled into the cellar for the long wait.

The cellar was ten paces long by five paces wide. Too restless to stand still, I paced it twice, soothed by the familiar ritual of walking wall to wall.

I couldn't stop thinking about what we'd heard on the radio. The Giruliai Forest was nearly twenty kilometers from here, if what Gulzifa said was true. Even if I'd run straight there, I knew it'd be too late. There would be no survivors.

Rickety shelves were cluttered with jars of pickled beets, tomatoes, and mushrooms. Other containers held liquidlike contents that glistened in the lantern light, casting ruby reflections across the wood when our candlelight struck the glass. I walked over to study them.

"Jams," Miriam said, joining me. She held the lantern up to them. "Bilberry and lingonberry. My mother used to make them from the bushes that grew along our fence."

"Jam," I echoed softly. My lips puckered around the word. I remembered sweet bilberry jam spilling from hot blintzes or enveloped in cold, satiny cream. The memories were not my own, but it soothed me.

She cocked her head. "Have you had it before?"

"No, not me."

She snuck a glance back toward the ladder leading up to the ground level then set her lantern on the shelf and picked up a jar. She twisted off the lid and handed it to me. "Try it."

I stuck my fingers in the jar and spooned the thick, sticky jam into my mouth. Closing my eyes, I savored its sweetness.

"What do you think?" Miriam asked.

I inhaled another mouthful before I could stop myself. "It tastes like summer."

"Summer?" Miriam asked.

I nodded, though I couldn't find the words to explain why exactly it made me think of the warmer months.

"Hey, Vera, toss it to me," Akiva said from his spot on the old potato sacks piled in the corner.

I walked over to him instead, afraid that I would turn the jar into a deadly projectile if I tried gently punting it.

"It does taste like summer, I suppose," Miriam admitted.

Akiva took a gob of jam and thrust it into his mouth. "No, this tastes like winter evenings, served with some strong black tea. Summer is, ah, beef shashliks grilled on charcoal, or cold

borscht, or a whole leg of lamb roasted over an open fire, surrounded by your friends. That's summer."

A hint of a smile touched his lips as he spoke. He swallowed another mouthful of the jam before passing it to Miriam, who sampled it in turn. By the time the jar returned to
me, we had eaten nearly half the thing. I felt a twinge of guilt
as I returned it to the shelf. Unlike Gulzifa and the others, I
didn't need to eat to survive.

They took a couple minutes to settle into their separate
corners. Miriam offered me one of her blankets, but I assured her that it was all right. I had been born on hard wood
floors and had spent every night of my short life on rougher
surfaces since.

Long after Miriam had fallen asleep, Akiva shifted restlessly in the corner.

"Can't sleep?" I asked, and he shook his head.

"Can't stop thinking about the distress call. What even
was that?"

I had no answer to that. This violence was new to me, but
I had so little to compare it to, other than the long months
in the hayloft. It felt natural to me, to always be prepared.
To be ready to fight. To kill. It was what I was created for.

"You should get some rest," I said. "I'll keep watch."

"In a bit." He took out his revolver and wiped it down
with the corner of his shirt. "I don't know how Miriam can
sleep like this. My nerves feel like they're on fire. You'd think
after a year with the Volkov Brigade, I'd be able to sleep anywhere and through anything, but it's different here. I don't
like being this close to the city."

"May I see that?" I asked as he gently set his revolver on the dirt floor beside him.

He passed it over.

I ran my fingertips over the smooth metal. Working on some vague intuition, I clicked open the gun's cylinder, revealing the brass shells housed within. There was no confusion this time. The words came to me in an instant—*cartridges, shells, bullets, revolver, gun, weapon, shoot.*

Akiva glanced at me casually, but in his eyes, I caught a trace of suspicion. He had been studying me. "Have you fired one before?"

"No, not me."

"You opened it like you knew how to use it."

I gave the gun back to Akiva, deciding it was safer not to answer. He wouldn't understand that I had Chaya to thank for that. As he settled into the horse blankets with a sigh of contentment, I leaned against the wall. Within time, I sunk into a dim state between waking and the darkness of the riverbed, lulling myself into a haze of memories that were both comforting and sad.

I watched Akiva through heavy lids. In sleep, his features subtly changed. The harsh cast of his mouth softened. He groaned, muttering something so quietly, I couldn't catch it even when I leaned closer.

"What is it?" I touched his shoulder without thinking, and it felt so right, I could almost believe that my hand had been molded to fit this exact place. Instead of shying away from the chill of my skin, he leaned into me.

The heat radiating from him shocked me. He seemed even warmer than the lantern we'd brought for light, and I couldn't help but feel a visceral twinge of unease, fear even. If I stayed close to him for too long, his warmth might crack my surface.

"Chaya," he mumbled, his closed eyes flicking in the trap of a dream. "Don't go."

It felt like he had taken a pick to my gut, or a knife, or a scalpel, digging in and gouging away at me until he'd left a gaping hole. It was the closest feeling to human pain that I had experienced, short of my memories of Chaya's death.

But how could I refuse Akiva? I rested beside him, counting the measured breaths that lifted his chest. Once, he buried his face against his arm and wept forlornly as his body shuddered in the spasms of a dream.

Strange how these seemingly insignificant details made one human.

CHAPTER 18

AT DAYBREAK, WE SET OFF FOR VILNA. THOUGH the city was less than ten kilometers away, hours were wasted dodging villages, huddling in the underbrush, and wading through the dense mud that turned the roadsides into an inhospitable slurry. Carrying a rifle this close to the city was asking for trouble, and even though Akiva didn't say so aloud, I could tell he felt nervous leaving it behind with Gulzifa. He kept one hand in his pocket for most of the walk, his fingers clenched around his revolver's handle.

After a couple hours, we stopped for rest in a spruce grove, sitting on a fallen tree to avoid soiling our clothes on the wet earth. Gulzifa had given us a small rucksack containing lunch. Miriam carefully sliced the small loaf of dark-brown bread into thirds and then divided the cheese similarly. I sampled just a bite of the bread and cheese each and broke what remained into two equal portions that I held out to them.

"Aren't you hungry?" Miriam asked through a full mouth.

"No, you two have the rest. I just wanted to try it."

As they ate, I watched the clouds drift across the sky. They looked soft and fluffy, like the wool of the sheep we had passed several kilometers back.

"If you don't need to eat, that must mean you don't need to use the bathroom," Akiva said.

I nodded. "But I've seen Ezra do it."

"So, does that mean you don't have a—"

Miriam smacked his arm. "You don't ask girls these kinds of questions."

"A *stomach*, Miriam. I was going to say a stomach." He rubbed his arm. "You're both so violent."

His questions made me uneasy. I lightly traced the toe of my boot through the dirt. I didn't want to think about the parts I lacked. If I dwelled on it for too long, I was afraid I might slowly crumble back into my base elements—clay, and straw, and rebar, scattered across the ground in a pile of rubble.

"Miriam, where do you plan to go after this?" I asked, eager to direct the conversation away from me. "After the war, I mean."

Miriam pondered it over, and a smile spread across her lips. "America! I want to listen to jazz and go to their beaches. It all sounds very exciting there. What about you, Akiva?"

He blinked, looking baffled. "To be entirely honest, I haven't given it much thought."

"But you must have an idea," she said.

"Really, I haven't." A strain of annoyance entered his voice.

"Not anywhere? You don't want to go anywhere?"

"Back," he said. "I want to go back home, okay? To Yashny."

For a moment, no one spoke, and then Miriam shrugged and yawned, seeming rather bored by the response. "I don't know about you, but I can't wait to get out of this country. I mean, just think about it, those warm, glistening white beaches. Vera, I bet you'd like it there. You've never seen the ocean, have you?"

I shook my head. But someone deep within me must have visited it once, because at the sound of that word, *ocean*, a vision filled my head of a vast and churning expanse of water even bluer than the Vokė, frothed up with waves and crested with glistening white webs of seafoam.

"What will you do once you get there?" I asked, mesmerized by the thought.

Miriam considered it more and chuckled. "Open a bakery. No, I'll teach piano lessons. You two can come, too. We'll have a cottage along the beach, and my brother will be there as well."

"Sounds nice," Akiva said, and despite the frustration that I'd detected in his voice moments before, he actually appeared somewhat warm to the idea.

"But don't think you can just slack off and live there rent-free," she said playfully. "You'll need to find a job, too."

The way she said it, it was as though she was extending an invitation to the both of us. Offering us a dream of the future.

"Fine." He shrugged. "I'll help out at your bakery."

"I don't think so. I can tell just by looking at you that you'll burn all the bread. You'll need to get your own job."

"I'll build stuff," he said, and she arched an eyebrow.

"Funny. You didn't strike me as a type to build stuff. More like demolish it."

"I'll take that as a compliment," he said dryly. "It was hard work building the dugouts back in the forest, but I liked being out in the woods, watching it come together piece-by-piece."

Miriam turned to me. "What about you?"

Her question took me aback. I couldn't see myself building stuff like Akiva, and I knew that if I tried baking bread, I'd be lost surrounded by so much delicate glassware. But then I thought of Ezra and the long days in the hayloft, and something about the memory of all those books, their dusty scents and the silken feel of the aged parchment, it soothed me.

"Books. I want to work somewhere with books."

"A librarian?" Miriam mused. "Or maybe you can own a bookstore. You can restore antique books. Or is it just the Hebrew text you're interested in? Maybe you can be a scribe."

"Those all sound good," I admitted, even though I wasn't quite sure what the occupations would involve.

"Next year in America then!" she said with a smile, and I chuckled. I looked to Akiva for a response, but he was already in the process of cleaning his revolver, his gaze on the gun, as though it was the only thing real.

Despite all that Miriam said, I couldn't imagine him on a sunny American beach, or even leaning over a carpenter's table, or on his knees setting stone by stone. He existed, both here in the present and in the remains of Chaya's memories, in the forest, the wilderness, streaked with dirt and his hair in a wild tangle, gun in hand, gaze boring forward. Angry, and alone, striding through the darkness like an avenging angel.

And similarly, I couldn't imagine being anywhere but here

in this moment. The idea of having a future without a purpose both excited and frightened me. And though Miriam spoke of a life beyond this war so fondly, it seemed as if that future was meant for someone else, for someone human.

Rather than approach the city from its main throughway, we crossed groves and fields, straying far from the roadside, until a low roar filled my ears. The sound grew louder with each step. We fought through a tangle of snow-encrusted trees, and suddenly the Neris unraveled before us like a black serpent. Scales of ice lined its banks, gleaming in the ruby glower of the rising sun.

I froze, watching the river flow along sluggishly, as though it were just awakening. Tendrils of mist wafted off its cracked surface. I wanted to sink my feet into the mud along its shoreline, but even through my shoes, I could feel the hardness of the ground. The shards of ice would cut my feet to pieces. Wouldn't that feel strange? To be cut by what had once been—no, what still was—my own body?

A choking sensation built in my throat, as though Ezra had forgotten to pry out a stone, a boulder really, before shaping my neck. I stepped forward until I was at the river's edge.

I knew that simply getting moisture on my mark wouldn't harm me, not when the ink had already set beneath my surface like glaze on a kilned vessel, but it made me on edge being so close to my source. As if something might call to me the moment I stepped foot in the shallows, and I'd give in to it and find myself oozing back into my natural element. That was what truly terrified me—I didn't know that I could trust myself or the emotions and urges that guided me. How could I, when I wasn't even sure if they belonged to me?

"Vera."

I flinched as a hand closed around my shoulder. Turning, I met Akiva's blue eyes—in the smoldering dawn light, they were almost as dark as the river itself.

"Are you all right?" he asked.

"It's beautiful." My voice came to me faintly. "I've never seen it this way before. Not in person anyway. Only in memories."

As I leaned down to touch the ice, a gruff voice rang out: "Hey!"

A man struggled to climb down the embankment fifteen meters upstream, his dark pants sheathed in snow. Black coat, black cap, a leather belt snug across his waist. The Auxiliary Police.

Akiva swore. "We need to go now."

I couldn't move. Akiva seized my shoulder and tried to drag me, but my feet were rooted to the ground. Two other men appeared at the top of the embankment, their hands reaching for the guns holstered at their sides. My own hands flexed, straining with the impulse to tear, rip, crush, kill.

"Vera, don't," Miriam said, her voice strained. "Not here."

I turned, unable to believe her. "But these are..."

The men who killed Chaya, I wanted to say, although that wasn't quite the truth. They wore the same uniform, but they were strangers to me. And Kazlauskas was already dead.

"It doesn't matter!" she said and took off at a run with Akiva close behind her. I followed after helplessly, as though I was bound to them.

Why? Why was I going with them?

Rapid footsteps crunched through the snow behind us, and the police officers shouted for us to stop. Gunshots cracked out, sounding small and hollow with the pale sky above and the river flanking us, black as though it weren't water at all, but a crack in the shell of the world, plummeting into a darker reality.

A stone-lined crevice emerged in the embankment, choked with rubbish and dead weeds. Miriam bolted through first, but Akiva paused at the mouth of the tunnel long enough to see that I was coming. As I followed after them, I glanced over my shoulder. The men were closing in on us, fumbling with their guns as they ran.

It would be easy to pivot on my heel and close the distance between us. I would get the truth about Dr. Brandt out of them, even if it mean drawing it out in blood. But I trusted Akiva more than I trusted my own emotions, and with a twinge of bitter regret, I forced myself to keep going.

As I ducked through the opening, the darkness folded in on me. My feet slipped over the frozen mud. I gripped onto the walls to keep from falling, ducking my head low and folding my chin against my chest. Three steps in, one of my heels punched through the ice, soaking me to the ankle. I reeled forward but kept going.

Deeper in, the air smelled of the river and rotting leaves, a scent nearly as comforting as the darkness. Back at the safe house, Gulzifa had described Vilna's sewage system to us in detail. Although most of the infrastructure had been constructed in the 1800s, the oldest tunnels dated to the seventeenth century, deteriorating shafts of wood and stone. More recent tunnels had been built during the first three decades of our century, some incomplete and others trailing off to dead ends. In total, it formed a labyrinth over a hundred kilometers long.

The auxiliary policemen must have known this, because within moments of breaching the tunnel, three sets of footsteps became one, and soon even the last man's sounds of pursuit trailed into hollow silence.

I continued deeper, following both the glistening trail of footprints and the same vague prey drive that had led me to hunt the two men through the midnight orchard. Turning the corner, I spotted Akiva and Miriam crouched in an alcove.

Akiva gripped his revolver tightly in both hands and flinched as I approached, pivoting in my direction with his gun raised. My eyesight wasn't perfect, but for the two of them, this darkness must've been even greater.

"It's me." I sank to my haunches beside them.

"Vera." The relief in Miriam's voice was palpable. She reached out blindly, found my hand. Her fingers were cool and damp, her palm gritty with soil. "I couldn't hear you. I thought you…"

I curled my nails against my palms. The clay refused to yield, no matter how hard I pressed. I wished it would. "Why didn't you want me to kill them? I could have done it. I could have taken care of all of them."

"We're in the city now, Vera," she said. "If you killed even one of those men, you know who would pay for it? Either the Jews in the ghetto or the Christians outside of it, depending on who the Nazis blame first."

Her words weighed on me. There was still so much I didn't

know about being human. Why did it have to be so complicated? At the very least, Ezra should have taught me these things.

We crouched in silence for a minute or two longer, until we were certain the policemen had moved on. Akiva struck a match and built a small fire from dried twigs he tugged from the alcove's masonry. He held the map that Gulzifa had drawn to the firelight, tracing out our route with his fingertip. We had only strayed a little ways off course, it seemed. Luckily, we hadn't been forced to run too far in.

Once we had found our general location, we made a makeshift torch using a scrap of coat lining tied around a branch. Akiva smudged the small fire to ashes underfoot. The tunnel was too narrow for us to walk side by side, so we proceeded in single file, hunched over so the ceiling wouldn't scrape our heads.

The tunnel we had entered was a relic of the original sewage system, with the masonry broken up by age-blackened timbers. Dead moss formed a thick gumline around snaggleteeth of stone. Someone, perhaps one of the original builders, had etched his name into the wall. I trailed my fingertips over the pale scratches. He was probably dead now, like Chaya. Maybe Ezra, too, though the possibility weighed on my chest like a boulder. Dead like so many others whose names I'd never know.

Minutes later, the cracked stones smoothed into a gullet of new red bricks. Our wet boots squeaked with every step. Each time Akiva exhaled, his breath left him in small puffs of smoke or fog. I tried to catch the vapors in my hand when he wasn't looking, but I couldn't even feel it. It was just air.

We turned down one branch then another. Distant voices filtered down to us; they came from no apparent direction or source, as though they had materialized from the air itself. Laughter. Crying. Once, I heard soft music that Akiva told me belonged to a piano.

"That's Satie. *Once Upon a Time in Paris.*" He lifted his chin, closing his eyes only for a moment. "It was my mother's favorite song of his."

His fingers, until now hanging loosely at his side, drummed silently against his pant leg, tracing out the notes.

After a few more notes, the music stopped. Silence descended over us, silence so deep that I could almost believe the piano's delicate notes had come not just from beyond the curved brick walls, but from another world entirely, through a crack made in our own. And before Akiva turned away, the firelight glazed the unshed tears in his eyes.

CHAPTER 19

I EMERGED FROM THE DARKNESS, BLINKING against the searing glow of the midday sun. Lifting the manhole cover, I pushed it out of the way, along with the broken plywood boards that had been arranged strategically over the opening, and crawled onto solid ground. Akiva and Miriam emerged moments later. As Miriam kept guard, Akiva and I moved rubble over the hatch to conceal it.

"Here," Akiva said, and handed Miriam and me each a yellow star Gulzifa had cut from a tablecloth. Already, the ink had started to run. We pinned the makeshift badges to our coats.

It didn't feel much different to me than the mark upon my brow, but Akiva gritted his teeth in disgust. Back at Gulzifa's, he had explained to me that after the Nazis had invaded, the

Jews in his town had been forced to identify themselves. The rules had changed day by day—first a patch with a yellow circle inscribed with the letter J, then a blue armband with a white star, before finally settling on the yellow star—and the Nazis and their collaborators had used the general confusion as proof of noncompliance, and an excuse for cruelty.

"I hate this," Akiva muttered as we left the alley, fingering the edge of the badge. "I never thought I'd be wearing one again."

The ghetto's streets were barren of life and begrimed with rubbish. Only one or two of the people we passed glanced our way with drawn-out faces, but the rest kept their eyes cast downward or turned straight ahead, as if we didn't exist at all.

"I want to look for my brother," Miriam said, and Akiva nodded.

"Do you know where he might be?"

"Our aunt's house is over on Jatkowa Street." Miriam hesitated. "But I'm not even sure if we'll be able to get there now."

"Let's find out," I said, and she smiled faintly and nodded. I realized she didn't want to go off on her own, that this place might've been familiar to her once, but it was no longer her city or nation.

Down the street, a man lay along the curb, facedown in the dirt. His shoes were gone, and his feet were swollen and buried in the muddy snow.

"Is he all right?" I asked Akiva. When I paused next to the man and began to squat, Akiva took my shoulder and shook his head.

"You can't help him," he said.

"But he's just lying there," I protested. "We can't just leave him like this. What if someone steps on him?"

"He's dead." The lean muscles in his jaw tightened. There was something desperate in his blue eyes, something wild. "He's dead, okay? There's nothing you can do for him."

As he pulled me down the sidewalk, I looked back at the corpse, for the first time seeing the man's glazed eyes, the snow gathering on him. Ice covered his brow and lashes.

We continued down Jatkowa Street, past high buildings in shades of rustic brown, russet, and tan. The structures were even taller than the barn where I had been born, and I stopped to marvel at them.

Miriam sighed. "How am I going to find my brother here? There're so many people."

"Don't give up," Akiva said, ruffling her hair the way Ezra had done to me once. "We've barely even started."

"Touch my hair again, and you won't have enough fingers to do it a third time," Miriam said, but past her annoyed scowl I caught a hint of relief, even enjoyment.

There was something comforting in the banter, something that even I could find pleasure in. I found myself smiling. I wanted to see what it felt like to touch a person's hair, so when Akiva turned ahead, I stepped up behind him and entangled my fingers in his hair.

"Ah, Vera!" He jerked back in surprise. "Ow, let go!"

I did as he asked.

He rubbed his head. "You're brutal. I think you just tore out a fistful."

There were a few stray hairs in my palm, but hardly what I'd call a fistful.

"What were you trying to do?" he asked as Miriam chuckled.

"She was trying to ruffle your hair, schmuck."

Akiva shot her a disgruntled look. "More like scalp me."

"Here." Miriam took my hand and placed it on her head, moving my palm back and forth. "This is how you do it. But don't be impolite like him and do it without asking."

Gently, I ran my fingers over her hair. The auburn strands were as thick as Akiva's unkempt locks, but more silken to the touch. As I lowered my hand, Miriam smiled.

"May I touch yours?" she asked.

I nodded.

She didn't riffle her fingers through my hair, but simply traced her fingertips across the side of my head, snared a loose curl, teased it between her thumb and index finger.

"It feels so real," she said in wonder. "You can't even tell it's clay."

I didn't answer, afraid how her expression might change if I told her the truth. She might veer away from me. Her face might contort with the same revulsion that I had caught glimpses of in Ezra's features when he thought I wasn't looking.

A desecration, she might say, *but necessary.*

"Let's keep going," she said instead. "Max has to be here somewhere. I'm sure of it."

As we continued down the street, a passing girl seized Miriam by the sleeve.

A thin, choking sound came from Miriam's throat. The noise sounded so pained, I thought the girl had hurt her and stepped forward. Before I could intervene, Miriam latched her arms around the other girl in a tight hug.

"It's so good to see you, Miriam," the girl said.

"You too. I'm so glad you're alive." Miriam pulled back, wiping her eyes. She turned to me. "Vera, Akiva, this is my friend, Shula. She lived next door to my grandparents in Lentvaris."

Shula offered us a small smile, which I returned. Her black hair was plaited into two neat braids.

Akiva's face remained placid, and from the way his gaze had started to drift, I could tell his attention was already waning. I wanted to get close to the two girls, step into their orbit and become a part of the conversation, but for Akiva, it seemed like the opposite. He had already taken a step back from Shula, and as I watched, he retreated even farther still, his gaze on the street.

"I wish we could meet under better circumstances," Shula said.

"Likewise," I said, and I was surprised by how much the response felt like my own. It wasn't just Chaya anymore.

Shula turned back to Miriam. "Wait until Max finds out you're here. He thought you were dead."

"You mean he's here?" Miriam's voice rose in excitement. "Where is he? You have to take me to him."

Shula nodded. "Follow me."

As they hurried down the street, Akiva and I followed after them. When we had first entered the ghetto, the streets had seemed barren. It wasn't until we passed through the spaces in between—those courtyards, the corridors of old houses, the nooks and vestibules now crammed with hollow-eyed figures with snow melting in their hair and their lips blued from the cold, that I realized how crowded the ghetto actually was. There were people everywhere, some resting on mattresses set up in the halls or just piles of blankets and pillows. They seemed less like people than like a scribe's recollection of people he—I—had once known. Ghosts becoming.

As we searched for Max, the gleam of excitement in Miriam's eyes began to dull. She nibbled at her lower lip, and when that wasn't enough, gnawed at her thumbnail until she ripped the edge off with a shred of skin.

"He *has* to be here," she muttered after we had stopped at the third building where Shula knew he frequented. He hadn't been in the soup kitchen on Strashun Street or helping with the children at the school, while Miriam's aunt's apartment sat just blocks outside the ghetto's gates. Shula had explained that Max didn't have a labor certificate, so he was technically not legally permitted to live in the ghetto, but he earned his bread rations by doing odd jobs for others, including helping Shula with her sickly grandfather. He could be anywhere this early in the day.

"We'll find him," I said, and Miriam flinched as if she hadn't even seen me. Glancing in my direction, she favored me with a weak, distracted smile then turned back ahead.

At last, an old man pointed us in the right direction, to where Miriam's relatives were now staying. We entered the foyer of a home and followed the winding stairway to the garret room above, a dim space lit by dusty shafts of light peeping through the drapes.

A boy sat on one of the mattresses on the floor, carving a piece of wood. Curls of wood landed on the floor at his feet. He was so absorbed in his task, he didn't raise his head as we entered, and it was only after Miriam had taken three steps into the room that he spoke.

"Sarah, I'm almost finished…" He trailed off as he looked up. His carving clattered to the ground. It was the head and bust of a human. A doll.

"Max," Miriam choked, tears flooding her eyes. She rushed to his side and hugged him fiercely. "I can't believe it's you. I'm so glad you're okay."

I stood in the doorway and watched them embrace, their frenzied laughter and words echoing dully in my ears, only half-distinct. I should have felt happy for Miriam. I should have felt something. But when I said her name, and she looked back at me, a buried twinge of resentment rippled through at the joy in her face. My anger both shocked and disturbed me, and as swiftly as the bitterness came, it fled, leaving only sinking shame.

Silently, Akiva slipped out of the room, brushing past me without a word. I followed him into the hall, watching as he restlessly paced and drummed his fingers against his leg. Gaze on the floor, jaw set. And when he glanced my way, I recognized the envy in his eyes as the same emotion that had twisted like a knot of barbed wire in my chest.

"Maybe your family is here," I said, not realizing how cruel the suggestion was until he drew in his breath sharply.

"They're not," he said.

"Do you want to look?"

"They're not," he repeated, firmly, putting the idea to rest.

"Vera," Miriam said, and I looked over to find her standing in the doorway, her brother beside her. "Max says that if you want to find people from YIVO, you should go to the library on Strashun Street. It's not the main archives, but someone there might be able to connect you with one of the members of the organization."

"Let's go then," Akiva said.

"I'd go, too, but…" Miriam began.

"It's all right. We'll meet back here in a few hours." He turned to me. "Yeah?"

I nodded.

"Come on."

He seemed strained, taut, and it wasn't until we were back outside that his shoulders loosened.

"I'm not a big fan of reunions," he explained, catching my eye. "Too much talking, too much hugging. I never know what to do in those kinds of situations."

"Me too," I admitted, and he chuckled, then winced. His fingers strayed to his side, over the wound Dr. Reznikoff had bandaged, but his smile remained.

"Yeah, I figured," he said.

"Does your wound hurt?"

"Don't worry. It's nothing." He shoved his hands into his coat pockets as if to hide the gesture. "Although I doubt wandering through the sewers helped it much."

As we walked down Strashun Street, I searched the faces of everyone I passed, but they were all unfamiliar to me. Strange that I expected them not to be. Stranger still that I should feel at home here, even though I had never walked these cobblestone streets in my own life. But in many ways, it was like touching the calligraphy on my wrists. Vilna was a part of me. It was sunken deep below my surface.

The library was a modest building, and though it was midday, its reading rooms and narrow stacks were well occupied.

Handwritten fliers on the wall advertised upcoming plays and discussions.

"YIVO?" the woman at the counter asked, blinking thoughtfully. She tucked a stray strand of brown hair behind her ear, her fingers smudged with ink from the ledger in front of her. "There are a few people here who once worked there, but if you're looking for the archives, they were all removed. We mostly just have fiction books here, some nonfiction, and a small children's selection."

"What do you mean 'removed'?" Akiva asked.

"They were taken, a few weeks ago. Nathan will know more." She gestured to a teenage boy organizing books in the corner. He was so focused in this task that he didn't notice us until we were right next to him, and startled, adjusting the round spectacles dangling from his narrow nose. His sandy-brown hair was brushed back neatly from his brow, and behind his round glasses, his hazel eyes were slightly unfocused, as if he were lost in a daydream.

"May I help you?" he asked.

As Akiva explained to him our dilemma, the boy listened thoughtfully, his fingers drumming against the book he held, forgotten.

"Any valuable documents were taken by the Einsatzstab Rosenberg," he said. "Every morning, we go to the old YIVO building and prepare the books for transport."

"Transport where?"

"Germany, for the most part. Anything they consider to be valuable. They pulp the rest."

"Valuable?" Akiva scoffed. "Since when were the Germans concerned with preserving Jewish heritage?"

"I don't think that's what they're concerned with," Nathan said, but didn't elaborate. Instead, he turned his attention back to his task of sorting books. "Anyway, lately, it's changed."

"Changed how?" I asked.

"They're looking for specific materials now. Things related to Kabbalah and mysticism. And these ones aren't going back to Germany."

"Is there a way we can get inside?" I asked, and a thin chuckle escaped his lips.

"Yeah, if you have a work permit and a good grasp of Hebrew." He turned his attention back to his sorting. "Look, if you really want to get in, I might be able to help sneak you onto the crew. Give it some thought, and if you decide you do want to go, meet me here tomorrow morning at six o'clock sharp."

CHAPTER 20

BY THE TIME WE RETURNED TO MAX'S HOME, the sun had started to set. I sensed something had changed in the several hours that Akiva and I had been gone, although I couldn't place exactly what, except that as Miriam carried a pot of broth across the kitchen, she wouldn't look me in the eye.

Miriam's aunt had returned home from the garment factory where she had been assigned to work, and Max had gone to the ghetto school to retrieve her five-year-old daughter, his cousin Sarah. They shared the cramped residence with several other families, and when we entered the small kitchen, I had to dodge stray elbows and resting bodies.

I tugged down my hat and tugged up my gloves, wary of the strangers' glances, and kept close to the door. It made me uncomfortable to be surrounded by so many people—and more importantly, so many hands and sharp objects. I felt much more at home in the countryside, as if wading ankle-deep through the snow or striding along the riverbank brought me closer to my baser elements.

A pair of candlesticks waited for us on the table, the candles themselves just stubs and the wicks almost all ash. It startled me to realize it was Shabbat, and it was just as disorienting to know that even in the ghetto, the day and time mattered. Whereas to me, it meant nothing at all.

"Would you like to join us in lighting them?" Miriam asked, catching me off guard. Ezra had never offered to let me light the candles he burned in the hayloft, perhaps wary of spilled wax and an accidental fire, but more likely because he hadn't considered the ritual to be of any importance to a creature like me.

"Really?" I asked. "I can do it?"

"You're a woman, aren't you?" she said with a smile.

It dawned on me that she saw me as I was. There was no doubt in my identity. I was not just a monster to her, but a girl and a Jew.

"I'd love to!" I said, joining her and her aunt at the table.

"Shouldn't we invite Akiva?" I asked, glancing over at where he sat in the parlor, gaze on the door.

"Normally, the women light the candles," she said, "or at least when there are women to do it. I mean, you can invite him, if you'd like."

Nodding, I crossed the room. Akiva glanced up as I approached.

"Would you like to join us in lighting the candles?" I asked.

"Why bother?" he asked. "Nobody's listening."

Something in my features must've given away my disappointment, or maybe he'd realized the matter of prayer had never even occurred to me, simply the novelty of joining them on Shabbat.

He sighed, rising to his feet. "Yeah, sure, why not?"

We stepped into the kitchen. There were no matches, which I imagined were in short supply here as well. But Miriam had a fire striker, and within seconds had lit a third smaller candle that could be used to ignite the others.

She turned to me. "Would you like to do the honors?"

It made me nervous to be so close to fire, wary that it might crack my surface. But as I stepped forward and took the candle from her hand, a different kind of anxiety rose up inside of me, a prickly sensation in my core like the static in the air before a storm. Excitement.

I lit the candles, and while Miriam and her aunt recited the blessing, they covered their eyes. I realized too late that I was expected to mimic the gesture, but that was all right. There was so much I didn't know or hadn't yet recovered from within me, and yet with each moment, I felt myself coming more in tune with the memories I had inherited through my teeth and ink. The prayers rose to my lips, unbidden, and the strangest sense of relief slipped over me, as if the words themselves were a soothing hand.

Ezra had always acted as if the words of our people were forbidden for me, as if just by reading from our texts, the very texts written upon my skin, I would be committing a transgression. I would crumble and cease to be. And I had believed him, that my nature, my being, my *existence* was a crime. An abomination. A desecration.

But what did that make of the Nazis? How could they consider themselves pure and whole beings when they were capable of such terrible things? Whereas for me, my first and greatest crime was to be brought into this world.

The more I thought about it, the angrier I became. Although I wasn't sure anymore who exactly I was angry at. I had never asked to be born, but I wasn't willing to simply crumble back into clay. I didn't know what I wanted or where my future waited for me. The only thing I could do was keep moving, and maybe someday this world would make sense to me.

As the final words of the prayer slipped from my lips, a faint wailing echoed from the attic above. Everyone fell silent. Miriam and Akiva glanced up at the ceiling, while the others in the room made a clear effort to look everywhere else, their gazes shifting about in unease.

"Is that a baby?" Akiva asked tensely as her aunt hurried out of the room.

"Come on," Miriam whispered, and followed after her aunt. We trailed her up a narrow stairway into the attic above. Drafts intruded through the vented windows and the roof's small decorative domes.

There was a nook in the corner carved out of the wall itself, insulated by old cushions and hidden behind a false wall. A makeshift cradle had been set up there, heated by a copper bottle at the foot of the crib and softened by even more blankets. An infant squabbled from its swaddling, but when Miriam's aunt rocked it gently, the baby's fussing quieted into happy babbling.

"Do you two know of anyone outside of the ghetto who would be able to hide a baby?" her aunt asked, glancing at us.

"It's not yours?" Akiva asked, and she shook her head.

"The Levin girl's. She died a couple weeks ago. There's a woman across the street who's helped us nurse, but I fear it's only a matter of time before her own child is discovered, and then..." Miriam's aunt trailed off.

"Is it a boy or a girl?" Akiva asked.

"Why should that matter?" I asked.

"If he's been circumcised, it will."

His words dawned on me. That out there, it wouldn't matter if the infant was only months old, or that it was so young it couldn't even speak yet, or that it had done nothing wrong. The only thing that mattered was that it was a Jew.

"A girl," Miriam's aunt said as we came up to the cradle. "Her name is Dvosye."

Such a small human. I stared down at the infant's chubby features. A few locks of flaxen hair coiled over her brow, framing eyes even bluer than Akiva's.

"Don't get so close, or your ugly face will scare her," Miriam teased, and Akiva rolled his eyes as he leaned over the makeshift cradle. Instead of bursting into tears, the baby reached out to him with a low coo of delight. When he picked her up, she giggled and grabbed at his hair, and he chuckled, surprising us all.

"She likes you," Miriam's aunt said with a weary smile. "I'm going to see if our neighbor is home. Will you watch her for me?"

Akiva was too busy trying to untangle the baby's fingers from his hair to answer, so I nodded in his place.

"We'll protect her," I promised.

The aunt laughed, seemingly taken aback. "I'll be back in just a minute. Hopefully protection won't be necessary."

As the woman left, Akiva held the infant out to me. "Can you take her before she rips out my hair?"

I hesitated. The baby was so fragile, and it scared me that I might drop her. I couldn't trust my own strength either.

I swallowed hard, too afraid to admit this to him. He'd never be able to understand that there were parts of my body that were strangers to me. But Miriam must have sensed my unease, because she gave me a reassuring smile and placed her hand on my arm.

"I get scared holding babies, too," she said.

Just when I worked up the courage to take Dvosye from Akiva, the baby snuggled in the crook of his arm, propping her thumb in her mouth. Akiva rocked her gently, his vague smile creasing the scar slashed down his cheek.

"I never expected you to be good with children," Miriam said, and he rolled his eyes.

"I helped take care of my baby brother."

Miriam's face drained of color, and my smile slackened as his words struck me with all the force of a gut shot. If he'd told Chaya about that, the memory was buried too deep for me to excavate. It had come as a surprise to realize he had parents, a professor father and a mother who loved Satie, but I hadn't even wondered if he'd left siblings behind, too.

If Akiva registered our shock, he showed no sign of it, just kept rocking the baby, who cuddled against his chest in a deep slumber, a bubble of drool forming on one corner of her mouth. It was only when Miriam cleared her throat that he looked up.

From the way she frowned, I could tell she was weighing something internally.

"There's something we need to talk about," she said. "I've decided I won't be returning to Gulzifa's with you two."

"Wh-what?" I stuttered.

"My family needs me. My aunt says she can get me a work permit and register me as a member of her family." She spoke the words slowly, carefully, as though reciting them from script. She must have practiced this, or replayed it over and over in her head during the hours we were gone, the way I'd imagined all the conversations I'd have with Ezra, before he'd given me a mouth. "I spoke with Max, and he has no intention of leaving. Not in winter, at least."

"But you all can come with us," I said as Akiva placed the baby back in the cradle and tucked the blanket in. "There's a family camp in Rudniki Forest. Akiva and I can take you there."

She listened calmly, with a vague half smile, and even as the words left my mouth, I could tell from her serene expression that she had heard this before, and that she had already made her decision.

What I couldn't understand was why. This place was no different than a hayloft. No, it was even worse than that, because at least in the hayloft, there had been an unspoken expectation that at some point, Ezra would slowly open the rest of the world up to me—first by showing me to the area of the hayloft beyond the hideaway, then by leading me down below among the cows and horses, and after that, the inevitable moment I stepped into the outer darkness to fulfill my purpose.

"While I appreciate the offer, I'd rather stay," Miriam said.

"But you'll die here!" I said it before I could stop myself. Her mouth twitched in what might've been a grimace, but her face smoothed over before the expression could fully form. In the cradle, the baby began crying again.

"I'll die if I leave." She turned away. "At least in here, it'll be surrounded by family. In my community."

As she left the room, I turned to Akiva, who had watched the exchange in silence, his smile gone now, features chilled over once more.

"Can't you do something?" I asked, startling myself with the bite in my voice.

He scuffed a floorboard with his heel. "There's nothing to do."

"Convince her!"

"Vera, she's made her choice." At last, he looked at me. "It's what she wants."

"How can she want to stay here?"

Akiva was quiet for so long. Just when I thought he wouldn't respond, he answered my question with one of his own: "What do you really want, Vera?"

"I told you."

"You told me why you were made, but that doesn't mean it's what you want. You don't have to do this, you know. Not any of this."

His words awoke a fault line inside me. He was right— with Ezra dead or missing, I had free will, the ability to decide my actions. But Ezra had infused his hatred and desire for vengeance into my flesh; with each slice of the pick and gouge of the awl, he had driven his rage deeper and deeper into my body, until it wrapped around the steel armature of my skeleton like a choking vine.

I could not simply turn my back on the war and go my own way when more innocent blood was spilling into the ground. The ability to choose to ignore or fight against evil was a gift of human mortality.

I had no such choice.

"Why are *you* doing this, Akiva?" I asked as his gaze returned to where the infant lay in her cradle, and for the first time, I saw the harsh edge of envy in his gaze. Something cold and jealous, and I realized maybe he'd been so kind to the child because he wished he could have someone hold him like that, to be safe and warm and know someone was there to protect him.

"Why me?" he echoed, not meeting my eye.

"You're a human. You have free will, do you not?"

He swallowed hard, and I could tell that I had pierced him, exposed something deep inside of him.

"Why?" he murmured, gazing down. "I… I don't… Vera, we're living like animals, and I hate it. I hate it so much. This isn't how things should be. This isn't how any of us were raised. It's disgusting. It disgusts me."

Akiva's voice broke on the last word, and he turned away quickly, as if the crack in his voice had revealed a fracture that went even deeper. He crossed the room, brushing past Miriam's aunt and another young woman on his way downstairs. I didn't know if he expected me to follow, but I did anyway. We walked outside, the air so cold that each breath I took seemed laced with ice, freezing me from the inside out. Snowflakes swirled down, gathering on the cobblestones.

The winter chill seemed to rejuvenate Akiva. He closed his eyes and craned his head to the sky, snow settling on his hair and lashes. Even at rest, he had seemed filled with tension, but now his rigid shoulders slowly loosened and slumped down. He exhaled softly, his breath flowing from his lips as fog.

"The snow. It's beautiful, isn't it?" Akiva kept his eyes closed. A frigid wind tousled his hair, unfurled it behind him like the wings of a crow. "We all have the seasons we feel most at home in, and it's the winter for me. The snow, the scent of hot oil, fried latkes, firewood, burning candles…"

I wished that I could share in his memories and talk about the beauty of a Lithuanian winter. But when I thought back to the time before this, there was only snow encrusting the top of the river, and silence down below, fish dead or hibernating, and the clay of my riverbed veined with ice as white and delicate as a skeleton's fingers.

"It's beautiful, isn't it?" Akiva repeated.

"It is," I said, but I didn't think that was the answer he wanted to hear.

"Snow like this, you think it'd cover all the filth in this place," Akiva said, opening his eyes. The darkness robbed his irises of their blue intensity, left them dark and unlit. "But it doesn't. It'll just melt into a brown slush, and it'll get into our shoes, and I hate it, and I hate myself. I hate myself so much. I didn't used to feel this way. They're the reason for it, so I hate them even more, and I want to make them pay. They deserve to pay. And that's why I'm doing this, Vera. Because they turned us into this. They're the ones making us live this way, and killing us, and now when I look in the mirror, I don't see myself anymore, I see what they want me to see, and I can't stand it. And if we don't change it, it'll just keep going on, and on, and on like this, forever. Until they kill us. Because that's the endgame, you see? It always has been. Chaya knew that. Miriam knows that, even if she won't admit to it. And that baby, you think she'll survive here? She'll be dead before winter's over. When they find her, they'll pick her up and smash her head against the wall, the way they did to my brother."

Moisture welled in Akiva's eyes, trickled down his cheeks. At first, I thought it must be melted snow, since the snow simply gathered on me, while it turned to beads of water once it got trapped in his thick lashes. Then a sudden convulsive noise racked him, and he bowed over himself and pressed his hands over his eyes, and I realized he was crying.

"Shit." His voice came out sharp and abrupt, like broken glass. "Shit. Shit. Shit."

I reached for his shoulder to try consoling him, but he tore away from me with a low, wounded groan. Stumbled against the wall. Bowed over it. I was afraid he was going to fall, but then he just slammed his fists into the wood, swore, and sobbed.

No matter how much he had hardened himself, he was not a golem at all, just a fragile being of blood and bones. So, this was the difference between us. This was what it meant to be human.

I didn't know what I should do. I dredged through all my memories, searching for a kind word or a comforting phrase. I could wipe the tears from his cheeks, let them freeze on my fingertips. I could cradle him against myself, but I knew my body would be so cold, it'd be like embracing a gravestone.

So, I stood back and I watched Akiva weep. And as he curled on the ground, his side and shoulder against the wall, a revelation slowly dawned on me. His face was so sharp because he wasn't eating nearly as much as he should've been, and those shadows under his eyes were because he couldn't sleep. And he was slowly dying. He was dying. Like the man we'd come across in the street, with no shoes and his face in the dirt.

Like everyone in this place, except for me.

When Ezra was still alive, I had been afraid that if I stepped out of line, he would destroy me so that he could recreate me in a better, more obedient image. But now I was not afraid of dying. I was afraid of being the only one left alive.

"Akiva," I said softly, wanting to soothe him. I knelt down beside him, not touching him. I had a feeling that if I were to touch him, it would be excruciating as any blade. "Akiva, please don't cry. It's going to be all right."

"You say that, but it isn't." He blotted his eyes. "Don't you understand, Vera? Nothing's going to be all right. Not for any of us, except for maybe you. This is the end. The end of everything. Don't you see? That's why Miriam wants to stay here, with her family. Because at least she still has a family." A tortured smile came across his face. "No matter how hard we try, we can't change a damn thing, because there's a million of them, and they've got our backs against the wall. And all we can do—the only thing left to do—is try to take as many of them down with us."

"But—"

"Just go away." He curled tighter into himself. Snowflakes landed on his shoulders and gathered in his hair. "Please. Don't say another word. Just go back inside."

"Akiva—"

"I said, 'go!'"

I said nothing. Golems were creatures of command. So, I did what I was told.

CHAPTER 21

WHEN WE WALKED TO THE LIBRARY THE NEXT
morning, it was as if nothing had changed at all. Akiva had
built up his barricades overnight and gave me a muted smile
as he ate the rest of the bread we had brought from Gulzifa's.
He offered me a chunk, like a peace offering, but I shook
my head.

"If only we were all like you," he said, and there was an
edge to his words that hadn't been there before. "There'd be
no need for the Jewish Council's food stores here."

Miriam accompanied us as far as Strashun Street, but even
she seemed aware of the tension that lingered between me
and Akiva, because she kept her distance. "I'll be back at
the flat, when you return," she said, except there was a hes-
itance in the words themselves, and doubt and fear lingered

in her gaze. Maybe she was already preparing for the possibility that we wouldn't return. It must've been commonplace here—and in the world outside of here, for that matter—for people to just vanish. Their history cut off, unresolved, like a torn page.

"What about America?" I asked as Miriam turned to leave, and she flinched and looked back at me.

"America?" she repeated in a whisper, as if it were a prayer.

"You said that you wanted to go to America one day." With each word, I could feel my chance to change her mind slipping between my fingers like sand. I began to speak quicker, louder. "That you wanted to go to the beaches. That you'd open a bakery."

"Vera," Akiva began, but I shook my head, stepped forward. Kept my gaze boring into hers. For once, I wasn't worried she'd recognize the gleam in my eyes as human. I wanted her to.

"What we talked about," I said, "was that all a lie?"

"I won't find America out in the forest, Vera," she said quietly.

"But you said—"

"I know what I said." Her word was firm, final, shutting the conversation like a slammed door. My own lips eased closed. I saw no way to argue with her. The debate felt impossible. I had already lost.

I turned away and made it several steps before she said my name again. I looked back.

"After the war," she said, offering me a thin smile. "We'll go after the war, just like I said. You, me, my brother, and Akiva. All four of us, in a cottage along the Pacific Ocean."

"Really?" I said.

She nodded.

"Next year in America then," Akiva said, and like the bread he'd offered me, I sensed that this too was a kind of peace treaty.

"Next year in America." Her smile never quite reached her eyes. It dawned on me how frail human life was, and how quickly it could be snuffed out. This was why she had to stay here, why she had to be with her brother. This was what separated us.

"She's made her choice, Vera," Akiva said, once she had continued back the way she came. "She's no longer part of this, and we shouldn't involve her anymore."

"You don't have to come either," I said. "It would be safer if you just stayed behind."

He chuckled. "And let you have all the fun?"

The boy from the library, Nathan, waited for us under the library's eaves. He ushered us inside without a word, into the shadow of the stacks.

"The other workers will be here shortly, and we'll all be escorted to the old YIVO building," he explained. "You're on your own after this. I won't be able to help you if you're stopped."

"We'll take our chances," Akiva said, and Nathan nodded reluctantly. I could tell he was already regretting his decision to assist us.

Before more could be said, the rest of the workers began to file into the foyer. Most of them were older men and women, but there were a few teens as well, and Akiva and I gravitated toward them. As distant bells tolled the hour, two members of the ghetto police came to escort us to the gates. Akiva and I merged with the crowd, cocooning ourselves in the middle. Eyes down, head bowed, shoulders drawn inward as though in preparation for a blow. It was easy to mimic the postures of those around me, until I realized my unease had nothing on the fear that hung over them.

I wondered if I was missing something. I wasn't human, true, but maybe it went even deeper than that. Maybe there was something in my core, my very being, that was deeply wrong with me.

The ghetto gate rose before us—a wooden wall topped with coils of razor wire and guarded by men with rifles and dogs. As I passed, one of the hounds strained against its leash, his dark, glistening eyes boring into me. I fisted my hands at my side until we passed, and the dog's whines and panting diminished behind us. I didn't want to fight the animal, not just because it would ruin everything we had come here for, but also because the dog had been *made* for this.

We stopped to allow for the guards to open the gate. One of the men, with flinty eyes and a face as hard and broad as the blade of a shovel, gestured for us to step forward. My muscles tensed as I followed after Akiva, afraid something in my face might reveal my true nature or the stiffness of my body would betray me. If a harsh wind blew, I would be exposed in an instant. And once that happened, I would have to make a choice. To fight. To kill.

I wished I knew how I was supposed to behave. Why couldn't these things just come naturally? It had been so much easier out of the wilderness, where violence was the expected response. In here, there were layers to each conversation and gesture, and I was once more a stranger.

Only after we had emptied into the street beyond and the gate rattled shut behind us did the tension in my shoulders loosen. I stopped metering my breath, allowed my fingers to unfurl. Beside me, Akiva exhaled slowly, raking back his hair.

"Thought you'd end up dog food there," he whispered, catching my eye. A smile curled one corner of his mouth, cutting his scar deeper into his cheek.

"I don't think clay would taste very good."

"Hate to break it to you, but dogs eat their own shit sometimes. Clay would be a delicacy for them compared to that."

The old YIVO headquarters was only a short walk from the ghetto, and though I prickled under the gazes of the soldiers who escorted us, we reached the building without confrontation. It was a simple two-story brick building with a gabled roof and white limestone pillars. I expected it to be guarded as well, but there was only one police officer waiting for us in the lobby.

As we entered the archives, a strange calm settled over me. I had never been here before, or at least not in this short lifetime, but there was something oddly soothing and nostalgic about walking down the stacks of books piled haphazardly on the floor, arranged in a sprawl even more chaotic than the hayloft's disarray.

I longed to tug off my gloves and trace my bare palms over the books' leather covers. Flip through their pages. Test the words on my tongue, slowly and tenderly, the way Ezra had guided my finger over the letters he'd chalked on the floor. אמת for *truth* and מת for *dead*.

At the memory, I bit my inner cheek, testing the clay. A part of me wanted to see how deep I could dig my teeth, how far I could strain the reliability of my form. Ezra. I missed him. He had to be here, right? If the papers were taken here, he must've been, too.

As we reached the second-floor landing, our group was split into two. Akiva and I followed a handful of others into a room filled with even more books than those below. Crates lined the walls nearly to the ceiling, and documents covered every available surface. I searched for any clue that they were the ones from the hayloft, but the boxes could've come from anywhere.

The rest in our group got to work immediately, but when I began to follow Akiva to a private corner, someone cleared their throat behind me. I looked back, meeting an older man's keen maple-brown eyes. No gun, shoulder-band, or badges. So, not a soldier.

"Excuse me, but I don't believe we've met," he said. "Are you two new here?"

"We were chosen for the work detail," Akiva cut in before I could answer. He offered the man a smile, but his shoulders were stiff with coiled tension.

"I see. Well, I imagine you already know the importance of being quiet and respectful. No chattering, no slacking." He nodded to the other end of the room, where books overflowed from wooden crates. "Begin by sorting the materials. Set aside any materials that look older, handwritten, or Kabbalistic. Put anything from the Talmud or Tanakh in another pile. Census and birth records and civil paperwork can go in the pulp bin."

As the man returned to his sorting, I took in the sight of the stacked books and scattered scrolls. They looked so much like the ones back in the hayloft, that my heart ached for Ezra and for those long days we had spent together. He had never been kind to me, but he was still my creator, and some of the love I felt for him must've remained behind, because his absence felt like an open wound that had been left to fester. The most painful part was that there was no resolution. He was just gone as if he had never existed in the first place, and all those who knew him were likely dead as well.

I got to work, hoping that the monotonous task of rifling through the pages would eventually dispel him from my thoughts. But as I sorted through the papers, I couldn't stop thinking about the hayloft or about the books he had taken from his shul's genizah. Kazlauskas had said that they'd taken the papers here. So where were they?

My fingers froze over a well-worn book with a blue cloth cover. *Archanioł jutra*. It was a book of poetry by Franciszka Arnsztajnowa, out of place among the twine-bound scrolls and scraps of paper. As I turned to the first dog-eared page, the words of the poem's stanza were already welling on my lips.

I had read these books before. And those scrolls, their very Hebrew was written upon my skin.

I turned. It took all of my self-control not to cross the room in a single lunge, seize the guard posted at the door by his collar, and demand to know where Ezra was. The soldier might not be able to hurt me, but the others in the room would suffer for my outburst. Akiva would suffer.

I breathed in, breathed out. Human. I needed to act human.

"Akiva."

When he didn't answer, I looked over at him. He leaned over the table, frowning at the scatter of yellowed parchment strewn out before him. He had scarcely gone through half of his stack in the time since we started, and as he shifted a new leaf into place, I realized he wasn't sorting it, he was reading it.

"This feels wrong," he muttered.

"What we're doing?"

"No. This text. It's not Kabbalah. I don't even know what it is." His fingertips traced over the faded ink, and then he wiped his hand on the seat of his pants. At first, I thought it was to keep from darkening the vellum with the oil of his skin, but then I caught a glimpse of the unease in his face, disgust even, and I realized it was as if he'd touched something dirty. "I've been trying to read it for the last hour, and every time I look at the letters, it feels…it feels like they're moving inside my head. Like something. Like maggots. Some of it's written in Hebrew. I can read that, a little, but the rest… The rest is—"

"Kishuf," I said quietly, and he looked at me, not understanding.

"Sorcery?"

"These are from the hayloft," I whispered. He just stared at me, not comprehending. I sighed. "They're from Ezra."

"Oh."

"So, where is he?" I looked around us once more, as if acknowledging his absence would make him materialize from thin air. "He has to be here. Doesn't he? I mean, his books are here. He *has* to be."

"Vera, calm down." His fingers strayed to my arm. "You're talking too loud."

"But Kazlauskas said—"

"No chatting!" a guard barked, and I stepped away, gritting my teeth.

Akiva leaned down to pick up a fallen book, wincing as he reached for it. His hand strayed to his side, and as he straightened again, I met his gaze. Sweat dewed on his brow, and something about the way he moistened his lips, or leaned to rest against the table, made me realize he wasn't feeling well.

I gestured to my side and mouthed, *Your wound?*

He shook his head, but I couldn't decide whether he meant something else was bothering him or if he just wanted me to let it be.

"Vera," he said quietly, "there was never a guarantee he was here. Look around. There are other people fluent in Hebrew. It's possible that…"

He trailed off, but I knew what he meant to say. The weight of his unspoken words hung over me like a guillotine blade.

There was a possibility, perhaps a very good one, that Ezra was dead. That he'd never made it out of the gestapo's custody. That somewhere in Lithuania, there was an unmarked grave, or a pile of ashes, and that was all that remained of him.

The anger drained out of me, replaced by exhaustion so great, I thought I might collapse. So, this was it then. A dead end. No path for me to follow.

"So, he's dead."

Akiva didn't answer.

"What am I supposed to do? I…" I swallowed hard, feeling myself waver. I leaned over the table, staring at the scatter of papers. This was all that was left of him. "What is my purpose?"

As I gripped the edge of the table, Akiva placed his hand over mine. Slowly, I looked up, meeting his piercing blue eyes.

"Vera, you don't need someone to give you a purpose. You create your own."

CHAPTER 22

FLURRIES OF SNOW SCRAPED AGAINST MY FACE, finding their way into my collar and dripping down my back. Even in the shelter of the buildings' eaves, the storm managed to find its way into the alley, the gusts mercilessly cold and abrasive. As I knelt down to shift the rubble from over the sewer hatch, Akiva lingered at my side, holding the slumbering infant in the fold of his coat. She had woken only once on the walk over, but her soft mewls of protest had been drowned by the howling wind.

Voices rose from beyond the alley, accompanied by the heavy clump of boots. Leaning down, I wrenched the metal plate covering the manhole and held the lid up for Akiva.

He climbed down with care, cradling the infant against himself. I eased shut the manhole cover on my way down, catching a glimpse of a man's heavy boots through the opening just before the lid groaned into place.

Miriam had given us candles to find our way, and Akiva lit one. He took the baby, and I took the candle. It made me nervous to hold the candle, even with my glove protecting my hand from hot wax. Ezra had never told me what would happen if I was burnt, and somehow heat seemed even more treacherous to my form than brute force.

The infant began to cry as we headed deeper into the tunnel, scared by the darkness maybe, or the skitter of rats in the walls. I could sympathize—when I had first been created, such noises had frightened me as well.

There was something about the darkness that made it easy to lose myself, to feel the fragile hold I had over my body begin to slip away, until I could no longer quite recall the shape of my feet or the length of my legs, or even discern where the floor began and my body ended. It made me anxious enough that I held the candle close and hurried after Akiva.

The tunnel seemed even darker than earlier, the air so thick and cold that it felt sodden. Akiva paused and began to cough with such force, I was worried he'd drop the infant.

"Let me hold her," I said, once he stopped. His gaze met mine, dark hair framing his cheeks like ragged feathers. Something about the way he wheezed in catching his breath, or how his other hand lowered to his side, made me shift in deepening unease.

"Just be careful you don't drop her," he croaked, and handed me her swaddled bundle.

Even though I loathed having to give up the candle's light,

somehow feeling the infant's breath warm the side of my neck was more soothing than the flame. It reminded me of what it was like to be human, or at least what I thought it must feel like.

I was finally beginning to realize. Everything I felt was simply a reflection of an even older feeling or memory. I wanted to believe that Chaya had given these feelings to me, or even that the scribes—decades dead if not centuries—had known what their scriptures would be used for. I wanted to believe these things were gifts. I needed to.

The moment we entered Gulzifa's cottage, her dog came up to Akiva, tail wagging furiously as it sniffed at his coat hem and tried to prod its wet nose up against the slumbering infant. Gulzifa's reaction wasn't nearly as enthusiastic—she stared at the child, mouth agape, looking almost as shocked as when Miriam had introduced me to the business end of an ice pick.

"Is that a baby?" Gulzifa whispered.

"I'm sorry, but I couldn't resist bringing back a souvenir," Akiva said.

She just stared. It wasn't until Dvosye stirred that Gulzifa stepped forward, holding out her hands to take the swaddled infant from Akiva.

"What am I supposed to do with a baby?" she stammered.

"Would you have preferred we leave her in the ghetto?" Akiva asked.

She had no response to that.

With a sigh, he sank into the rocking chair by the fire and kicked his feet back. It had been a long and miserable hike from the ghetto back through the sewers, and near the end of it, he hadn't even tried hiding how much pain he was in.

"I could carry you," I had offered the third time we had stopped, when he had paused to tap his feet against the ground to work out the soreness. I had plotted out the logistics in my head, and figured if he rode on my back, I'd still be able to cradle the infant against my chest.

"Over my dead body," Akiva had shot back, but from the way he now removed his boots with infinite care, I could tell he regretted not accepting my offer. The moment he unrolled his woolen socks and began to unwrap the rags he'd wound around his soles, Gulzifa veered back with a groan.

"Are your feet rotting?" She crossed to the other side of the room to put some distance between them.

"Probably."

"They don't look like they're rotting," I said, squatting down to get a better look. But they were covered in scabbed blisters, and his wrappings were stained with blood from fresh sores.

He snorted, pressing a hand over his face. "You're hopeless, Vera."

It would've upset me, except he said it with warmth, and he even chuckled, although in his pain and exhaustion, the laugh trailed off into a wheeze.

While we recovered from the long journey, Gulzifa warmed some evaporated milk for the baby and gave her a rye rusk to teethe.

"She's old enough to be weaned," Gulzifa said quietly.

"So, can you take her?" Akiva asked.

Gulzifa sighed, brushing her hand over the flossy flaxen

strands cradling the crown of the infant's head. "Do I have a choice?"

Akiva's shoulders loosened, and I felt my own body relax. That was confirmation enough.

"Thank you," Akiva murmured.

The infant drifted off with a low, contented murmur, snuggling into the crook of Gulzifa's arm.

"Last night, I was able to get through to General Volkov's brigade," Gulzifa said as she brushed the stray crumbs from the child's face. "He again refused to give us soldiers, but he said that if we recover any weapons from the shipment, he'll be glad to take them off our hands."

Akiva turned to me. "Vera, will you help us?"

I didn't know what I wanted anymore. Back at the library, he had made it sound so simple—creating my own purpose— but the truth was, I couldn't see a future for myself beyond this war. Beyond fulfilling Ezra's desire for revenge. In any case, I needed to see this through to the end.

I nodded.

"What do you think is in the shipment?" Akiva asked. "Guns? Or explosives?"

"I wouldn't rule out chemical weapons either," Gulzifa said.

"Chemical weapons?" I asked.

"Toxic gas," Akiva said.

I was struck by a sudden memory of the slow encroachment of rolling gray clouds across a barren steppe of thorny wire and trenches. Men writhing in throes of agony on the muddy earth, others stumbling forward in masks and drabs. Not my memory. A scribe, one who had come of age in the electrical lights and rumbling automobiles of modern Vilna.

His works' vellum had still been supple, the ink still fresh when it had sunk into my skin.

Like Ezra, the scribe had lived through that desolate landscape. And like him, he was probably dead now.

"Whatever's inside it, once the train reaches Vilna, we won't have a chance," Akiva said. "If it's coming from Germany, the last place it'll stop would be the Uzberezh-Senové border crossing, and even if we travel all day and night, there's no way we'll be able to get there before Wednesday night. The safer bet would simply be to mine the tracks and derail it."

"And if it is something like toxic gas or explosives, what then?" Gulzifa said gravely.

"We'll be far enough away from the tracks by the time the mines are detonated."

"But villagers might not be," she said.

Akiva gave her a cold, lingering look. "Why should that matter?"

I turned to him in disbelief. "They're innocent."

"Not all." He scoffed. "Not enough."

The anger in his voice made me uneasy. It ran in a vein even deeper than my own, and unlike me, his resentment belonged to him fully.

"If it's a supply train, there must be food on there as well," I mused. "Medicine. Warm clothes. We can bring them to the family camp."

"Even if we could hijack the train, how exactly do you plan to transport the supplies?" Akiva asked dully. "Carry them on your back?"

"A sleigh," Gulzifa said, drawing our attention across the

room. "I have a spare sleigh in the barn. It's small, only for a single horse, but it'll be enough."

Akiva sighed, resting his forehead in his hand. "The only issue left is how to get aboard."

I thought back to the night Akiva and I had fled through the orchard, the night I had joined him with a man's blood drying cold and tacky on my palms. When we had watched the train cross the moonlit field, it had seemed to hover above the tracks, its movements as fluid and effortless as an eel through water.

"Does the train ever slow?" I asked.

Akiva turned to me. "At turns and as it's approaching stations, but even then, they'd spot you if you tried jumping aboard."

A smile curled my lips. "Not from above."

CHAPTER 23

THE SNOW-DAPPLED TREES GLISTENED IN THE moonlight. Quivering birches regarded us, their black-scabbed trunks like a multitude of eyes.

From Gulzifa's house, the walk on foot had taken Akiva and I several hours, mostly through fields and forests. Though I could have made that journey in half the time had I gone alone, it soothed me to have another person by my side.

No, not just that. To have *him* by my side.

We had hiked parallel to the tracks, though not near them. The Germans had bunkers set up along the railroad and patrolled the stretches to deter partisan attacks.

"With Chaya, we derailed four trains," Akiva told me with a touch of bitter pride. I couldn't remember the details, but as we neared the tracks, I dredged a remnant of Chaya's exhilaration from within me—the bulk and heft of the explosive charges, the blind rush through the woods to put some distance between herself and the explosion, the knowledge that this was *vengeance*.

Ahead, the train tracks gleamed darkly, the crisscrossed rails as ominous as the bars of a cage. Akiva had kept his finger against his rifle's trigger guard all throughout the hike, and even now, he continued to trace that band of metal restlessly, thoughtlessly.

"Are you sure you want to do this?" he asked as we lingered in the forest's shadow.

"I'll be fine."

"You say that, but..."

I narrowed my eyes. Did he doubt me? "But what?"

He just shook his head, as if to put the question to rest. "Forget it. Listen, this is just a supply train, so it likely won't be guarded as heavily as one transporting soldiers or heavy artillery. I suspect you'll be dealing with five, perhaps ten guards, along with a seven-member Deutschbahn crew."

He passed over a cloth-wrapped bundle stowed inside his coat's inner pocket, along with a brass lighter.

"Do you remember what I showed you?"

I nodded, taking the supplies from him. As I began to pull away, he took my wrist. I stared him in the eyes, my teeth sinking against my lower lip. A part of me expected him to lean forward—the way he'd once done, the way he would have done with *her*—and kiss me deeply, like he meant to draw the breath from me. Instead, he just held my arm in an uncertain grip.

"Don't use it until you see the old mill and lake on your right. That's where we'll be waiting." His fingers slipped away.

The warmth they left behind made me acutely aware of their absence. "In this weather, with the way the tracks are, the train will be going slow. Still, you'll have less than twenty minutes."

"I understand," I said, the words rising mechanically.

He nodded. "Good."

I waited for him to say more, and I supposed he must have been waiting for something, too, because he didn't move. Our stillness and silence felt fraught with a tension of its own, as if we were two wolves circling each other, eyes glued to the pulse.

I didn't know what I wanted, just that it felt as if there was an unreconcilable difference between us, but that we were also somehow of the same nature. I wondered if he felt similar.

"Just be careful," he said, stepping back.

"I will."

"Your life is important. Don't waste it on a stupid mistake."

"I could say the same for you."

As he retreated into the undergrowth, I regarded the trees surrounding me. The brush near the track was trimmed down, but the canopies of the nearby trees had been allowed to flourish. I climbed up the largest specimen, an ancient oak whose branches nearly reached the wires.

As the branch swayed, I clenched my teeth in anticipation. It would be a three-meter jump from the end of the bough, and farther if I leapt from my stable perch in the middle. If I missed and slammed my forehead against the metal ties, the force of impact would be enough to wipe out Ezra's careful sculpting, and the word אמת along with it.

I settled against the crook between the branch and trunk and began the long wait. Being aboveground made me uneasy, my skin prickling as if it might crack. At least in the hayloft there had been an illusion of solid ground under my feet, and below that, the same earth from which I had been dredged.

I gripped onto the branch until the scabby bark fissured beneath my fingers and I reached the tender wood beneath. Better.

Twice within an hour, a small group of soldiers passed through the shadow of my tree's outstretched bough. From above, they resembled fragile constructs of leather and cloth, no more human than me. I thought how easy it would be to leap down on them from above. Drive them into the earth. Gouge, strike, and crush. I shuddered, recalling the crack of bones. I couldn't tell whether it was disgust or excitement that made my body tense.

Why did you have to make me feel this way? I wanted to ask Ezra that. Why hatred? Why anticipation? Wouldn't emptiness have been enough? But more than anything, I wanted to know—why *me*?

As soon as the second patrol disappeared along the track, I freed my fingers from the cracks I had made in the tree. Minutes later, a low rumbling filled the air. I shifted onto my haunches and eased down the branch until the wood groaned beneath my weight. Leaning forward, I squinted down the track.

A white glow materialized in the distance. As the radiance grew, the trees cast branched shadows across the tracks, each quaking like disembodied hands.

The train was upon me in an instant, rushing past with a shrill howl and a blast of frigid wind. For the briefest moment, a tremor of fear seized me. But Ezra had not made me to hesitate. I leapt from the branch, springing forward with such force, the wood cracked beneath one heel.

As the bough crashed to the ground, the train passed beneath me. Instead of coming short as I had feared, I nearly overshot my target. My waist slammed into the roof of the train, while my upper half curled over empty space. I began to tip forward over the side of the train, fingers slipping across the frosty metal hull in desperate search of purchase.

At the last moment, I seized hold of a rivet with my right hand. My left hand dug into the seam between two of the curved panels, disfiguring my fingers as the metal bent inward beneath my grasp. Once I was certain I wouldn't fall, I pulled away. Clods of clay remained behind in the sharp lip.

I waited with my chin and stomach pressed against the roof, afraid to look at my hand. I took shallow breaths to convince myself I was alive. Yes. This was my form now. These were my hands. Once I would look down, my fingers would be as they were, because I was designed to be human.

Slowly, I lifted my left hand, and a low groan escaped my lips. Horror washed over me in a nauseating wave. My fingers were curled inward. Several had bent at the first digits, the nails crooked or buried beneath curls of clay.

It's alright. I could fix this. I could fix this.

Gritting my teeth, I forced them back into place. There was no pain, but the sensation of being contorted sickened me on its own. I rubbed the clay down and flexed my hand. After a moment, the damage smoothed over on its own, and even the nails resurfaced.

A small smile wavered on my lips. There. Back to normal.

I carefully turned myself sideways so that my body was pressed flat against the roof, facing toward the rear cars. Once I was certain a harsh gust wouldn't hurl me from my perch, I eased onto my hands and knees and crawled forward.

As I neared the other end of the car, the creak of hinges

made me freeze, body pressed against the roof. Coiling back on my haunches, I listened keenly.

A man coughed below. There was a metallic rasp—the sound of a lighter wheel being thumbed. Yes. I knew that sound, and the scent of smoke that billowed up to me moments later was even more familiar. I remembered sitting in an earthen room lit by the hesitant flicker of a candle, sharing a cigarette with Akiva. In the gloom, his eyes had been as dark as bruises, his mouth swollen and lip busted.

Chaya, don't hog it, he'd teased, plucking the cigarette from between my—her—lips. The way he said her name made my face tingle, though maybe it was only the melting snow.

I shook my head, stirring myself back into reality. No matter how close that version of the past felt, the truth was this: when Chaya and Akiva had huddled in the dugout, close enough that their shoulders brushed and their shared smoke mingled in the air, I had still been part of the river. These memories didn't belong to me, and the pleasant warmth they stoked in my chest was no more mine than my hair or teeth.

But this savage anticipation welling up inside my core, hotter than blood, was all me. This rage. This hunger. I would claim it as my own.

I edged forward until I reached the overhang. Below, a soldier stood on the small balcony between cars, one hand on the railing, the other holding a cigarette to his lips.

He lifted his head as I rose into a crouch. I expected him to draw his gun or shout out, but instead, he reacted by stumbling back, nearly crashing over the railing in the process. I leapt to the platform, exhilarated by how the metal shuddered violently upon impact.

"*Was zum Teufel?!*" As he reached for the holster at his side, I drove my shoulder into him, putting the full weight of my body behind the blow. He tumbled over the railing. If he made a sound, it was lost to the howling wind and the crunch of his bones breaking upon the track.

Immediately, I pivoted to face the door he had come through. It was closed, the round window etched over with frost. The milky gleam of electrical lamps filtered through the glass. Light meant people. If I went that route, I would encounter more soldiers and bring them the retribution they deserved, but that wasn't why I had come here. I needed to keep going.

I crossed the space between cars, reaching the platform on the other side. It was hardly more than a shelf to stand on. Throwing open the door, I left behind the turmoil of the winter night for a dark, silent interior burdened with the scent of dust and machine oil. Wooden crates were bolted to the floor with chains and ropes. Stacks of barrels formed pyramids.

There was no exit on the other side of the car, only broad sliding doors along its side, accessible by iron bolts. Overhead, a small window admitted paltry light. I walked up and down the rows. Some crates were marked with numbers, while just as many had been marked with a strange and familiar symbol:

ᛗ

The black paint had dripped down the wood and dried there, as though each symbol had been a gaping wound. I traced my fingertips over the mark, recalling the silver pin I had torn from the soldier's coat.

But this badge is…new, Akiva had said at the time. Not SS, not Auxiliary Police.

Something even worse, I thought, lowering my hand. I didn't know what was in these crates, but it scared me to open them. It was the same lead-heavy fear that had weighed over me the first time I descended from the hayloft ladder, testing each rung beneath my feet. Anything could be waiting for me inside these boxes.

Returning to the front of the car, I carefully knelt on the rickety platform and removed the bundle Akiva had given me from my coat pocket. Inside the handkerchief were several lengths of neatly-coiled wire and a burlap pouch containing a small but potent explosive charge.

Inching forward, I fastened the pouch to the train car connector, being careful not to stick my fingers in the gaps between the metal bars. One simple jolt and I would be left with a hunk of disfigured clay where a hand had been. I didn't know if I'd be able to recover from that, and I wasn't ready to find out.

The car shifted beneath me as we rounded a turn. I held onto the low railing for support, searching the dark blur of landscape for a mill.

Old mill and lake on your right, Akiva had said.

I was so caught up in my own head, I didn't see the mill until we were nearly upon it. It rose out of nowhere, a beacon of wood and gray stone. I hooked my finger through the charge's metal ring and yanked it free, scrambling back through the open door. Five seconds. I had five seconds. I threw myself across the floor on my hands and knees. Four seconds. At the other end of the car, I found refuge behind a stack of crates, gripping the chains bolting them to the floor.

The explosion was loud but contained, barely jolting the car. The chaos came with the aftermath—the shrieking of train wheels on the metal rails as the car broke free of the procession, the sudden jolt when one wheel slipped free of the track, and the screaming protest as the detached cars came to a halt.

Slowly, I picked myself off the floor. I had gripped the chain so tightly it had imprinted its shape in my palms. A few barrels had fallen over during the derailment, spilling grain and dried beans across the floor. Through the open door, I watched the train pick up speed, receding into the darkness, until its light was only a memory.

CHAPTER 24

CHICKENS PECKED THROUGH THE HAY AT MY feet as I eased the first crate onto the barn's dirt floor. Within moments of the detached train car coming to a halt, Gulzifa and Akiva had emerged from the forest with a horse-drawn sleigh cutting through the darkness behind them. We had worked rapidly to load the crates; although the train hadn't stopped, the noise of the explosion would have driven the German soldiers from their bunkers along the stretch and sent every patrol within two kilometers scrambling for the train tracks. Only now, with the barn's doors bolted tightly behind us, and a single lantern to cast its glow, did I feel safe and secure.

I could have lifted the crate's lid on my own, but I held back as the others fought at it with hammers and crowbars.

The wood groaned in protest beneath their onslaught, until at last the lid crashed to the floor, teethed with nails.

"What...?" Gulzifa stepped forward, peering into the crate with her brow furrowed.

The box was lined with cloth and packed to the lid with a beige substance. Blocks of it, glistening in the lantern light.

"What is it?" I asked.

"I can't believe it," Akiva murmured, raising a brick so carefully, almost reverently. He tested it under his fingers then lifted it to his nose and smelled it. "Earthy. It's some kind of explosive. It has to be."

"You can tell that just by smelling it?" I picked up a block to take a whiff. Dense and minerally, the smell reminded me of my own past below the water.

"The British use one that smells like almonds. This one must be made with another material. A mineral perhaps."

"With this much, we could stage a simultaneous attack on the gestapo headquarters, the railway station, all major outposts," Gulzifa said. "We could cripple their control of Vilnius in an instant."

I parted the brick's material beneath my fingers. Inside, it was wet and slick, threaded here and there with the same strands of algae and pebbles I occasionally found emerging from my own skin.

"These aren't explosives," I said, setting the crushed block on the table. "They're clay."

For a moment, neither of them moved, shock stark in their faces. Gulzifa was the first one to speak.

"That's impossible," she said. "They *have* to be explosives.

These came from Germany. They wouldn't transport building materials all this way..."

She trailed off.

"Unless these aren't for building," Akiva said quietly, giving me a sidelong look.

There were two uses for clay: to build and to bring to life.

"But why bring it all the way from Germany, when there is plenty of clay here?" I asked.

Akiva shrugged. "German soil, German soldiers. It fits their ideology."

"You can't be suggesting that the Nazis are trying to build a golem, too," Gulzifa said in disbelief.

Gritting his teeth, Akiva paced the room. "All for nothing. All that for nothing." He raked a hand through his hair.

He sounded so upset, when he wasn't even the one who had gotten onto the train in the first place. Maybe it wasn't what was in the crates that mattered, as much as what could have been in them. Maybe he thought that there would be something in there that would end the war.

I didn't know what to think. It both chilled and electrified me, the idea that there might be another golem like me out there.

"There has to be something more here," he said, shoving aside the blocks of clay.

The second and third crates revealed more of the same, and as he turned his attention to the fourth and final crate, I stepped forward. "Akiva, I think that's all there is."

The lid came crashing to the ground. Instead of neatly-molded bricks of clay, large tin canisters were insulated in a bed of wood shavings, each about the size of a bucket. Frowning, Akiva picked up one of the containers and weighed it in his hands thoughtfully.

"*Familien-u. Vorname: Lang, Arnold*," he read, tracing a thumb over the label pasted onto its side. "*Geboren am 18.5.1920 in Leipzig.* Does anyone here know German?"

I stepped close to get a better look. I had spent so much time being surrounded by Hebrew, both the verses that had sunk beneath my skin and those written across the sprawl of old scrolls and books stored in the hayloft. It disoriented me to read German, but with each word I mouthed, the language surfaced inside of me.

"*Truppenteil: SS-Panzerartillerieregiment 3.*" On my tongue, the German felt as stark and serrating as shrapnel, though the language would always be a part of me. "SS Panzer Artillery Regiment 3."

"This has to be the weapons then." Using the hooked end of the hammer, Akiva pried open the sealed lid, which gave way with the pneumatic hiss of air. My nose prickled at the sharp, strange scent of chemicals that rose from the container.

"What is it?" I asked, leaning in close. It was filled nearly to the brim with cloudy amber liquid. As Akiva held it to the glow of the lantern, the container's contents slowly resolved from the murk—a rounded surface covered in glistening brown tendrils that wafted in the liquid like algae.

No. Not tendrils. Hair.

"It almost looks like..." Akiva trailed off and upturned the contents onto the floor. A human head sluiced out in the flood of liquid, rolling across the dirt, before coming to a stop face-up. Its cataract filmed eyes confronted me, its mouth gaping dumbly. The arteries and tendons of the throat had been severed with surgical precision, bleached by the liquid to a livery gray.

"I would imagine," Gulzifa said, "that this is Arnold Lang."

A queasy feeling passed over me, as if someone had dug their hand into my stomach, unsettling the clay there. Staring down at the severed head, I felt as if I were looking at a part of myself, torn free and dripping.

"Klaus Preuß," Gulzifa read, rolling over the next container. "Alek Jung. From the look of it, they were all Nazi soldiers killed last month in Demyansk. All SS."

German soil, German soldiers. It fit the ideology.

Akiva frowned. "I don't understand. Golems are supposed to be just clay. Why would the Nazis be collecting body parts if they wanted to create…?"

He trailed off, staring at me as if seeing me for the first time. The puzzlement in his face dimmed, and his jaw loosened, and for the first time, I caught a trace of horror in his eyes. Because he saw it now. He understood completely what I was. What I was made of.

"No," he murmured, stepping away from me. "It can't be."

"Akiva," I began, and then stopped, at a loss of words. What would I say? What could I possibly say? All I could think of was Ezra and how he had looked at me. My first hours on earth, exposed to his horror, his rage, his disgust. But even then he had known full well what I was, and what had been sacrificed for my creation.

Recognition flared in Akiva's eyes, flanked by another emotion I had no name for. "Vera, did Ezra…did he… Your eyes. Your teeth. They're not clay at all, are they?"

I couldn't answer. From the way he asked it, he seemed to

value those meaningless bits of flesh so much, as if they were the sum of my parts. The most important thing about me.

"Tell me! Are those Chaya's?"

"I…" The burning intensity of his gaze made my voice shrivel in my throat. All this time, I had been so eager to show Akiva that a part of me, however small, was human. But it was not truly a part of me. It was merely an inheritance.

Here was the cruel truth: I was everything but my own person. My clay had come from innumerable places along the river, settled over the centuries. The calligraphy that had sunk into my skin had been written by strangers. And even these eyes and hair that I valued had never really belonged to me.

"They're mine now," I whispered, but the words felt shallow.

"No," he said tightly, stepping closer. "No, they're not."

Suddenly, it dawned on me. That emotion burning in Akiva's gaze—it was anger. And he had his teeth bared in disgust.

He took another step, his ice-blue eyes fixated on me. "They're not yours at all."

Before I knew what I was doing, I thrust out my hands, catching him across the shoulders. At the last moment, I remembered my strength, and pulled back the force of the blow, toppling him to the floor in a light shove instead of slamming him into the stall wall. Even so, he landed with enough force to drive the air from his lungs and send a scatter of dirt and sawdust spraying behind him.

Mortified, I sunk to one knee to help him. Reached out my hand. "Akiva—"

Cold steel pressed against my brow. Teeth bared, eyes wide,

he confronted me. One hand raised, his finger already curled through his Nagant's trigger guard.

I froze, conscious of the icy metal curve of the revolver's muzzle. I couldn't see the barrel's hole, but I felt it resting like a void against the mark on my brow.

"Akiva," Gulzifa exclaimed, but he didn't move, just kept the gun raised and stared me down. His ice-blue eyes pierced into me, as sharp as scalpels; they seemed capable of carving away at me.

"The old man in the forest camp, he was right," Akiva whispered harshly, as a curse. "You are a monster."

His words struck me as hard as a bullet, bowed me inward, sent me stumbling back. I could have answered, but I sensed that no matter what I said, Akiva would remain unwavering in his condemnation. How could he know what it was like to be born in bits and pieces—first a head, then a torso, each part carved over the span of weeks? And aware throughout it all. No eyes, no ears, no mouth or limbs. But aware. And writhing inside.

How could he possibly know?

I spun around on my heel and fled the room. If I stayed for much longer, something might come over me. I might hurt him, or worse—I might take his hand in mine, press the revolver harder against my brow, and guide his finger to the trigger.

Through the barn door, down the dirt path. My arms were uncovered, but that didn't matter. Let the enemy come for me. Let them see me for how I truly was.

I surrendered to the thrilling power that rushed through my limbs, daring myself to see how fast I could go, how far I could go. Maybe if I ran fast enough, I would be able to put this all behind me.

I didn't realize that I had a destination in mind before I burst past a line of trees and found myself at the brink of the Neméža River. Just a few steps across a dirt shore.

I came to the edge, staring into the dark water. The current cast the moonlight into quivering silver streaks. For how often I thought of the river, it had never dawned on me until now how close it had been this entire time—just a tributary of the Voké, true, but its winding route would guide me home, to the place of my creation.

"Vera," Akiva said from behind me.

I could run, I thought. As far away from here as I needed—down under and across the river, through the woods and fields. I didn't need to be around other people. I wasn't born for that. And though there were parts of me that were human, or had once been, the bulk of my being was simply soil and water. Maybe I didn't belong here among other people. Among the living. Maybe the wilderness was my true home.

It would have been easy to give in to the impulse, to run and not look back, keep going until the sound of his voice was drowned out by the blustering wind. But I turned instead.

Akiva stood close enough to reach out and touch me. It shocked me to realize that I hadn't heard him approach, let alone felt the warmth of his breath against my nape, as if the differences between us were already beginning to soften and lose their form.

As he stepped forward, I took a step back, wanting to keep my distance. We were incompatible beings. Get too close, and the heat of his body might crack me. And he was so fragile next to me, his bones as weak as cinders compared to my iron frame.

"I'm sorry, I shouldn't have said that," he said.

"It's the truth." The words burnt like acid on my tongue. He was right, and that was the worst part.

"That doesn't make it right. You didn't choose to be created." Akiva's eyes lowered to my hands, looking at the calligraphy maybe, or my nails. "When we first met, you recognized me. I thought it was because of Ezra—that somehow, you gained that knowledge through him—but now, I need to know... Do you have her memories?"

I nodded, not trusting myself to speak.

"How much do you remember?"

"It's just fragments."

"But you're not her."

His gaze burned into me. This would be my one chance to lay claim to my identity. I could take Chaya's name for my own and step into the hole her death had left behind. I could take what belonged to her—not just her memories, and the bloodier parts of her, but also his love and attention. And he would accept it. I could see it in the desperate hunger in his eyes, the way he leaned forward like he thought I might disappear if he even looked away just for an instant. He would accept it without question, because the alternative was infinitely worse—that Chaya was truly dead, gone forever, and all that was left behind was this monster. This crypt. This desecration.

"I'm not her," I said, and he drew in a sharp breath, as if my words had cut deep. I couldn't do it. Deceiving him would only hurt him in the end, and any affection he gave me would be unearned. "I'm sorry, but I'm not."

"I know." A tentative smile rose to his lips. "You're Vera the golem, killer of Nazis."

"To be fair, you've racked up a bit of a body count yourself."

He chuckled, shaking his head, and I couldn't help but smile, too. This felt better. It felt genuine.

"Akiva, do you think this was what Chaya would've wanted?" I asked as we turned away from the dark, gurgling river.

Just when I was beginning to think his silence was an answer of its own, he said, "In the end, I think she wanted to live."

CHAPTER 25

BACK IN THE BARN, ONLY A PUDDLE OF LIQUID marked where the head had landed, and Gulzifa was in the process of nailing down one of the crate's lids. She glanced up as we entered. I expected her to look at me with disgust, anger even, but instead she offered the thinnest smile.

"I was beginning to think I'd have to chase you two down." She set aside the hammer and brushed off her hands on the seat of her coat. "I hope you've reached a...resolution."

Akiva looked at me. I nodded.

"More or less," he said, sliding shut the barn door behind us.

Gulzifa nodded, before turning her attention back to the crates. "We'll dump these in the river. They're useless."

"Where was the package going?" I asked as she picked up the hammer once more.

"Trakai Castle."

"What did you say?" Akiva asked suddenly.

"It's going to Trakai Castle."

He swore softly under his breath, shaking his head. At first I thought he was even more upset, until I saw a smile lift the corners of his lips. "I don't believe it."

"What is it?" I asked.

"I know that place. It was one of the Soviet partisans' targets." His fingers drummed restlessly on the side of his leg. "The castle is falling apart and half-ruined, but our camp's leader got news from sources in Vilna that there was going to be some sort of big event being hosted there. There are officials coming all the way from Germany. It's one of the reasons an airdrop was arranged. We were going to target it."

"Do you think the two could be connected?" I asked.

"There's only one way to find out." His gaze lifted to me. "Feel like going to a party?"

Flames seethed against the fireplace's grate, their ruby light pooling in the jars of rouge and powder. Somehow, Gulzifa had managed to put together a stockpile of beauty products, along with a luscious silver-fox coat and matching hat to go over a sleek evening gown. The clothing was strange compared to what I was used to, all soft silk and thick fur, designed for luxury rather than practicality.

"That dress looks like it hasn't seen the light of day since the '20s," Akiva said, leaning against the doorpost as Gulzifa mixed the powders and blended pastes. He cradled Dvosye in his arms, the infant lulled asleep by his gentle rocking. Arslan wagged its tail beside him, having spent the entire evening following him around like a ghost. "You never told me you were a flapper once, Gulzifa."

She glanced up with a hint of a smile. "You never asked."

"And here I thought you were just a degenerate communist."

"You say it as though the two are mutually exclusive."

She added scanty pinches of powder at a time, testing each color against her own inner forearm before comparing them to my own muted complexion.

"She'll be under candlelight," Akiva said. "So, don't be excessive and turn her skin orange."

"Would you like to do this?" she snapped, brandishing a pot of foundation at him. "Be my guest!"

"I think I'll pass." A hint of a smile curled his lips. "Unless you want her to look like a pumpkin."

"Then step back and let me work in peace."

Shrugging his shoulders in defeat, Akiva backed from the room.

Gulzifa sighed and turned back to me. "Let's hope this is enough to cover those marks."

She carefully spread the cream over the letters encircling my wrist. The ink showed through the first coat of makeup like a bracelet of bruises, but after the second coat, it faded. By the third coat, it was impossible to tell that the letters were there in the first place.

She only needed to cover the parts of my body that would be exposed. My shoulders and calves, the nape of my neck, my throat and chest. As she worked, I flipped my hand upright and down again, studying the way her makeup had touched my skin with a warm glow. A mimicry of living flesh.

I was so different than her and Akiva. As she moved on to my face, I rolled my lower lip between my teeth, tested the unyieldingness of the sculpted clay.

"How do you see me, Gulzifa?" I asked.

She dabbed at my cheeks with greasy red cream and worked it into my surface. "What do you mean?"

"Do you think I'm a monster?"

She sighed. "If you must know, I'm jealous of you."

"Jealous?" The word felt strange on my tongue, sharp and spicy.

"We do what we can do, but the impact we make...the difference... It's so small. It's almost nothing." She rubbed the bridge of her nose. "And if we make a mistake, we're not coming back. But you can keep on going. And you can truly change things. That is the difference between you and us."

I sat back and absorbed her words, turning them around in my hands like waterworn pebbles. I envied humans like her for their flesh and bones, their warmth, their mortality. And all this time, I had been the source of their envy.

"But enough about that." She opened her small pocket compact and gave it to me so that I could see myself. "Tell me what you think."

The girl that stared back at me was a stranger, so different from the distorted reflection I would study for hours in the mirror Ezra used for shaving. Her skin was as smooth as silk, her cheeks aflush with life. On her brow, not a trace of the mark remained.

I lifted my fingers to my face to be sure it was really me.

"Well?" Gulzifa asked, a corner of her mouth rising in a smile. "How did I do?"

"I look…" Human, I wanted to say, but I couldn't bear to utter the word.

"Beautiful," she finished for me, leaning over my shoulder to tuck a strand of hair behind my ear. She smiled at me in the mirror. "If I had a daughter, I'd want her to be as brave as you. Just wait until Akiva sees you."

Akiva was sitting by the fire when I entered. He froze, taking in the sight of me. I shifted uneasily, feeling as if I was standing on thin ice. Since he had learned the truth about my creation, being near him felt like a tentative truce.

"What do you think?" I asked, fingers knotting up in the fox stole.

"Vera, you look—" He took a deep breath and set his jaw, as if the words themselves had physical weight to them. And I knew then he wouldn't say what he wanted to, what he truly meant. "Your disguise, it'll do."

CHAPTER 26

IT HAD BEEN A WARM DAY, AND AN EVEN warmer night. The snow we crunched through had turned halfway to slush, slopping across the rubberized waders I wore over my bare calves. My heels were stowed safely in the sack Akiva had slung over his back, with clean rags and extra powder, too. The bag's contents clinked together as he squatted down on the planks of the crude jetty built alongside the shoreside of Lake Skaistis.

"Keep an eye out," he said as he worked to free the rope tying the rowboat to its mooring. I scanned the tree line, body tensed like a live wire, although I wasn't sure anymore if it was fear that rippled through my core or exhilaration at what we were doing, and what I would do soon enough.

The shutters were latched in the fisherman's cabin, but

as Akiva cut the rope and reeled the boat in closer, a light gleamed at the front of the property.

"Someone's coming," I said, and Akiva swore, clambering into the boat.

He gave a hard jerk of his hand. "Get in."

I swung myself into the boat, finding a stable perch as he pushed off from shore. A man shouted for us to stop, and Akiva shocked me by chuckling. Before I knew it, I laughed, too, even though it wasn't funny. Even though there was a chance neither of us would come back from this.

The layer of ice atop the lake had melted in the sun's heat, dissolving into thin, dark lozenges that broke harmlessly against the prow of our rowboat as Akiva guided us downstream. From here, it would be a winding journey down the wide channel connecting the smaller lake to Lake Galvė.

He sat at the boat's helm, his rifle angled across his lap. As he rowed, his pale-blue eyes confronted me, silvered in the moonlight. A hint of a smile remained, but it didn't last.

We didn't speak, but there was something so familiar about our silence that I welcomed it. It was almost as if we were the separate halves of the same animal, working in tandem, muscle to clay and steel to bone. We didn't need to speak, because we could feel each other.

Overhead the arch of tree branches parted, revealing the broken circle of a moon, one edge bitten out. I wished that there'd been no moon at all, that the sky had been as black as a grave. It felt safer that way.

Akiva must have thought the same. As we passed through a meadow, he glanced up at the star-speckled sky and frowned, a crease forming between his brows. "I used to love nights like this. My father and I would go on walks sometimes. During summer, he would point out the insects drawn to our lantern— the March dagger moth, the sphinx, and so on. And during winter, it'd be the constellations."

"I'm sorry."

"I hate it now," he said, after a long pause. "Nights like this."

Every so often, through the trees growing along the banks, I caught a glimpse of nearby houses, lights burning in their windows. The homesteads seemed to belong to a separate world, somewhere where we didn't have to fight, where the glow of fire meant safety, not danger. I drew my fur coat around myself, even though the cold bothered me no more than the darkness or the silence.

Akiva shivered, ducking his chin as a bitter wind swept over us. His grip faltered on the paddle, and it nearly slipped into the water, would have if I hadn't grabbed it at the last moment.

"I can row," I offered as he repositioned his fingers across the worn handle.

He shook his head, stifling a cough with his fist. "It's okay. Let me."

"You're cold." Of their own accord, my fingers strayed to his face. Just for a moment, I touched his cheek and felt the warmth of his breath brush against my skin. He shied away from me as though I had harmed him, his gaze veering down.

Touching him felt so good, but at the same time, it felt like a terrible transgression. We were not meant to be. This affection didn't belong to me. I wish I could uproot it, tear it from myself as though it were nothing more than a thorn or a fishhook.

Akiva began coughing again and leaned over himself. His dark hair fell over his face, tumbling over cheekbones as sharp as bayonet blades.

This time I didn't ask him if he was okay. I simply slipped off my coat and passed it over to him. He took it wordlessly, wiping his hands on his pant legs before daring to draw the voluptuous folds of fur around himself. When I picked up the paddle, he didn't argue.

"Much use I am," he said sarcastically, from the depths of silvery fur. "Even a lousy chauffeur."

"I'm glad you came," I said, and it surprised me how true the words felt.

He stared at me intensely, his eyes piercing in the darkness. He looked as if he wanted to say something, and his lips parted. Before he could respond, a searchlight skimmed over the water. Instantly, we ducked low, pressing our bodies against the worn wood. Akiva scrambled for his rifle, jacking back the gun's bolt. As I slid the paddle from the water, he shifted the rifle's barrel toward the searchlight, tracking its source. We floated freely, tugged this way and that by the channel's swirling eddies.

Searchlights brushed over the water's surface, painting it in shades of silver. The glow refracted against the snow lining the banks, setting it alight, as if the entire world were conspiring to expose us. Akiva held his breath, his body so still, even I might have mistaken him for simply another mound of snow.

I grasped hold of a dead log extending from the water to still our passage, stopping short of the moving lights. German voices echoed through the underbrush. Laughter. It was just aimless talking, the kind of chatter that seemed more suited for beer halls and town squares. I remembered once listening to people talk like this, joking, prattling about their families and their first loves. I remembered it clearly now, through Chaya's eyes—back at the camp when she and Akiva were on patrol. Yael and the others, they had talked like this. They had turned that place into a home.

Slowly, the light beam shifted away from us. I glimpsed it riffling through the trees, illuminating a stretch of meadow strewn with snow. In the darkness, the blades of sedge glistened like individual filaments.

Gently, Akiva pushed off, guiding us farther down the winding channel. He took control of the paddle, steering us away from the nets of waterlogged branches, the dead snags.

The channel grew wider, and the current picked up. There was no ice now, only the treacherous rapids and the frigid mist that dewed on my lips and eyelashes. I visored my hand over my face, afraid the wind might scour the makeup from my skin.

Then the banks melted away behind us as if they'd been no more than snow themselves, and we drifted through the dark glistening waters of Lake Galvė. A multitude of lights shone in the distance. Trakai Castle.

Akiva's shoulders loosened. He exhaled slowly, even though the worst of the danger was yet to come. He glanced in my direction, and for just a moment, I saw him for what he truly was—a terrified human boy.

It was too dangerous to speak now. I sank my nails into the soft wood along the boat's ram, and splinters began to tumble away and flake. Before I could accidentally capsize us in my anxiety, I moved my hand to my own knee, and waited.

We slipped across the lake's surface as soft and smoothly as an eel, the moonlight illuminating our passage. The only sounds were the soft lapping of the waves and the rustling of the branches, but as we headed deeper out to the lake, those noises grew fainter and fainter, until all I could hear was the liquid slosh of waves against our boat's prow.

More searchlights skimmed over the basin's surface, their movements as predictable and smooth as clockwork. They were not searching for a single boat, but a fleet of them, or the approach of partisans from the bridge that spanned across the water. They would not expect this.

We slipped into the shadow of the castle, the boat gently rocking against the ancient embankment. I traced my fingers across the pockmarks and pits gouged in the stone. The structure was not as old as me, but it didn't feel that way.

"Are you ready?" Akiva whispered, resting the paddle in place along the side of the boat.

"I'm ready."

He lit a match, just for an instant, to study my features. His fingertips brushed my hair away from my brow in a touch as light as the batting of moth wings.

I tensed as his thumb traced over the inked mark, those three simple letters that kept me tethered to this world. It was risky to let him get so close, but I didn't feel in danger. If anything, a part of me deeply wanted to close the space between us until there was nothing but clay against skin, cold against heat. But what he saw must have satisfied him, because all too soon, his fingers dropped away, leaving behind a patch of warmth that ached like a wound.

"The makeup's still there," he said, flicking the match into the water.

Easing forward, he found a place along the embankment where a series of stairs had been cut into the hillside, leading up to the grass above. I grasped onto his arm for support, afraid the weight of my body might drive me over the edge of the boat and send me plummeting into the water. My feet touched down on solid ground. I began to let go of him, but something stopped me. I looked back at him, and before I really knew what I was doing, found myself leaning forward—close, closer.

As my lips brushed against his, Akiva froze in absolute stillness, like a deer trapped in lanternlight. Then he reached up, cupping my cheek, and kissed me back, tenderly.

This felt so right, like claiming the desire I'd felt for him from the first moment I saw him. Chaya's love would always be a part of me, but that didn't mean I couldn't hew my own way. I didn't need to follow in her footsteps.

"Be safe, Vera," Akiva murmured as I pulled away.

I couldn't promise that, but I smiled as an apology and nodded. While I changed into the dress and heels, he kept his back to me, his gaze drifting across the lakeside. It wasn't until I said his name that he looked back and took my spare clothes and rubber waders.

"We'll meet back at Gulzifa's," he said, and I nodded again, knowing he might be left there waiting. That come morning, I might just be another pile of lifeless clay settled at the bottom of Lake Galvė. That it didn't matter, because what I was doing tonight, this was what I was made for. This was why I had to keep going.

"Next year in America," I reminded him. "You, me, and Miriam."

A wry smile touched his lips. "Next year in America."

As I strode across the lawn, I thought I heard Akiva's voice rise behind me, but his words were lost to the wind. I didn't look back.

CHAPTER 27

TRAKAI CASTLE ROSE BEFORE ME, ALL SOARING battlements and narrow windows. Red brick upon red rooftops, crested by a tower on the verge of collapse. Moonlight pierced through the ruin's void windows, while electric floodlights illuminated its base.

I crossed the lawn almost silently, as though the snow and soil were my conspirators. As I entered the structure's shadow, the bushes rustled.

A large dog slunk from between the shrubs. On all fours, it stood nearly to my waist. Its ears pricked at the sight of me, black eyes glistening in the moonlight.

As it advanced toward me, the dog's powerful muscles rolled beneath a pelt as dark and sleek as oil. From deep within its throat came a low warning growl, and its ears flattened against the hard shelf of its skull.

"Go away," I said sternly.

The dog stopped abruptly, studying me. Its breath steamed in the air.

"Go away," I repeated. "*Geh weg!*"

The dog's ears prickled up again. It came closer, close enough that I had to force myself not to clasp my hand over my forehead instinctively. It nudged its slick nose against my legs, rubbed its snout along my dress. Whatever scent it had caught, it was not my own.

I rubbed the dog gently behind the ears and scratched it under the jaw, the tension slowly draining from my body. The animal's body was so warm, and even its breath was hot. I wondered if I'd ever get used to the heat of living things, or if it would always feel dangerous.

"Good," I murmured, and stepped away.

The hound came forward again, tail wagging.

"No, stay here."

The dog whined and settled down. I continued backing up until I was sure the animal wouldn't follow, then turned and continued on my way.

The gardens must have been beautiful during the summer, but now the rosebushes were a warren of thorns, and the ivy hung dead on the arbors. In the darkness, the brambles and shrubbery held far too many shadows than I cared for.

As I proceeded through the garden, I tensed, expecting at any moment for someone to shout out. They might not even warn me. For all I knew, the moment a guard spotted me, I'd be met with a volley of gunshots. Instead, only silence prevailed, and even the soft sinuous movements of the prowling dogs failed to elicit alarm.

As I neared the entrance, I adjusted my dress and coat. Going in through the ground floor would raise too many questions. I climbed the ivy trellis to the floor above, grimacing each time the scaffold groaned under my weight. Yet in spite of the noise of my intrusion, I managed to make my way in undetected.

I swung over the balcony railing and sank to my knees on the frosty stones. My shoes refused to endure my abuse for long, and as I advanced forward, one heel snapped beneath me. I caught my balance before I could fall and swore at the sight of the wooden peg dangling like a broken limb from the leather sole.

Instead of hobbling on uneven footing, I tore the heel off and brutalized the second shoe to match it. Deprived of their heels, the shoes made for an awkward fit, but I endured it and strode into the room beyond.

Though the balcony had been deserted, the room overflowed with people dressed in all manner of finery. Silk, lace, rippling cascades of satin and velvet. Only a few men wore ash-gray uniforms and armbands, but as far as I was concerned, everyone here was my enemy. They laughed and talked while my friends waited with guillotine blades poised above their heads. Compliance was no different than collaboration.

Before emerging from the shadows, I checked my clothes to be sure that no incriminating evidence marred the fur or silk. The soles of my shoes were muddied, but that would have to do.

"I've heard it's something truly marvelous," a man said to his companions, passing by the alcove without even glancing in my direction. "That it could spell the fall of Stalingrad. It will change everything."

Drawing my coat tighter around myself, I stepped into the room. A woman glanced my way as I brushed past her. My fingers tightened into fists at my side. Could she see the unnatural smoothness of my features? Had the makeup Gulzifa so carefully applied been worn away, rubbed off to expose the unnatural grayness of my complexion?

Fingers curled around my shoulder. "Enjoying yourself?"

I turned.

The man had spoken in unaccented German, so I felt no surprise to see the bent cross emblazoned on his shoulder-band. As his hand slipped down my arm, I fought the sudden compulsion to seize it and break his fingers one by one until I turned his hand into a swastika of its own.

Instead, I lifted my gaze to his face. Unremarkable, with light-brown hair neatly combed back and pale blue eyes rimmed in pink, the eyes of a hare. He was older than Chaya had been, older than any of my friends.

My body froze, fingers straying reflexively to my chest. I knew him.

I *knew* him.

I hate killing women, he'd said, his features cloaked in the forest's darkness. Regretful smile just a gleam of white teeth. And then he'd pulled the trigger.

As I met his gaze, his smile faded by a degree. My fingers sank into the fur coat, curling tight.

"Is something the matter?" he asked.

He didn't recognize me. Slowly, I released the breath I'd drawn in out of habit. Of course. Why would he recognize me? Chaya's face had just been one in a sea of them. She'd meant nothing to him.

"Yes, I'm enjoying myself," I said blandly, when I realized he expected an answer. I tried to keep my voice light and airy, but instead it came out in a flat monotone.

He quirked an eyebrow. "You don't sound as though you are."

"Perhaps that's because I haven't found the right company yet," I said, stunning myself. These were not my words. It was as though someone else—*Chaya?*—had taken hold of my steel armature, twined her fingers through my clay. The presence inside me played puppetry with the tongue and teeth I had inherited from Chaya and smiled cunningly at him. An invitation.

"Is that so?" His fingers slipped away, but the way he looked at me, it was as though he was still touching me. It filled me with revulsion. "I believe I have the cure for that."

"Wonderful," I said, and allowed him to guide me deeper into the room. Men and women laughed and sipped drinks.

A man came by, carrying a tray stacked with high glasses so thin and delicate, I was afraid they'd shatter if I merely touched them. The soldier took two and handed me one. Unsure whether it was polite to drink, I held the glass at an awkward distance and waited for his lead.

He tapped his glass against mine. "*Prost.*"

Part of me wanted to say *l'chaim*. Another part whispered

na zdrowie. And the remnants of Chaya's conscience just wanted to shove the glass down his throat. I simply echoed his phrase: "*Prost.*"

We drank. In the candlelight, the liquid was rose-gold and fizzled like sparks on my tongue. Bitter, with just the faintest fruity tang.

"Thank you for the drink," I said, wishing for Chaya to step back into her role and regain control of my tongue and teeth. But I was alone here. Not even the scribes' memories proved useful in this place.

"You haven't told me your name," he said.

"You haven't told me yours."

"Günther."

"Ana," I said, and he waited, looking at me expectantly. "Ana Richter."

"That's a lovely name. How old are you?"

"Eighteen." It was months older than Chaya had been when she died, but I didn't think he would care. He was, I suspected, at least fifteen years her senior.

I laid the glass down before I could break it. He touched me again, very briefly, on the arm. His fingertips were damp with condensation. The moisture lifted the upper coat of makeup from my skin, exposing a dark bruise-like blur when he slid his hand away.

I took a step back, clasping my palm over my wrist. By the moment, my smile felt like it might crack apart and fall, taking parts of my face with it.

He studied me closely. "Is something the matter?"

"No." I swallowed, suddenly hyperaware of the stillness of my chest, the way the air I drew in fell upon dense clay.

No lungs to breathe, no heart to pound, no sweat to course down the nape of my neck—and yet, as my unease deepened, I couldn't shake the feeling that there was something inside me, buried within the clay of my chest. Something *growing*.

I couldn't stay here. Couldn't pretend to be human. As I began to turn, fingers locked around my sleeve.

"Hey, not so fast," Günther said.

At my side, my fingers curled into a fist. I could punch him in the throat, probably collapse his windpipe in a single swing, if not snap his spine outright. As I pulled my hand away, a little harsher than I should've, he smiled.

"Why the rush?" he asked.

"I want to meet Dr. Brandt."

"Is that so?" There was something low and cunning about his smile. "May I ask why?"

"I've heard about his work. What he's doing to help the fatherland. I want to see it for myself."

Günther didn't answer. His gaze had shifted to my forehead, and the smile that had teased his thin lips had begun to fade.

"You have some dirt on your brow," he said, but by then I was already turning away.

"Excuse me," I said hastily, hurrying from him. I slipped past the few people lingering in the hall, bowing my head in fear they'd spot my mark. Not that they'd even know what to make of it.

"Wait—" he began, but when I glanced back, he had been swallowed by the crowd.

"Excuse me, but where is the water closet?" I asked the guard stationed at the door.

He pointed across the room toward another corridor. "Two doors down. It's on the left."

I thanked him hastily and hurried into the hall, only relaxing once I reached the water closet and latched the door securely behind me. The toilet was of no use to me, but I sat down on the porcelain lid and studied my forearms. Only a few letters had appeared after all.

After calming myself, I rose to my feet and studied my reflection. The red pigment that Gulzifa had rubbed into my cheeks had begun to fade, leaving my complexion ashen. I gripped onto the sink basin. To ground myself, I whispered the words to Oyfn Pripetchik, the lullaby Ezra had taught me before I'd even had eyes to see him. I wished he was here right now. I wondered if he'd be proud of me.

Once I had stabilized myself, I left the water closet and continued down the hall, chin raised, as though I belonged there. It relieved me to see Günther was nowhere in sight.

During my walk through the gardens, I had realized that although the southeastern wing of the palace was maintained, the rest of the complex appeared on the verge of collapse—crumbling towers and holey walls, terra-cotta roofs caved inward like ruptured blisters. Maybe Dr. Brandt had chosen this location for its seclusion or access to clean water, but in any case, I doubted he ran his project from the ruins.

If this building contained a secret, it would be down below, out of sight. I needed to go lower.

I followed the corridor along, leaving my damaged shoes and fur coat next to a decorative urn in an alcove. From here on out, violence was likely inevitable. I had scarcely been able to blend in out there, and I knew that with each minute I stayed here, my disguise would become increasingly difficult to maintain, both from the dampness of the environment and from my own inexperience with what it meant to be human.

As a twin set of footsteps approached, I froze in an alcove, pressing my back against the wall. My fingers snapped into the plaster, making a sound like the crack of a brittle twig. Jaw set, gaze straight ahead, I waited, thankful I didn't need to breathe. It felt unsafe just to dispel the air I drew in reflexively.

"Did you hear that?" a man said.

I flexed my fingers, curled them inward. Waited. The men came closer, closer—their footsteps grew louder, and I knew they were almost upon me.

I stepped quickly into the hall, prepared to tear and gouge and punch, but the corridor was deserted. The footsteps receded.

Instead of pursuing the guards, I went in the opposite direction, following the route they had taken—around the corner and through an archway reinforced with wooden scaffolding, the floor littered with broken masonry. This wing of the castle was incomplete, and as I continued down the corridor, it grew increasingly dim and dilapidated. Caged electrical lights were set up along the route, strung to a softly rumbling generator.

The floor had been cleaned recently, the dust swept into the corners, but the floorboards groaned with each step. It wouldn't have surprised me if one gave way beneath my weight, sending me plummeting into the nether regions of the castle, or lower still, into the lake itself. But I made it across the hall unscathed.

I stopped at an open door, peering down at the stone stairs trailing into the darkness below. As I stepped onto the landing, from behind me came the low metallic click of a gun's hammer being cocked.

CHAPTER 28

I TURNED SLOWLY, FIGHTING AGAINST MY NAT-
ural impulse to go straight for the throat. Günther smiled at
me, pistol in hand. He didn't look angry. He didn't even look
menacing, despite his finger on the trigger and the detestable
uniform he wore with pride. That was what I found truly
puzzling—that I wore my true nature on my forehead, as glaring as any brand, but humans were able to lurk unseen in their
monstrosity. They could smile, the way he was smiling now,
and act friendly, and even reach out—reach out, just like he
was doing—and lightly brush the hair from over my brow.

"Emet." Günther's teeth were tidy and white. I would've
liked to rearrange them. "You must be the one who killed
my men at the farmhouse."

"Dr. Brandt?" I whispered, and his smile only grew.

He looked so weak. So normal. So human. How could he possibly be the architect behind this?

"Before I return you to the dirt, there's something I'd like to know. Thanks to the materials, I figured out how to awaken your kind, but how do I control you?" When I didn't answer, he chuckled. "You see, my prototype—"

I never gave him a chance to finish. As I lunged at him, he drew the pistol up. I ducked as the barrel veered toward my brow, and the first gunshot cracked the stonework centimeters from my head. The second bullet tore open the side of my head at point-blank range, would've killed an ordinary human being, but instead only staggered me. Growling, I drove him to the ground. He struggled beneath me as I wrestled the gun from his hands and cast it across the floor.

Günther's fingers gouged at my face, coming dangerously close to the mark on my brow. I snapped at him in reflex and caught his index finger between my gnashing teeth. He screamed as I gave a sudden violent jerk of my head, a hot spurt of blood flooding my mouth. He writhed against me in a desperate struggle to escape, his cries turning raw and guttural.

Either I must have fallen, or he must have caught me by the arm and dragged me down with him, but suddenly the floor gave way beneath me and I found myself rolling down the stairs, entangled in a knot of limbs. We landed in a heap on the stones below. I rose in an instant, grimacing at the slick pop of my iron scaffolding shifting back into place, my joints reforming.

I swiveled around on all fours, my knees skidding in liquid. For a sickening moment, I thought the moisture had come from my body. Something wet and fragile within me had ruptured, and any moment now, my chest would cave inward and my limbs would give way. I'd spill across the floor, a shapeless muck.

No. I looked down. It wasn't river water. Blood inched across the grout.

"H-help me," a voice croaked centimeters from my ear.

Günther lay in a heap on the floor. The force of impact had catapulted him nearly a meter from where I'd landed, and unlike me, his contorted body hadn't simply flowed back into shape. His limbs were bent worse than a swastika. One knee was grotesquely twisted beneath him, and below where his elbow began, a piece of bone had pierced through the pressed wool of his uniform jacket.

"Help," he repeated, his voice waning even as I spat out his finger.

"No." As I wiped his blood from my lips, the makeup stripped off the back of my hand, revealing the calligraphy twined up my surface. There was no longer any point in pretending to be human. I didn't want to be like them anymore, I didn't want to be mistaken for one. Humanity was cruel.

Humanity was the source of all suffering.

"I'm ordering you—"

"You can't order me," I said. "You didn't create me."

"You think—you think this will change anything?" Blood welled from his mouth and the sockets of his lost teeth. "You think I'm the only one?"

I didn't answer.

"Someone will take my place in Project Mökkurkálfi."

"Then I'll kill them, too," I said as the life faded from Günther Brandt's eyes.

CHAPTER 29

DR. GÜNTHER BRANDT WAS DEAD. AND THE Nazis' victims were not resurrected. Günther Brandt was dead. And Ezra was still missing. Günther Brant was dead. And nothing had changed at all.

As his blood inched across the floor, no relief came. No resolution. I didn't crumble back into dirt and water. I simply stood there and watched.

This was how it was in life, I realized. One enemy down, but why did it matter? There were enemies all around me. And beyond these walls, there were hundreds—no, *thousands* more. And I was just one person. And I couldn't stop it.

How did Akiva cope with this knowledge? How could he keep fighting, knowing that everything he did was just a drop in the bucket, that no matter how many people he

killed, he couldn't change the world? Couldn't repair what
had already happened.

I felt petrified by the realization. Ezra had created me for
vengeance, but how many others would I have to kill in order
to achieve my purpose?

I looked back the way I came then turned, peering deeper
into the basement. Electrical lights emitted a stark white glow.
Pale clay slickened the grout in the pavestone floor, and clods
of dirt littered the double row of wooden tables, where lumpish forms were shrouded beneath stained sheets. Skin prickling with anticipation, I neared the shape nearest to me—a
silhouette I could almost imagine was the torso of a man. I
yanked down the sheet, expecting to uncover the bulging eyes
and mealy skin of a corpse. An abrupt laugh escaped my lips.

The object underneath the sheet was shaped like a person,
but instead of ears, there were lumpy knobs of clay. No mouth
or nose. Deep hollows where the eyes should have been, rudimentary holes thrust by a thumb.

I pulled down the next sheet. Just a pile of river clay shaped
into an arm, the fingers jointless and as thick as sausages.
Down the tables I went, uncovering piecemeal bits—legs,
arms, heads with half-finished features or no faces at all. As
I reached the end of the row, something crashed behind me.

I swiveled around.

Broken glass lay on the ground. The water carafe used
to wet the clay and make it malleable. Beside the shattered
pitcher, an arm twitched sluggishly.

Mouth dry, I approached the limb and flipped it over with
my foot. Written on its palm was a single word.

אמת

"Truth," I whispered.

On my forehead, the inked letters ached like a scald burn. We were the same after all.

I picked up the hand, expecting it to feel cold and slimy, like something plucked from the riverbed. But the skin was as firm as my own, and the same temperature, too. Of course, it would be. We were made from the same matter.

The fingers curled in response to my touch, grasping weakly at my hand. I dropped it. To leave it like this would be a disservice, when it would never be whole. I shivered at the memory of crawling across the hayloft's floorboards when I'd had no legs yet, reduced to moving on my belly. Now, try that, but without eyes or a face or even a torso. Just five fingers and a stump of a wrist.

I had no doubt that, to some degree, the hand was aware of its surroundings. Its world was confined to what it could touch, but that didn't mean it couldn't suffer. And for us, the worst kind of torture wasn't physical pain—it was waiting. It was time.

I took a deep breath, preparing myself. As the fingers flexed and curled, I stomped down on the arm, grinding the heel of my shoe into the letters carved in its skin. When that wasn't enough to obliterate the engravings, I brought my foot down once more, smashing the clay into a shapeless mound and turning אמת into מת. *Met.* Corpse.

The moment I removed the letter *aleph*, the arm went still. But my mercy killing didn't go unnoticed. As I returned the lifeless hunk of clay to the table, the sheets began to rustle all around me. Fingers twitching; toes curling; eyeless, mouthless faces contorting in rage or horror.

They were awake.

I froze in the center of the room, staring in shock down the rows of twitching parts. Clods of dried clay, disrupted by the incomplete golems' motions, scattered on the floor.

A head on half a torso twisted toward me, its mouth a gaping hole. Its lips puckered, working in silent urgency. Was it trying to speak to me, or was it just growling like a beast?

Horrified, I backed away. I wasn't like these creatures at all. This wasn't who I was deep down. Right?

"Stop it," I whispered. "Just stop. Stop moving."

My legs stiffened into ice at the thought of having to walk down those rows, blotting out letter after letter with my bare hands. Tearing out fistfuls of clay, the same clay from which I was made.

I couldn't do it.

I had to do it.

If I left them like this, I would be abandoning them to an even worse fate. Aware, but unable to move. Mouthless, but screaming inside. At least by returning them to clay, the rain might wash them down to the lake and settle them at its bottom once more. And there would be a kind of peace in that.

I picked up a shard from the broken carafe and turned my focus to the golem nearest to me. Just the stump of a leg, affixed with wire to a wooden base, writhing. I carved out the Hebrew letters engraved on its thigh. It went still the moment I turned the word *Emet* into *Met*. Next. A bust a little more defined than the others, chest heaving, the head lolling dumbly, deprived of its eyes or mouth. I cut it down like all the rest.

Met.

Met.

Met.

My palm grew slickened with clay. I wiped it on my dress hastily, afraid that if I let the muck linger on my skin, my victims' consciousnesses would become a part of me—half-formed, seething with animalistic hatred, their wrath strong enough to fissure me from the inside out.

I reached the end of the room, still gripping the shard so tightly that it cut into my palm. Mud squelched beneath my feet, the only sound aside from the grinding of my teeth. Even though I'd left a trail of broken parts in my wake, my mission here felt incomplete. Clay could be reshaped, and golems could be remade. To our creators, we weren't people. We weren't even living things. We were simply the bullets in a loaded gun. If he'd used Shachna's ancient manuscripts, I needed to make sure no one else could get their hands on them.

Through a pair of double doors, I entered a part of the basement that was more medieval than modern—an arched hallway with mortared stone walls that glistened with condensation. Dangling from the ceiling at uneven intervals, naked bulbs cast amber discs of light across the floor.

The first door I came across was bolted shut but not locked. I wrenched the bolt free and strode into the chamber, eyes adjusting to the darkness even as my fingers clenched in preparation to tear and punch.

The light intruding from the hall weakly illuminated a woman strapped to a chair. My fist loosened, and I stepped forward uncertainly, put on edge by the scent of gore and chemicals that hung in the air.

"Hello?" I said.

She didn't move, not even when I went to her side. Bloodied bandages were affixed over her eyes, the gauze hiding the worst of the devastation.

A crude clay head had been set on a stool in front of her, its ears and nose just rudimentary ridges, but its eyes—I shuddered. Its eyes.

"Enough," a voice croaked so close to my ear, I stumbled back with a low cry. Trembling, the woman lifted her head. Her parched lips moved with excruciating slowness, only to repeat herself in faint Polish. "Please. Enough."

If the head—*the golem*—had a mouth, maybe it would have formed the same word. Maybe it would have just snarled at me or sobbed. But instead, it confronted me unblinkingly, its eyes pleading silently, and I should have carved out the words on its brow, I should have done something, but I was already fleeing from the room, grinding my palms against my own eyes, wishing I could blot out the image from my mind, because I was not like that. *I was not like that.*

I turned the corner, nearly blind with panic, and passed through a caged nook crammed with crates overflowing with books and old parchments, including the medieval lead box I recognized from the hayloft. Passed the open door of a room, where covered forms lay on metal tables, and if not for the blood staining the sheets, I wouldn't have known whether they were golem or human. On one, the sheet had slipped down to reveal the corpse's naked back, its skin peeled away to expose the yellowed ridge of its spine. A single word had been scrawled on the chalkboard beside crude chalk sketches of the human skeleton: LUZ?

At the end of the hall, I reached the final door. I wrenched the bolt open so frantically, the metal groaned and twisted beneath my palm. I didn't know where I was going or what I wanted, only that I needed to get away from the memory of the woman, and the brutal reminder of what I was.

It wasn't a stairway or escape route past the door, just another cell as dismal as the first. The room's sole occupant stirred on the cot, his leg jerking out like a dog in sleep. Slowly, he lifted himself as I entered.

His gray eyes met mine, as familiar as my own reflection.

"Ezra!" I cried, flinging myself at him. He startled as I grabbed for him, flinched away like I was a stranger. It was strange to see his cheeks and chin unshaven, but even stranger to take in the sight of the fresh bruises marbling his face, one eye nearly swollen shut.

"Vera," he whispered, shock dawning across his features.

"Ezra, I thought you were dead." Moisture blurred my vision; the water level was rising inside me. "What are you doing here?"

"All this time, that Nazi bastard has been trying to create golems." His hoarse voice failed on the last word. "He just needed to figure out how to awaken them and endow them with the ability to seem human. Listen to me, you must find him. Find Dr. Brandt and kill him, and destroy the papers. Destroy all of Shachna's materials."

"I've already killed Dr. Brandt."

"What?" Ezra whispered.

"I killed him. I'll do as you ask and get rid of the papers, but first, we need to get you out of here. Get you to safety."

"No."

"I'll carry you. You can ride upon my shoulders. I'm strong, Ezra. Stronger than you ever thought."

"If what you say is true, there's only one thing you can do for me, Verochka. Only one thing left to do." He took my hand and lifted it to his throat, pressed my thumb over the slow, steady throb of his pulse. "End it."

His order shocked me. "I can't!"

"You can." A thin smile touched his lips. "You will."

"No. Please, don't make me do this." My voice came out strained and cracking. For the first time in my new life, I felt choked and breathless, as though I actually had lungs. The room's stifling atmosphere seemed to crush me on all sides, squeezing my chest into putty. "We can find another way. I'll get you out of here."

His trembling hand brushed away an errant strand on my brow. The gesture shocked me, seeing as he'd spent my short life until now avoiding touching me unless absolutely necessary, cringing away the moment I got within arm's reach.

"I was going to have this be the final lesson I'd teach you before sending you out into the world, but you have already learned what it means to spill blood. So, it will be my gift to you—a future without a master, without the need to fulfill another person's order."

His fingers stroked the mark on my brow, the word drawn by his own hand. I wanted to press my palm over his mouth, crush the order that was forming on his tongue, but I couldn't even move.

"Kill me."

CHAPTER 30

MY BODY MOVED ON ITS OWN. THE MOMENT the command left his lips, my fingers tightened around his throat of their own accord.

Kill me. The command was simple, direct. No loopholes, no need to prolong it.

I squeezed tighter, cutting off Ezra's air flow. He struggled beneath me. His leg grazed against my calf. Just for a moment, his mouth contorted in a grim smile, as if he wanted to convince me that it was okay, I was doing the right thing.

As he writhed in my grasp, my spirit thrashed against its own restraints, fighting to break free of the control his command had over me. But I couldn't stop it. It was as though my hands weren't even connected to my wrists anymore.

"You truly are—" he gave a choked gasp "—of my blood. My daughter."

Something cracked deep inside of him, and a thin line of blood trickled from his lips, gathered in his stubble, dripped onto my wrist. His body went still. Slowly, I eased him back onto the cot. His eyes confronted me, bulging and sightless. I eased his lids shut and held his jaw until his mouth stayed closed.

"Why did you make me do that, Ezra?" I wanted to scream at him, but my voice came out sounding very small, as though it might disappear at any moment. With each word, it grew fainter, fainter. "Why? You knew I was strong. I could have saved you."

He lay on the sheet like a golem himself, his face waxen in the sallow light. Somehow, his features seemed softer now, as though the moment his life had left him, so had some rigid strain. A tiny hope inside me whispered that if I stayed there long enough, listening very closely, he might answer. I could sit with my ear next to his mouth, and he would tell me things, forbidden things about the world, and the secret art of Kabbalah, and profane kishuf, and the Master of the Universe. As my own creator, Ezra might even explain to me what it meant to be human, and what it was I lacked.

But I couldn't stay.

I backed away, folding my arms under my elbows. My hands felt like traitors. I wanted to scrub at them with salt and sand, until I removed the careful lines Ezra had etched into their surface, a mimicry of humanity. Except that wouldn't change a thing. It wouldn't erase what he had made me do.

As I hurriedly left the room and retraced my steps back

the way I came, I rubbed my hands on my shirt, wiping his blood from my wrist.

I had been prepared to kill from the moment I had stepped through these doors. It should have felt natural. After all, it was what Ezra had made me for. But this didn't feel like my purpose. How could killing my creator be my purpose? How could he have *wanted* this?

I reached the caged alcove that contained the lead box and tore the door from its hinges, the metal screeching in protest as it gave way beneath my fingers. Compared to crushing human bone or bending metal, Shachna's manuscripts yielded far easier. I knelt on the floor and tore them, tore them, ripping at the vellum until each page fell to the floor like a thousand dead rose petals. I didn't realize I was sobbing until moisture splattered across the floor, landing on the scatter of ripped parchments. Not water, just mud. I couldn't even cry like a real human being.

Weeping, I bent over myself on the floor and held the ancient papers to my face. Bit and tore at them, like I would've liked to do to my own features, to my hair, to these worthless things he had given me.

In the middle of my destruction, wood groaned from back the way I came. I froze, listening to the footsteps. Someone was coming down the stairs.

When I entered the basement, a flaxen-haired soldier stood by Dr. Brandt's corpse, considering it thoughtfully. He turned at the sound of my approach.

His skin was the same ashen tone as mine, the color of unpainted ceramic. Unlike the ruined specimens on the other tables, his limbs were well developed and proportional, his muscles clearly defined. Full lips, cheekbones as sharp as scalpel blades. Real eyelashes and hair, no doubt an inheritance from the dead.

No holes gouged into his face, but deep-set eyes. An eerie gold fringed by black. No whites. Not human. Upon his brow: אמת

"Who are you?" he growled in German, his voice dull and rough, like pebbles grated together. An uncontrollable shiver passed through me. The last time I'd heard that voice, it had been through the grille of Gulzifa's radio.

As he stepped forward, the light gleamed across his teeth— sharp and lupine, rearranged and filed down to fit a human mouth. His tongue might've been human, but he'd been given the kind of teeth made for shredding flesh.

We were the same. We'd both been created to kill the living, except that he couldn't hide his lethalness. Dr. Brandt had made it a visible part of him. And if he had the eyes and teeth of a wolf, maybe they had given him the nose of one, too. Eardrums that could pick up the thrum of a human heartbeat from many meters away, a nose that could detect warm bodies hidden in crawl spaces and behind walls.

It would be my friends he was after, their bodies he would tear his teeth into.

I made my decision in an instant. I couldn't spare him.

Snatching a slim metal stylus from the scatter of tools on the table, I lunged at him. He yanked away at the last moment. The pick slashed through his forehead, missing the *aleph* by millimeters, and instead cut a crooked line down his brow bone.

He reacted instantaneously, shoving the table with both

hands. It slammed into me with enough force to make me grunt. Crushed against the table edge, the stylus slipped from my hand.

I leapt back as the table upturned between us, the sheet puddling underfoot. Unlike him, my teeth weren't sharp enough to rip out mouthful after mouthful of clay or flesh. If I wanted to destroy him, I would have to blot out his mark with my own hands.

The golem stepped around the table, his golden eyes shining like searchlights in the buzzing electrical lamps. Framed by thick ash-white lashes, his irises were as eerie as they were mesmerizing.

"You're like me," he murmured, sounding almost thrilled. The scratch on his forehead began to close up instantly, the clay flowing in. "Not a dumb, twitching part. You're actually alive."

"No," I said. "We're not alive."

"Is that what you were made to believe?" He grinned, flashing his fanglike teeth. "Who made you? Whose eyes are those?"

I didn't respond. I continued backing up, testing the floor with each step. I winced as I stepped down on a hunk of clay, which gave slowly beneath my shoe and made a wet *pop* when I tore my foot away.

"Where were you dredged from?" he asked.

"The Vokė."

"Ah, so that's why you smell like river water and algae."

"And I suppose you came from Germany?"

"From the ground of the *Externsteine,* or so I've been told." His gaze never left mine.

For every step I took away from him, he took one closer, until we were less than a meter apart. Close enough that if he lunged at me, I'd have to touch him. Have to get close to his teeth and ripping fingers.

Suddenly, the golem leapt toward me. I swung my foot up without thinking, striking him in the thigh. A useless blow, considering he had no ability to feel pain.

"Get away from me." My voice trembled uncontrollably as I backed away, retreating back the way I came.

He approached me with teasing slowness, his lips curled in a smirk. Just as Ezra had endowed me with his wrath and fury, Dr. Brandt must have given him something, too. Confidence, sadism, or indifference. The ingredients for a perfect killer.

Fear turned my gut to a bubbling mud-pot. I was in the hayloft again, forced to crawl legless across the floor.

"You're the one who destroyed the others." He stepped on a ruined torso, smeared it to clay beneath his bootheel. "Why?"

"This was no existence."

"Do you think you have the right to decide that? What gives you the power to choose whether something deserves to live or die?"

His words struck me like a blow to the chest.

"That's—"

He made a lunge for me. I pulled back, but I wasn't quick enough. He seized hold of my wrist, dragging me off balance. I shielded my forehead with my hand, terrified that at any moment I would feel his teeth bite through me. All it would take was a simple scratch to sever my connection to this world.

Instead of going for my mark, he slammed me against the cabinets. The force of the blow would have broken the bones of an ordinary human, but my body absorbed the impact, let it shudder through me. Deep inside me, the force reverberated in my steel armature. Even as the bars stilled, my legs shook uncontrollably.

"You're trembling." His lantern-bright eyes studied my face, as cold and sweeping as searchlights. Ready to uncover everything. "Are you afraid? Can you actually feel fear?"

"My creator gave me emotions. Empathy." I tried to keep my voice level. "What did yours give you?"

"Only the truth." His lips curled up in a smile, revealing a flash of those pointed teeth. "I was born self-aware. Aware of my creation. My purpose."

"And what would that be?"

"To destroy everything." His eyes weren't from a human, but there was human cunning in them. "They gave me knowledge, but they think they can control me. They'll soon find out that I am no one's dog. You are more sophisticated than the others. You can join me."

"Join you?"

"In destroying everything."

"No."

"That's a shame. Then you are the enemy."

His grip on my wrist tightened. I struggled to yank my limb free, strange growls coming from deep inside me. Then he gave a sudden twist, and metal twisted and snapped deep inside me. There was no pain as he shoved me back, only terrible pressure and a sense of being stretched until I tore.

I reached for the table to regain my balance, but I no longer had fingers to grasp with. The perfect illusion of my humanity was gone—the end of my wrist ended in a twisted lump of clay, fingers smashed into useless mounds against my palm.

The sight made me want to scream. It was just clay. Just clay, and a protruding knob of rebar where a wristbone should've been.

Nonchalantly, the golem wiped the mud from his palm.

Terror blacked out the edges of my vision. Swiveling around, I fled up the winding staircase. Down the first-floor corridor, up a flight of stairs, and then another. I didn't even try concealing myself now. How could I, when I was leaving behind a smatter of mud in my wake? Fear thrummed through me, resonating in my core like the memory of a heartbeat. If I slowed, the golem might catch up to me. Might take my limbs, or my eyes, or my mouth. Leave me like the others, alive but unable to move. Absolutely helpless.

I crossed paths with a uniformed guard. He gawked at the sight of me and reached for his gun. Before he could draw the weapon, I struck out at him with my uninjured arm. The force of the blow sent him crashing not just against the wall but into it, sending a shower of plaster across the floor.

The lower level of this wing had been renovated, but the upper ones were barren. Ancient masonry gleamed in the shafts of moonlight that pierced the damaged roof. In places the floorboards were missing, while a slick carpet of dust coated the rest. As I raced across the boards, they groaned beneath my feet, goading me on like the croaks of the dead.

The stairs rattled behind me. I lunged forward and springboarded off a pile of plaster sacks, seizing hold of the rafters and hauling myself through a gap in the ceiling. Snow and loose slates tumbled down to the room below, and a scalpel-sharp burst of wind flung my hair across my face as I found footing on the rooftop.

If he'd been human, I might have waited there, still as a statue, for the other golem to pass below. But we were of the same nature, and I suspected he would be able to smell the mud of me, if not Chaya's own remnants. I lurched to my feet and ran, and seconds later, roofing slates snapped like breaking bones as he followed.

I raced across the castle's pediments and leapt from rooftop to rooftop, tower to tower, harried by the crack of roof tiles and his urgent panting. He had no lungs, I was sure, but the forms we had been given slowly became us. Even I began to breathe heavily, drawing in air on empty space. Each time my feet slammed into tiles, the force of impact reverberated through the rods in my legs. I could almost believe that a pounding heart crashed against my steel rib cage.

The howling wind drowned out any noise of pursuit. I didn't risk glancing behind me to see if I had shaken the other golem from my trail. Even a single look back might slow me down. I needed to keep moving. Faster. Harder. Come on!

The basin shone below. At the other end of the rooftop, I took a running leap and gave myself over to the fall.

I closed my eyes as the water enveloped me, rejuvenated by its chill. The weight of my body dragged me down to the lakebed and sank me up to the ankles in the cushiony silt.

Above, the world rippled, the moon unspooled into a pale haze. Craning my head, I watched the golem's shape pass overhead. His eyes were made to see in the dark, not in water. And this far below, the lake's musky odor hid me. He landed hard on the bridge, disappearing from view.

Seconds turned into minutes. Too scared to look at my hand, I explored it by touch, tentatively tracing over the metal

rod that had burst free. Shifted it back into place. Shaped my
fingers one by one, reforming the smooshed joints. It wasn't
pretty, but it would do.

It soothed me to stand in the riverbed. I sensed that if I
stayed down here long enough, something might happen.
My legs would be taken first, dissolved up to the thighs, so I
could no longer stand. Then, slowly, kindly, the rest of the clay
would wash over me, until my iron bones were left to gather
rust. Until it would be like I had never existed in the first
place. Years later, someone might dredge me up in pieces—a
pile of useless scrap metal scattered with human teeth as white
and smooth as river pearls.

Give in, the water's soft gurgle seemed to say in a thousand
tongues. *Rest. Become a part of me again.*

I closed my eyes, swooning under a sudden sleepiness.
Strange, that. I had the scribes' memories of human sleep,
and my own memories of being put to sleep. And this darkness that lingered at the edges of my vision was like neither.
Not death, not life. Just...something else.

A part of me wanted to give in, settle down. I wouldn't
have to think or feel. Everything that I had witnessed above
the water, it would be as if it had never existed in the first
place.

But Akiva would still be out there, and down here, I
wouldn't be able to protect him.

My eyes opened. I forced myself to take one step forward,
then another, trudging through the mud. My iron skeleton
weighed me down. In my natural environment, I could tell
it wasn't a part of me.

The world above shifted and blurred. Fragments of the up-

side filtered down through the silt disrupted by my passage—
here the dark archway of a bridge, there the reflections of trees.
I allowed myself to fall back on an animal instinct, using the
subtle recollections of the scribes' past lives to guide me down,
down, following the channel's weaving bends toward Lake
Skaistis. I closed my eyes and moved through touch alone, at
peace in the sluicing, liquid darkness.

After some distance, I stopped and looked up again. The
moonlight unraveled on the river's placid surface. No sign of
the other golem.

I tried swimming upward, but my body was too heavy.
I waded to the edge of the bank instead and climbed up it,
digging my arms and feet into the frozen soil. At last, I broke
through the surface and rolled onto ice-slickened stones.

The black sky loomed overhead. My clothes hung on my
form, stiff and brown with mud. I looked down at my injured
hand and exhaled slowly. Two of my nails were gone, probably back at the castle, but at least I still had fingers.

As I sank onto my knees, the memory of Ezra's death
lodged like a boulder in my throat. Despair pounded down
on me like waves. I hadn't been strong enough. I hadn't saved
him. I ground my palms against my eyes, wishing to tear them
out. Tear out my teeth, my tongue. These were not parts of
me. These were human parts, human, and I was just a monster, not alive, never alive. Never alive.

I dug my fingers into the ground instead, sinking them up
to the knuckles in the cold earth. Tore out fistfuls of dirt, clods
of ice, dug a hole for myself. The brute violence soothed me
and allowed me to push my grief to a far corner of my mind,
somewhere I couldn't touch it.

Exhausted, I sank onto my side and pressed my cheek against the earth. The scent of soil filled my nostrils. Comforting. Familiar.

So tired. If I could sleep, I would have. I wished I could.

But I was still a long way from home. And there were people I needed to kill.

I forced myself to rise and brushed the dirt off my limbs. Ezra's words echoed in my ears as I advanced, grimacing at the waterlogged weight of my body. He had told me I wasn't human, that the only purpose was the one he had given me. That the reason I had emotions was so that I could feel hate.

So, when the other golem had stepped toward me, why had I felt an ice-cold tremor pass through my steel armature, like he had reached into my chest and crushed something deep inside of me? Why did the idea of Akiva's dead body make me want to squeeze my eyes shut and cower, grind at my eyes and temples until I blotted the terrifying images from my head?

I couldn't stand the thought of anything happening to him. I thought it might destroy me.

As I reached Gulzifa's house, a sudden debilitating exhaustion fell over me. I collapsed on the frozen earth, wings of darkness furling over the edges of my vision. It wasn't sleep, but it was something like it. It sucked me down and held me under.

For the first time, I dreamed, as if a little of Ezra's humanity had leached into me the moment I'd taken his life. We were back in the hayloft during summer, and gnats and mosquitoes wavered through the air. Ezra was sitting on the pallet, reading aloud from a book.

He closed it with a sigh. When he lifted his eyes, tears glistened in their depths. "Do you understand now?"

When I awoke, my face was wet, and Gulzifa leaned over me with her hands on my shoulders. Her dog crowded close, nudging my cheek and neck with its moist snout. At first, I thought the dampness was gathered snow, but then I wiped my hand across my cheek, and my skin came back glistening with muddy water.

Overhead, the sky was marbled pink and purple to the east, with the sun rising beyond the dark trees like the crest of the rooster. It stopped snowing during the night, and when I sat up, I disrupted the thin layer of white that had molded my body.

"Vera, what happened?" she asked as I settled onto my haunches. "What are you doing out here?"

I looked around, still groggy. I felt as if I'd been asleep for ages, unsure of the year or the season. "Is Akiva asleep?"

Her brow furrowed. "No, Vera, he never came back."

CHAPTER 31

SUNLIGHT FRACTURED AGAINST THE NEWLY fallen snow, as bright as the fragments of a broken mirror. The snow had swallowed my tracks during the night, and if not for the sun's eastern climb, I wouldn't have been able to find my way.

Panicked, I raced through fields and groves, searching for any sign of Akiva's presence. But the only footprints to mar the snow were my own, and if he had left any trace of himself, it was lost beneath the fresh new mounds.

"Akiva?" I called.

Only the wind answered.

"Akiva?!"

Dread pressed down on my chest, its weight so distinct that if I'd had lungs, it would've crushed them to raw pulp.

Even now, my breath grew harried, rapid, driven by Chaya's muscle memory. I didn't need to breathe, but I felt as if I was drowning. This was the same thing that had happened with Ezra. Here one moment, gone the next, and I hadn't been able to stop it.

I wanted to scream. What was the point of my creation if I wasn't even strong enough to protect the people close to me? Ezra should have just left me in the riverbed—not feeling, not thinking, just thoughtless and foolish clay. I never should've been made in the first place.

Dawn broke as I reached the shoreline of Lake Skaistis, not far from the small fisherman's hut where Akiva and I had stolen the rowboat the night before. Now the craft lay upturned, half-sunken in the shallows. It had been left that way for so long that ice had begun to crawl up its sides, fusing it to the water.

Mouth dry, I turned over the rowboat, wrenching it up so roughly that the wood splintered in my grip. I expected to uncover Akiva beneath it, with his lips parted lifelessly and frost already creeping over his ice-blue eyes. There was only the glint of dark water, the sunlight rippling across it in bloodred skeins.

Wait. No. I bent down and reached into the shallows, tugging a metal pole from the mud—and with the pole, the oak stock and leather sling it was attached to. His rifle.

My mouth trembled and an unpleasant coppery taste rose in the back of my mouth. I told myself it was just a phantom memory, something dredged up by the terror, or the scent that hung in the air, a scent like...

As I turned back, a gleam of color caught my eye. Ruby stains glistened against the snow. Blood. Enough to lace the air with its thick, meaty odor.

The streaks penetrated the deepest layer of snow, turning it into a gory slush. The snowfall had been sparser here, and I could still make out the half-circle treads of bootheels.

I lifted my gaze to the treetops, half expecting to see the golem standing there among the black fir needles and scabby bark. Blue sky shone through gaps in the canopy, casting coins of sunlight across the fresh snow. I was alone. But for some reason, sickeningly, it made me feel even worse, on edge and destabilized, as if the pines were slowly collapsing in on me and the ground upheaving underfoot. At any moment, the earth might give way beneath me.

"Akiva?" I called.

My voice echoed back to me, bounding off the pines. I listened, frozen in stillness. Roosting overhead, the grackles croaked and cawed. I could almost believe they were mocking me, goading me on.

Already dead. He was already dead, wasn't he?

Dread building in my heart, I followed the trail of blood left in the snow, winding toward the fisherman's cottage. There was blood. So much blood. What had begun as streaks and sporadic droplets quickly became puddles of red, and then the frantic, dragging prints of someone struggling to flee.

I imagined that his pursuer or pursuers must have toyed with him, the way the barn cat had tormented rats back in the hayloft. Slowly, cruelly pursuing until he was too exhausted or too weak to keep going.

I passed between the trees and froze to a sudden halt. A motionless figure lay sprawled across the ground, the snow muddied with gore beneath him.

"Akiva!" I threw myself on my knees beside him, twisted him over, gagging at the limp grayish-purple coils of innards spilling from his torn stomach. No—it was not—it was not him. Dark-brown hair shorn close against the scalp, glazed brown eyes, the seamed features of a much older man. I swallowed hard at the bite marks on his throat and stomach, the way his flannel shirt had been torn with ease beneath claw or tooth.

The man must've been driven from the house, alerted by what? Screams of agony? Gunfire?

Slowly, I rose to my feet and continued toward the fisherman's hut, my despair mounting with each step. More blood speckled the path winding up to the cottage, and the door hung ajar like a broken jawbone, one hinge ripped free.

Inside, the air hung heavily with the scent of woodsmoke and spent gunpowder. I stepped past the threshold, entering the den. By the fireplace, Akiva sat doubled over, his form banked in the low, pulsating glow of dying embers.

His lips were blue from the cold, and I knew without looking down that frostbite would have left his fingers in even worse condition. And still—so still that I feared he was dead, was almost certain of it, until I knelt down beside him and he stirred. His lids cracked open, and he regarded me through clouded eyes, too weak to even speak.

His nose was freshly broken along the old fault line, one nostril crushed into a gory slit, blood bubbling from the second. Blood slickened his lips, froze in a line down his face. I could tell from the way he looked at me—pupils dilated even in the glow of the fire, so swollen that I knew I must be just a shadow to him, that the damage was more than skin deep. And that was just his head.

"Akiva." His name left me in a croak of despair.

"It was a monster," he said, his lips rising in a pained, humorless smile. "He—it came looking for you. I guess he could smell you on me. Just my luck, huh?"

Closer now, I could see the wet shadow bloomed across his coat, over the place where his wound had been. And I knew without peeling back the wool folds, that the stitches would be torn open, gouged at with fingers made of clay, or a wolf's filed teeth. And there were more teeth marks, too—an entire chunk of shoulder shredded, and another bite taken out of his forearm. The splintered end of a bone pierced through his pant leg, and with a sickening jolt, it dawned on me that was his femur.

"We need to get you to a doctor!" I leaned down to scoop him up but hesitated as my arm encircled his back. There was so much blood. I was terrified to move him. If I even touched him, something else might break.

"It's too late for that, Vera. No one will help us." Akiva struggled to get the words out, his voice wet and thick, as though mud was welling up inside of him.

"We'll go to the family camp. Doctor Reznikoff—"

"We'd never make it in time anyway."

I pressed my hand over his stomach wound to stanch the bleeding, but it was no good. The hot liquid coursed against my palm and escaped through the gaps between my fingers.

A ghost of a smile passed over his lips, only to vanish as a sudden violent spasm racked his body. Bent over himself, he coughed furiously, digging his nails into the cracks between the floorboards as if to prevent himself from plummeting into even darker depths. He spat onto the floorboards, his saliva marbled red.

"I'm sorry." His voice seemed very small.

"Don't say that."

"I—I'm scared." The words cracked brittlely in his throat.

The icy hatred thawed from his gaze, not permafrost at all but a thin veneer that drained to expose the terror burning beneath. "I'm so scared."

Something clenched up deep inside me, in the place a heart would have been. I held him against me as his grip weakened and eased us gently to the floor.

"Don't be afraid," I murmured, resting him on the ground.

He leaned against the wall beside the fireplace, struggling with each labored breath. A greasy sweat dewed his cheeks and neck. His skin was ashen, save for the bruised shadows gathering under his eyes and the swollen welt of his lips.

All this time, I had thought that Akiva was chasing death, but he had actually been running from it. Running as far as his body could take him, even as the infection consumed him, thinking that if he just kept going—hands on the gun, eyes straight ahead—and carved a path of blood and vengeance through Lithuania, death wouldn't catch up to him. But it had now.

"Is there anything out there?" Desperation gleamed in his wild eyes. He wanted so badly to survive; I could see the overwhelming need burning in his gaze. Except he was too weak to even lift himself from the floor.

I couldn't answer.

"There has to be. You would know, wouldn't you." His voice left him in a forceful gasp. I could tell how much it hurt him just to speak, how much he needed to get these words out. "You're a golem, so you must have seen God. Haven't you?"

The floorboards splintered beneath my clenching fingers. I dug my grip into the aged wood. It would be so easy to tell him yes, there was something out there. Someone was listening. This wasn't the end. And yet...

"You haven't," he whispered, sparing me from deceiving

him. He settled against the wall and laughed, a wet choking sound that ended with him retching blood until he crumpled over himself, trembling and breathless.

"I'm sorry," I said.

Slowly, Akiva regained his breath. Leaning against me, he traced the calligraphy winding down my arms. So cold. His skin was so cold that I could almost believe he was turning into clay himself.

"Please, when I die, take my eyes and teeth. Take them all. My nails, my blood, whatever you need. Take them and make me like you. I want to be just like you. I want to make the bastards pay."

"I'm sorry, Akiva," I whispered, my voice choking up. "That isn't how it works."

"But I can hunt them."

"It won't be you."

For a long moment, he just stared at me. Then, slowly, his lips rose in the saddest of smiles. "It's been a long time since I've been me. You can at least put what's left to use."

"You're not going to die," I whispered as his fingertips slipped lower.

"You are a memorial." A thin stream of blood spilled from the side of his mouth and unraveled down his chin. He rested his forehead on my shoulder and closed his eyes, his breathing slowing. His grip was like an infant's now, and by the moment fading. "Our history… Our faith. It's written all over you. As long as you survive, so will we."

CHAPTER 32

AKIVA'S GRIP FALTERED, AND HIS EYES SLID SHUT. He sank against me, his body racked by uneven gasps.

"You'll survive, too," I swore, scooping him into my arms. There was still time. He was still breathing, and the family camp wasn't far. "I swear. I'm not going to let you die. You'll survive this, Akiva."

He didn't answer, and after a few paces, I realized he had slipped into unconsciousness. I held him close against myself as I emerged from the fisherman's hut and broke into a run, wincing every time I landed hard or stumbled. But if he felt my missteps, he showed no sign of it. His arms hung loosely, head lolling heavily against my shoulder.

The world smeared into an endless span of snow, and scouring wind, and the slosh of mud against my bare feet. Now more than ever, I was acutely aware of the passing of time. Every moment mattered.

I needed to go faster. Faster. I felt the force of each stride thrum through my limbs, goading me to drop down on all fours and give myself over to the violent force raging inside of me. If not for the unmoving body I clutched in my arms, I might've succumbed to the impulse.

I sensed that this was what the wolf-eyed golem had done, and that after giving in to this vast hunger, any last shred of my humanity would be devoured. And yet…what did it mean to be human? The question taunted me like the twist of a knife. Humanity was responsible for this. They were cruel.

Maybe it would be better this way—to obliterate every speck of them from my body until I became something else, something better. Something that could protect Akiva.

But with each passing moment, I could see him slipping farther and farther away from me. His lips were ashen, and the fingers that weren't swollen and bloodied were blued from the cold. Despite my best efforts, snowflakes gathered on his hair and lashes. Blood hardened down the side of his face, drawing a crazed maroon path from his jawline to the corner of his mouth.

Desperation pounded away at me. I held Akiva closer to me, tighter. Something cracked with the brittle noise of a frozen branch, but it couldn't be him—it was my own body, surely. I was falling apart inside. I could feel it—my iron ribs corroding and tumbling into flakes of rust, the clay itself cracking and collapsing into a void, a howling black void. This was death. This was terror. And even though every impulse within me screamed to rip out my hair, my eyes, my teeth until there was nothing left, nothing human, just brute strength and hatred, I had to keep going. I had to save him. I was the only one who could.

At last, the swell of the forest rose ahead like a smear of ink on the darkening horizon. I entered the forest with my head bowed and my chest arched over his limp form, expecting to encounter the guards' bullets. Instead, as I neared the camp, a cry of alarm rose from the trees ahead, and Susannah emerged with her eyes flared in shock.

"Vera! Are you...?" She trailed off as I slammed to a stop in front of her. It vaguely dawned on me that there was blood on my face, blood on my arms, blood muddying the front of my dress, which had been torn and stretched until it was reduced to rags. The makeup had run from my skin, exposing the calligraphy that covered my body.

"Where's Dr. Reznikoff?" I demanded.

"I, uh..." As she stammered for an answer, her gaze remained on Akiva. All the color had drained from her face, until it was nearly as white as the snow itself.

"Akiva's dying! Take me to him, now!"

She nodded, and without a word, raced into the camp. I followed after her, nearly blind with panic. Everything seemed to sluice together into a wet smear, as if the world's structure had been eroded by the blood splatter, collapsing into shades of gray and green.

Someone reached out to me as I passed. I shoved them away before they could get too close to Akiva, my bared teeth keeping at bay the warning growl rising in my throat. I might not have the teeth of a wolf, but I would bite if I had to.

Down into the dugout, down into the candlelit darkness musky with the scent of ointment and gangrene. Dr. Reznikoff looked up from where he knelt arranging his small stockpile of medical supplies.

The blood drained from the man's face in an instant. "What happened?"

"Save him," I insisted, my voice rising in a snarl. "You were able to heal him before. Now do it again."

"W-wait…" His mouth trembled so fiercely, even his mustache quivered. Vaguely, it dawned on me how I must look to him, that for the first time, he must be seeing me for how I truly was. But I didn't care. I was not the monster in this world.

"Heal him. Do what you did then!"

Swallowing hard, he nodded helplessly. "Put him on the table. Carefully."

I did as he asked, laying Akiva down with infinite care.

As Dr. Reznikoff approached, a shadow passed over his face. He stopped at Akiva's bedside and placed two fingers upon his throat. Stood there, unmoving.

"What are you waiting for?" I demanded. "Why are you just standing there?"

Dr. Reznikoff looked at me, eyes welling with sorrow. "I'm so sorry, but there's nothing I can do."

"No! I don't believe you!" I stepped forward, feeling myself teeter at the precipice of a deep and uncontrollable rage.

Soft fingers closed around my upper arm, and I turned.

"Vera, he's already dead," Susannah said quietly, and I froze. It was impossible. I had carried him all this way, shielded him from the snow, clutched his head against myself to keep it from jostling. How could he be dead when we hadn't even had the chance to try saving him? When I hadn't been able to say goodbye?

"No, you're wrong." My voice came to me from a distance, as if I was already retreating back into the riverbed. I turned, searching for a sign to prove her wrong.

But Akiva's eyes confronted me, half-open and sightless. It dawned on me that he had probably been dead since I had entered the forest, perhaps long before that. And I had carried him all this way, a lifeless corpse. And that crack I'd heard—that had been his ribs snapping, hadn't it?

"His wounds were much too severe to be treated here anyway," Dr. Reznikoff said, as if that was supposed to console me. "Even at a regular hospital, he would have died on the operating table. I'm sorry, but there is nothing you could've done."

He kept talking, but his words were lost to the cold, brutal wind as I stepped outside. It had begun to snow, the air filled with the swirl of white flakes as fine and abrasive as sand. I made it two steps before I stopped, unsure of where to go from here. I could return to Trakai Castle and seek out the wolf-eyed golem, kill him, and carve a warpath across the entirety of Lithuania. I would root out my enemies in their bunkers and homes and offices and show them the reason for my creation.

But Akiva would still be dead, and I would be alone. No one who knew me, no one who'd known Chaya. Just utter loneliness and the thrill of the hunt. That should have been enough. It should have been sufficient for a creature like me. So why did I want more?

A crowd had gathered, drawn by the commotion. They stared at me, and I knew how they must see me—hair in a tangled frenzy, dress torn and drenched in mud and blood, calligraphy snaking down my limbs and naked feet, the word for truth on my brow.

In the far back, my gaze was drawn to a familiar face, and before I knew it, I was already striding forward. I shouldered roughly past those who had gathered, ignoring their sounds of protest.

Rav Oren stiffened as I approached him, his jaw tightening as though in preparation for a blow.

"When we first met, you said that you had met another like me." I stopped before him. "You recognized me completely."

He didn't answer. From the way he peered at me with his mouth cocked, I could tell my statement had taken him aback.

"Can you make one?" I asked, and his eyes narrowed.

"What do you mean?"

In the flinty sunlight, it was as though I was seeing him for the first time. That narrow chin, and those cold gray eyes. When Susannah had first brought me to him, in the gloom of the dugout, I had mistaken him for Ezra. In the short time since then, I had met so many other humans, but none who shared such an unmistakable resemblance to my creator.

"Have you made a golem before?" I reiterated.

He didn't answer.

"Have you?"

"I did, although it was not like you… Not a lump of clay masquerading as a human being." His voice was dull and hateful, his gaze even more so. "I made the right choice, and I destroyed it before it could walk. I realize what you want, but I will have no part in that. To attempt to create a golem in another person's image—to create one with a *soul*—it goes beyond the blasphemy of trying to shape one from mere mud and water. It is an abomination."

I reached out and seized him by the collar. "No, the abomination is you humans. You petty, cruel humans. You are the ones who caused this violence. You bring suffering and pain. And then you create creatures like me in order to fix it. It is you humans!"

For all the man's outrage, it dawned on me that a burial here would ultimately be no different than dumping Akiva into a mass grave or incinerating him into ashes. He would not be visited except by the scavenging wolves and ravens, and within months, the ground would level out from rain and runoff. Years later, people might unearth the bleached, gnawed-on scatter of what remained, but it wouldn't really matter at that point. They wouldn't even know his name.

"You will do this," I said, and for a long moment, we simply stared at each other.

"It's repugnant," he said.

"It's pikuach nefesh," I responded icily.

The man scoffed. "He's already dead. There's no life to preserve."

"There's your own."

His face blanched. "You wouldn't."

"We golems destroy all that we love, before destroying ourselves. Isn't that what you told me?" With each word, a cold, dark anger built up inside me. It would be easy to give over to the rage and prove him right. That I was a monster to the bone—that it was all I ever was, and all I ever would be. "Do you want a demonstration?"

"What you are suggesting is profane. It is desecration."

"It is what he wanted."

CHAPTER 33

THERE WAS NO BURIAL SOCIETY HERE TO TEND to the dead. No mikveh to immerse the met, no clean linen to sew a shroud, no pottery to lay over his face, and no soil from Eretz Yisrael. There was only Rav Oren and me in a darkened room, and Akiva on the table, and his blood drying cold and congealed on my fingertips.

Ezra had shaped me slowly, and with care, but I sensed a part of it was because he feared me as his own creation. He had taken it slowly because he was terrified of what he was bringing into this world. I didn't have the luxury of time or hesitation. And I was not afraid.

So, while the old Rav slept, I continued my work, laboring.

It was difficult to see this cold white body as Akiva, and even harder to view him as his disparate parts—teeth like a scatter of gleaned barley, hacked-off strands twined up in raven-black sheafs, his ice-blue irises even paler in death, rimed with a filmy haze.

It wasn't until I took his hand in mine and turned my attention to his nails that I realized how scarred and calloused his palms were. The nails of his index and middle fingers were split, and several of the fingers hung crooked, broken from trauma so recent that they hadn't even had time to swell. I wondered what the golem had done, if Akiva had scrambled across the snowy ground for his rifle, reached out this very hand, only to have it crushed beneath the heel of a jackboot.

I understood it now. *This* was what it meant to be human.

To repair something, it first had to be dismantled. That was the second truth of this world. So, I continued with my task of uncreating him.

Minutes became hours, hours became days, and the days themselves sluiced away into a candlelit haze. Time ceased to be important, and instead of charting the days and nights by the passage of the sun, I kept track by the progress I made with the golem.

His hands, smoother now than they'd been in life, stained at the nailbeds with his own blood. The tough, wiry muscles girdling his waist.

Shaping the clay we dredged from the river, I tenderly formed Akiva's features, the sharp curve of his cheekbones, the restless mouth I'd once kissed. When it came time to sculpt his nose, I straightened the crudely healed bridge into the shape I remembered from Chaya's memories, and then later, smoothed out the scar on his cheek. This golem had never suffered these injuries, had never endured the pain of a broken nose or torn cheek, but it felt like a kind of repair, as if I was correcting the wrongs of the past.

Only through my work on the golem did it dawn on me the nonchalant cruelty of my creation. Ezra hadn't been a kind creator, and even at the end, I still wasn't sure if he recognized my sentience. In any case, his pain and ignorance did not absolve him. Freeing me from my servitude did not absolve him. Turning me into his executioner did not absolve him.

Everyone who knew Chaya was gone. Akiva, her own father. Everyone. I would have thought that that would've been enough to loosen the bonds her memories had over me. But it wasn't that simple. I was beginning to realize that as long as I lived, I would have to accept that I would never be without her. These memories, these feelings, they were a part of me. They were an inheritance. And maybe that wasn't a bad thing. Maybe this was how the dead lived on.

I asked Rav Oren about it once, when he took a break from our labor and sat by the fire, wiping the clay from his hands.

"Where do you think she is now?" I asked, and he set aside the soiled rag. His stony gray eyes flicked up. "Chaya, I mean."

"Her soul?" he asked, turning to look at me.

I nodded.

For a long moment, he didn't answer, and then he said, "Did you ever see the body?"

The question took me aback.

"No," I admitted.

He nodded thoughtfully. "It is said that the soul is contained within the Luz bone, and that the dead will be resurrected from that bone. And to create a golem, one that can actually pass as human, one capable of speech—it needs a soul. Or the closest thing to it."

"You don't think..." I trailed off, my fingers straying to the back of my neck. The truth was, I didn't know what kind of man Ezra was, even now, or what grief had made him capable of.

What if it wasn't the teeth or the hair, or the eyes that gave an illusion of life, but the soul? If the Luz bone truly was the final key to unlocking the secret in creating golems, no wonder the incomplete golems in Dr. Brandt's lab had just been piles of crude, disparate parts. They had lacked the necessary component to maintain this guise of humanity that all this time I had taken for granted.

"We can take a look," Rav Oren said, nodding at the pile of tools left on the table. "All it would take is a little cut."

"It won't change anything," I said, and he nodded.

"It won't," he agreed.

I tested the clay of my nape. There was more I wanted to ask, but I didn't know if I was ready for the answer.

"Some believe the soul is reincarnated," he said thoughtfully. "I suppose if that were the case, the new body would be its own person. Although, this of course is just a theory. We can't expect to know what makes a soul or what one takes with it."

Rav Oren was right. As for this new golem, I didn't know who this being would be when he opened his eyes, but I didn't want him to enter this world unfinished, the way that I had. True, he would carry an inheritance of the dead—memories, dreams, feelings—but that didn't mean he needed to inherit Akiva's pain, too.

Sometimes, in the middle of the night as I worked on the

golem, I would glance over at where the twin body lay and watch the candlelight ripple across the stained shrouds. Someone in the camp had found or made tachrichim, perhaps sewn it from the same parachute silk that Akiva had once used to fashion his camouflage cloak. They had brought the burial shrouds to us and left them outside the door, like an offering.

When I had started, the shrouds had been clean white, but now they were dusty, and soiled with worse than dirt, and the contours his body created in the loose folds of linen had begun to slowly, inexplicably change. I wanted to pretend that as the golem's shape grew more and more detailed, the corpse's features were eroding, wearing smooth into ivory skin and dimpled impressions, the joints flowing into the bones. But I knew life wasn't that fair. Ruin only begot more ruin.

"You need to bury it," Rav Oren said one morning.

"Not yet."

"It's a health hazard." His gaze shifted to where the covered form lay in the corner. A yellowish-brown stain had dappled it in the night. "Tahara can't even be performed in this state. Not that there's anyone here who could perform it. And it's starting to stink."

He had a point. Besides, the corpse had long since lost its use as a model. I was beginning to discover that a model wasn't even needed, just my memories of Akiva and enough time to lose myself in the rhythmic motions of shaping clay. Hours could pass in that manner, and I'd stir to discover that what was once just a shapeless limb had become the perfect semblance of an arm, the fingernails already embedded.

The golem was almost complete. But Rav Oren was right. For now, I had to take care of what was left.

As I gathered the shrouded figure into my arms, I sensed Oren's eyes on me. He didn't speak until I turned, at which point he gave me a thin smile.

"It won't be long now," he said.

It made me uneasy to leave the golem alone with him, or even out of sight. It felt like nature itself was plotting to stop us. If I turned my back, anything might happen.

"What if it doesn't work?" I asked, weighing the corpse in my arms. Even bundled in its stained silk shroud, I swore it was lighter than it should've been.

"I don't think that's the only possibility you should be preparing yourself for."

"What do you mean?"

Oren hesitated, tracing his fingers over the edge of the table where the golem lay covered. He worked a clot of clay free from the wood. "He won't be the same."

"I know."

"It won't even be him."

"I know."

"Assuming it does work." His gaze lifted to me. "If he comes back, and he tries to kill the people in this camp, what will you do?"

I didn't answer. *You think too lowly of us*, I wanted to say, but the truth was, wasn't that question the same whether you were bringing a child into this world or a monster? Humans were capable of the same brutality and violence. My rage was simply a reflection of their own.

"Will you be prepared to kill him with your own hands?"

Cradling the shrouded body in my arms, I turned away. "I'll do what must be done."

CHAPTER 34

GOLDEN SUNLIGHT DANCED ACROSS THE DAMP pine needles coating the forest floor. It was warmer than I had thought it would be, the snow already melting into puddles. After climbing from the dugout, I froze for a moment outside, taking in the birdsong and rustle of the wind through the branches.

I felt strongly disoriented, like the first time I had emerged from the barn to realize the world was so much vaster than I had originally thought. Spring was coming, if not already here. How long had it been since that night at Trakai Castle?

As I made my way through the camp, the few people milling about stopped their tasks and watched me. Nobody approached, which was for the best. What would I even say? And if they tried shaming me, I didn't know if I'd be able to control myself.

I carried the body through the woods, through the marsh, until I reached the ice-crested edge of the Visinča River. I stepped into the river up to my knees, my hips, allowing the black water to wash over us. And then under, deeper.

The fish would eat Akiva, just as the worms and wolves would eat him if I were to bury him. He would rot. He would be tumbled clean and white by the river. And maybe that was profane or sacrilegious—it was not the burial that Akiva should've had, the one he deserved—but it was what it meant to be alive. To be in this world.

I weighed his body down with stones and smoothed the silt over him. Then, with my fingers still buried in the muck, I closed my eyes and knelt in the water, losing myself in the river's soft gurgle, its gentle currents.

Perhaps I should say a prayer for him or recite passages from Tehillim. I could rend my drenched clothes. But a clay form was waiting for me in the dugout, the skin not yet set. And I needed to keep going.

As I emerged from the water, the bushes rustled. I tensed, swiveling around, teeth already bared in preparation to bite and savage.

Susannah stood at the tree line, her rifle slung over her shoulder. I had almost forgotten that there were other people in the camp. That I truly wasn't alone out here.

"I'm sorry if I startled you." She offered a hesitant smile. "I just thought you might want some company."

She and Dr. Reznikoff had come and gone over the course of the days, but I had barely even noticed their presence. They had simply been more ghosts. Vaguely, it dawned on me that everyone in the camp must know to some degree what I was, and what had happened. She had told me during my first visit to the camp that nobody had believed I was a golem, but now, there was probably no doubt of it.

When I didn't answer, Susannah's weak smile faded, and she took a step away.

"I'm sorry," she said, turning away. "I don't blame you for wanting to be alone."

"Wait," I said, and she looked back. "It's okay."

She nodded, coming to my side.

"Would you like to say Kaddish for him?" she asked.

"You say Kaddish for the dead," I said, and she simply stared at me helplessly, not comprehending.

On the same night I had gathered his teeth and nails, Rav Oren had taken from the nape of Akiva's neck a small lozenge of bone no larger than a grain of barley, the final vertebrae upon which the base of the skull rested. I wanted to believe that when we brought Akiva back, all it would take was that little fragment and he would be resurrected whole, not a stranger. He would know my name. But in my short time on earth, I had begun to realize that what we wanted in life was seldom what we got.

As we retraced our steps back to camp, a din of harried voices filtered through the trees ahead, followed by hollow, agonized groans. My fingernails sank into my palms reflexively, and all I could think about when I heard that noise was Akiva—lying in a puddle of his own blood, with his palm pressed against his stomach to hold parts of himself inside him. I raced between the trees and emerged into the center of camp, blinking in the sunlight, searching wildly for the source of the uproar.

A bearded man had collapsed in the center of the glade. He wore a hand-sewn white cloak like the one Akiva had been wearing when we'd first met, only this garment was drenched heavily in blood. Already, a small crowd had gathered around him, and as I approached, the bystanders formed a wide column to allow me to pass.

As I squatted down beside the man, his glazed eyes rolled up to meet mine. With a jolt, I realized he was the general from the Soviet Camp. Volkov. The same one who had called me a zhidovka and spat on the ground at my feet. Except now, the only thing to leave his mouth was a thick ribbon of blood.

"What happened?" I asked.

"Some kind of creature," Volkov croaked, and was about to say more when a pair of explosions echoed through the forest.

Through the screen of branches, I caught a glimpse of a pillar of black smoke rising in the distance, cleaving the sky in two like a vivisection wound.

"That would be, I imagine, our artillery stockpile." Volkov struggled to rise. He failed and sank back to the ground. "Please. You have to help the others. That thing—it's going to kill them all."

As the man slumped to the ground, his eyes rolling back, I turned and looked into the faces of those who had gathered. Fear, resignation, anger. They stared at me as if they expected something, but I felt alone. Ezra hadn't anticipated this when he had created me, but perhaps he hadn't had to carve this will into my body—golems were known protectors. It was who we were.

"He's dead," Dr. Reznikoff murmured, sinking beside the body to place his fingers against the man's neck.

My gaze remained riveted on Volkov's lifeless form. I had seen this before. Over and over again, both in this world and my inherited memories. And with Chaya, I had tasted that blood and dirt in my mouth, felt the life drain from under my skin.

Rage welled up inside me, filling me with such heat, I thought it would crack my skin. As gunshots echoed in the distance, I strode toward the tree line.

Akiva had called me a memorial, but I swore to myself I would become more than that. I would be the Jew that the Nazis couldn't kill. I would show them and their collaborators that when they slaughtered innocent girls deep in the forest, those girls sometimes came back. And if they wanted to spill blood, blood was what they'd get.

CHAPTER 35

I RAN.

I had no need to stop, no lungs to weaken, no muscles to become sore. Twice, my legs were torn open by the outstretched branch of a thorn bush, but that barely gave me pause. The deep scratches filled in within moments.

With each stride, I felt myself becoming more in tune with myself, as if invisible chains were uncoiling from my body, their weight lifting. This was what I had been born for. This was who I was. This was where I belonged.

The wind changed direction, blowing the scent of smoke toward me. I leaned forward, going even quicker still. It felt natural to move at this pace, as though it was the river's current that tugged me to move faster, faster, pushing myself forward until the steel rods in my legs thrummed with the powerful force of my strides.

If I had a heart, it would've pounded, but instead, I felt my anticipation drum throughout my entire body, carried into the depths of me by the vibrations of my scaffolding. I understood now why I had chosen to come here, and why Akiva had sworn to fight until the end. Because this was life. This was all that was left.

I tracked blood through the snow. The droplets dried on my face, rapidly chilled and congealed. Deeper in came the steady, monotonous roar of a machine gun.

I encountered the first Nazi soldiers as they proceeded in a single file through the snow-caked trees. The one at the rear fell silently, his trachea crushed by a well-placed kick. At the hollow thud of his body striking the ground, the next soldier in line swiveled around, eyes flaring in alarm.

As the man raised his rifle, I was already lunging forward. Bullets peppered my chin and neck, and cold mud slicked down my ravaged chest.

"*Was bist du?*" he croaked as I wrenched the gun from his hands. What are you?

"*Ich bin—*" My tongue fumbled around the shapes of the words, gargling on clay. "*Vergeltung!*"

Retribution.

I slammed the rifle's butt against his stomach with such force, a crack raced up the wooden stock and a similar *crunch* resounded from within him. He fell, and I hammered it down once, twice more as the misshapen lead slugs emerged from my body and scattered to the snow. I took out the last two soldiers as they opened fire in a blind panic, driven by relentless violence even as their bullets tore up my body.

I was surprised by how much I detested them, not just for what side they were on, but for being *human*. Why use their time on earth to do this, when they could be happy? When they could fall in love? It wasn't fair that they had free will, while I was created solely to correct their wrongs.

As German voices shouted from deeper into the forest, I took to the sky. Bark fissured between my fingers as I grasped hold of a pine tree's trunk. I dragged myself up, forming my own handholds. My shoes struggled to find purchase, but after three meters, I reached the first branches and my climbing smoothed out.

I leapt to the nearest tree branch, wincing as it shuddered beneath me. The slender boughs of the upper canopy would never hold my weight. I kept to the thick branches no higher than ten meters up, moving from tree to tree. After the first few leaps, I found a steady rhythm. The drone of the machine gun drowned the strained groan of wood but couldn't so easily hide the cascade of needles and pinecones that fell each time I found a new perch.

Down below, a flash of light preceded a gunshot. I leapt down on the soldier from above, driving him to the ground with the weight of my body. His neck snapped beneath my folded knee. When I rose into a crouch, he remained still beneath me, blood oozing from his ears and mouth.

A burst of rapid gunfire pummeled the trees around me. I snatched the soldier's helmet off the ground and yanked it on, cocking it low over my brow. Darting from between the trees, I searched for the source of the gunfire. Bullets struck my chest and arms, but soon even their steady, forceful blows became easy to ignore.

I tackled one soldier firing at me from behind a tree, hammering my fist into his face and neck until something broke inside of him and he went still. Each blow only seemed to stoke the thrilling rage inside of me, until all I could think about was taking out the next Nazi.

As soon as the soldiers realized what was going on, their gunfire became erratic. Bullets thrashed the forest canopy and tore up the bushes around me. I loped from tree to tree, keeping to the shadows and the underbrush.

At last, I burst through the foliage. The golem stood at the other end of the clearing, over the mangled corpse of a partisan machine-gunner. He turned to me, his eyes as bright and searing as searchlights.

"I knew you'd show up," he murmured, his lips peeling back to reveal a gleam of white teeth. In the time since I'd seen him last, something had shifted in his features. His face was not quite as eerily symmetrical as I remembered. The left side bulged, peppered with half-healed bullet holes. "The boy who smelled like you, did you find him?"

My hands tightened into fists. I felt drowned by the rage rearing up inside of me, as if it might suck me down at any moment, send me sluicing to the ground in a puddle of clay. "I did."

"Alive or dead?"

"Alive, but not for long. You'll pay for what you've done."

"Not before you." He rushed at me. I ducked out of the way, and his fist slammed into the place right where I'd been standing, taking out a chunk of bark and wood the size of a human head. Splinters rained down on my skin. As I backed away, he swung at me again. I ducked beneath his arm and leapt several meters back.

If I was going to fight him, I would need to go on the offensive. As the golem drew back and began to turn, I rushed at him. My fist struck his chest with such force that I felt his sternum bow beneath my knuckles and the groan of metal bars echo from deep within him. I had thought that if I were to touch him, his body would feel hard and unyielding, but it was just clay in the end, no different than my own. No, softer even. He hadn't had time yet to set.

He slammed into a tree, icicles raining down around us. His eyes were wide with astonishment. He pressed a hand over his chest, testing the edges of the crater. "Not bad."

His smile had faded even if his voice remained clear and unaffected. A wary animal instinct lingered in his gaze. He moistened his lips, and drew forward, circling me slowly, like a wolf on the prowl.

I couldn't tell where he would aim next. I thought he might try to take out my limbs, but I had a feeling that the time was done for such cruel teasing. He would go for my mark, no hesitation.

I turned with him, keeping him in my sight at all times. The hole I'd made in his chest began to fill in, but his hand remained over the depression. Could he still feel the displacement?

He lunged at me. Instead of dodging like he might expect, I met him head-on. I seized his arms and drove him to the ground, landing atop him. His body writhed beneath me, his teeth gnashing mere centimeters from my face. I did the only thing I could do. I leaned down and sank my teeth into his forehead, tearing off a chunk of clay.

My bite missed the mark by centimeters, and before I could try again, he bucked me off him with such force, I rolled across the forest floor and struck a young pine at the other end of the clearing. The trunk gave way against my back, and pine needles rained down.

"Vera!" a familiar voice called through the trees as I lumbered to my feet. Susannah emerged, gripping a rifle in both hands. Blood streaked down her face, but aside from that she appeared whole.

"Susannah, don't come any closer!" His clay squelched on my tongue, the mineral lead taste sharp and unfamiliar, as though we are different being beings down to the core. It didn't even taste like clay.

As I began to say more, the golem lurched onto his hands and knees. His limbs had begun to lose their definition, the fingers melting together, and the elbow joints buckling until his forearms sagged nearly to the ground. Bizarrely, the ground itself began to bow, as if the entire atmosphere were distorting. No. The soil itself was being displaced. Veins of dark earth climbed up his body. A mouse, snatched from its burrow, disappeared into his chest with a squeak of terror.

He wasn't simply moving the earth. He was devouring it.

"I'll kill you. I'll kill you!"

His body rippled forward, no longer constrained by his scaffolding. I tried to dodge him, but one of his limbs shot out and slammed into my chest, throwing me across the clearing. I landed in a heap on the ground, my legs shaking violently, the rods in my limbs drumming like live wires.

He strode forward, as relentless as a landslide. As he reached me, Susannah opened fire on him. He turned to her and ripped the gun from her hands.

"No," I croaked as he shoved her to the ground. "Don't hurt her."

"So, these humans mean something to you." His voice left him in a gargled groan. "I'll deal with them later, and you will die, knowing that you will not be able to protect them."

He said more, or tried to. His voice came out thick and wordless, like the slosh of mud. I scrambled back, colliding with the bloodied corpse of the machine gunner as the golem lurched toward me.

"Run!" I shouted, and she darted through the trees.

My fingertips stroked a smooth, round form. I looked down. The machine gunner had dropped the object in his last moments, his finger still curled around the circular wire at its neck. It took me a moment to recognize what I was looking at.

A grenade.

I pulled the pin from the grenade. It yielded without force, so easily that I was afraid I had broken it. Even as I lifted my arm to hurl the grenade, the golem was already in the process of lunging forward. There was no time. His arms reached out for me, seizing hold of my limbs, my clothes, my hair. His face split down the middle, no longer a semblance of a human form, but a fragmented crevice lined with wolf's teeth.

The maw engulfed my arm up to the shoulder, grenade and all, took it in, began to feed. As an unbelievable force opened in my palm, I closed my eyes and welcomed the night.

CHAPTER 36

THERE WAS DARKNESS AND SILENCE, AS THOUGH I had returned to the moment of my creation. Memories peeled away, sensations faded, until nothing remained. I was nothing.

I allowed myself to settle into the darkness, sinking deeper and deeper, flowing in. I should have known all along this world was not meant for creatures like me. It wasn't as though I had ever been alive.

I waited for the final spark of my consciousness to fade, but it lingered stubbornly. A part of me wanted desperately to live. I wanted to see Akiva again. I wanted to feel the breeze on my face. Even something as mundane as the blue sky would feel like a priceless gift.

Gradually, I became aware of my fingers, though not my

palms. I strained to move them. Stillness, and quiet, and the darkness pressing down on me. I wanted to cry out, had no mouth. Tried to weep, but no tears would come.

Then, slowly, feeling flowed into an arm. Dry splintery wood beneath my back. I tested the surface, my nails picking away at the paint or varnish. Was I back in the hayloft? Maybe everything I had experienced up until this point had been a horrible dream, and I'd never left at all.

Warm fingers passed over my leg, restoring sensation up to my ankle. Cold slick moisture leaked through my skin, slathered over me until I could visualize clearly, by its chill, the back of my calf and the place where my knee met my lower hip.

The first sound I heard was a voice.

"I found another," a girl said. She sounded so familiar. "It's part of her arm, I think."

"Put it in the box." Hoarse and deep, this voice belonged to a stranger. "I'll need more clay, too."

A hand cupped my cheek sometime later, the fingertips stroking—no, reshaping—my inner socket. Then the touch moved lower.

"You're making her nose all wrong," she exclaimed.

I felt sudden relief. I knew that voice. Susannah.

"Would you like to try?" The man sounded harried. "No? Then she will have to make do."

The voices diminished, fading into a dark place inside of me. I allowed myself to drift, sluggishly conscious of the sensation returning to my body. My other leg materialized beneath me as though it were coming home from a long journey, so worn at the sole that I couldn't feel my toes, not at first anyway.

Then the hand returned to stroke my face, shaping my ear and cheekbone, and when it fell away, it brought light. Stunning light. Searing.

I blinked, struggling to adjust to the stunning glow. It wasn't sunlight—this light, it moved, coiling in shapes along the ceiling. The scent of…of melted candlewax hung in the air. Candles. Yes. I breathed in deeply, relishing in the memory of candles. Hanukkah. Eight tips at the end of a menorah's branched brass arms. The taste of challah dissolving in my mouth like butter in warm milk.

A face materialized from the glow—dark hair and gray eyes, a face as sharp and harsh as a scalpel. I wanted to weep. Ezra.

He leaned over me, and with the candlelight dissolving against his back, the illusion was shattered. Wrinkles creased his eyelids and cheeks, and his hair and beard were threaded with silver.

Rav Oren brushed his hand over my eyes and brow. "Rest awhile longer, child," he murmured, and the darkness folded in again.

After that, it wasn't quite as dark or quiet. Sensations came and went, but over time, I could tell that I was being remade. I tried speaking to Susannah and managed a few sounds, which were met by kind laughter and whispers from her.

When I was awake again, I knew Rav Oren finished because I could feel every part of myself. I sat up and looked down. Entire verses of calligraphy were lost beneath smoothed clay, the mended cracks where my limbs met body.

"So, you're awake," Oren said, resting against the table upon which I lay. His hair was shorter than I recalled, and more silver than before, the black blanched out.

"Old man." My voice was hoarse and dry, but it felt like my own now. "You brought me back."

"It wasn't easy. When we found you, the aleph in emet was nearly severed in two. A few millimeters more, and I wouldn't have been able to repair you."

"Why?"

He didn't answer.

"You thought I was a monster."

"Even monsters deserve to live."

"Does that mean… Akiva. Did you finish him?"

"No." A wry smile rose on Oren's lips. "We both will."

CHAPTER 37

THE GOLEM WAS BORN UPON LEAVES AND SOIL, on the first day of the first month of Aviv. A prayer shawl had been draped over him in his long sleep, and when Rav Oren pulled it down, we discovered the tekhelet ink had leached from the fabric and left a set of indigo lines running diagonally across his shoulder and chest.

We looked at each other.

"A small sacrifice," Oren said, resting his inkwell on the floor beside him. In preparation for this moment, we had mixed black ink from charcoal and water and cut a stylus from the reeds that grew along the Vokė.

During those long nights laboring over the golem, Oren and I had spoken of what was and what would come. With each week, the FPO was sending more and more young fighters from the ghetto into the forests, and while some joined the family camp, others simply passed through. The Jewish partisans traded news with the same eagerness with which they swapped supplies. The Siege of Stalingrad had failed. The Russians had retaken Kurst, and the Germans had once more reclaimed Kharkov, but it was a tentative hold. I knew that I could join in the fighting, but I was beginning to realize that no matter how many soldiers I killed, it wouldn't be enough. But saving a life? Protecting the people here? That was the way to make a difference.

As Oren stirred the ink to reconsolidate it, I studied the golem.

The candlelight drew a gleam of blue from his raven-dark hair. In his sleep—or the closest thing to sleep that us monsters were allowed—his features seemed softer somehow, kinder even. There was no blood to leave bruises, no bones to break. The worst this clay had suffered was being dredged from the river, and the only blade it knew was that of a shovel.

"Are you ready?" Oren asked, glancing up at me.

I nodded.

He held out the stylus. "Then you may do the honors."

I stared at him, certain that if I had a heart, it would've pounded. "Are you sure?"

Oren nodded.

"But I..." I trailed off, unable to find the words. But I was an abomination, I thought to say, except why did that matter? I was creating one anyway.

"You can do this," Oren told me quietly, with a sympathy I was unaccustomed to. In the days since we had started working on the golem, he had warmed to me, but the way he looked at me now took me aback. It was as though we were equals.

His words emboldened me. Taking the reed from him, I dipped it once, and with infinite care, brought it to the golem's brow.

א

מ

ת

As I painted the final letter, a draft passed through the room, stirring the flame of the candle and pooling shadows in the closed lids of the golem's deep-set eyes and the trough of his upper lip. I froze and waited—for what, I didn't know. One tentative draw of air he didn't need, or the twitching movement of those eyes beneath their closed lids.

A minute passed. Then another. My anticipation dimmed into a gnawing dread, and before I knew it, the stylus snapped in my hand. I swiveled around to face Rav Oren. "Why isn't it working?!"

"I don't know. It—" He was about to say more when the stirring of cloth drew our attention. I looked down in time to see the golem's hand flex and curl, and his eyes slowly open.

"Akiva!" I reached for him as he sat up. He shied away from my touch, scooting back against the log wall with his teeth bared reflexively and a low growl rising in his throat.

When he swallowed, I caught him flinch, glimpsed the pink flash of a tongue against the clay bank of his lower palate. I could sense what must be going through his mind—no lungs, no need to swallow, that wasn't saliva that welled in the back of his throat, it was only water from the Visinčia River.

"It's all right," I said, sinking to my knees before him. "You're safe here. It's over."

His lips moved, tongue struggled to form words. Faint, inarticulate sounds welled from deep within him, less like his cold, familiar timbre than like noises from the riverbed— the gurgle of water striking pebbles, the strangled glug of a beached pike, a pained grinding like stone against stone. His features contorted from the strain, or the pain of remembering.

"Akiva, it's..." I trailed off, looking into his blue eyes. They were stormy with confusion, the pupils just pinpricks, as if he were still looking back to the day he died, staring out across all that bright, sun-drenched snow. A slow realization came over me. "No... You're not him."

I knew that there was a fragment of Chaya in myself, a core of who she had been. But I was not a sarcophagus—I was a cocoon. I was something different than her, something one and only my own. And for Akiva, it was the same. This was not who he had been. This was someone else, someone I wanted to know.

"Don't be afraid." I smiled, even though it felt like a stone was lodged in my throat. Parting my hair, I showed him the letters on my brow. "We're the same."

"The same," he whispered, and just the sound of his voice brought tears to my eyes.

I took the golem's hand in mine. Our bodies were the same temperature, our skin the same ashen beige. Holding him was like slipping up against the Visinčia riverbed, or burying a corpse in its silt, mounding the half-frozen sludge over cold, lifeless skin. Bridging the gap between who we had once been and who we were now.

I wanted to believe that the same desire that had drawn me to Akiva in the first place, snared me like a thread and sewn me to him—I wanted to believe that it had survived his death, his undoing, his resurrection. I wanted to call it beshert. And I wanted to believe that whoever this being was, we would stumble close, reach out a hand, and find each other in this darkness.

This would be his first day.

"There is a mark on your brow," I murmured, leaning forward to rest my forehead against his. "And it means truth."

★ ★ ★ ★ ★

GLOSSARY

bubbe meise: The Yiddish word for an old wives' tale.

dybbuk: In Jewish folklore, a malevolent wandering spirit that enters and possesses the body of a living person until exorcised.

genizah: A storage area in a Jewish synagogue or cemetery where Hebrew books, papers, and other sacred objects are kept before proper burial.

golem: In Jewish folklore, a man-made artificial human, crafted from clay and given life through magic.

kishuf: Sorcery.

laumė: In Baltic folklore, a beautiful woodland spirit commonly known to tickle men to death and devour them.

met: Dead.

mikveh: A bath or water source used for ritual immersion and purification in the Jewish religion.

otriad: Commonly used during WWII to refer to partisan groups who fought the Nazis, derived from отряд (*otrjád*), the Russian word for a detachment or troop.

panzer: A German armored vehicle, specifically the series of tanks used during WWII.

pikuach nefesh: The principle in Jewish law that declares the preservation of human life is more important than any other law or religious obligation.

Schuma: Abbreviation of Schutzmannschaft.

shul: A Jewish synagogue or temple.

tati: Yiddish for father.

tekhelet: The special blue dye historically used in the High Priest's clothing and the tapestries of the Tabernacle, and which is still used to dye the tassels on prayer shawls.

Vilna: The capital of Lithuania.

ziz: In Jewish folklore, a griffin-like bird that God created at the dawn of creation, whose wingspan was said to be large enough to hide the sun.

ACKNOWLEDGMENTS

Every book is a journey, and *Wrath Becomes Her* was no exception. Over the course of my writing career, I've come to appreciate and understand that each book's path to publication is different. What connects each one is the support and enthusiasm of the people who help bring the books into the world.

I would like to begin by thanking everyone at Inkyard who made *Wrath Becomes Her* possible, including my editor, Stephanie Cohen, whose enthusiasm and excitement for my story made working on this book such a joy.

As well, I want to thank the marketing and publicity teams, notably Brittany Mitchell and Justine Sha. I am also deeply grateful to Bess Brasswell for her support and encouragement.

In addition, I would like to thank my critique partners, Laura Samotin, Laura Creedle, and Brenda Marie Smith.

Lastly, I'd like to thank the booksellers who've helped get this book out to teens who need it, as well as readers who've followed me since my earliest books.

ACKNOWLEDGMENTS

Every book is a journey, and *Wrath Becomes Her* was no exception. Over the course of my writing career, I've come to appreciate and understand that each book's path to publication is different. What connects each one is the support and enthusiasm of the people who help bring the books into the world.

I would like to begin by thanking everyone at Inkyard who made *Wrath Becomes Her* possible, including my editor, Stephanie Cohen, whose enthusiasm and excitement for my story made working on this book such a joy.

As well, I want to thank the marketing and publicity teams, notably Brittany Mitchell and Justine Sha. I am also deeply grateful to Bess Brasswell for her support and encouragement.

In addition, I would like to thank my critique partners, Laura Samotin, Laura Creedle, and Brenda Marie Smith.

Lastly, I'd like to thank the booksellers who've helped get this book out to teens who need it, as well as readers who've followed me since my earliest books.